GOOD RIDDANCE TO BAD RUBBISH . . .

Fred didn't want to rest. He wanted to get to the bottom of this. But it wouldn't do him any good to argue—he'd seen Enos in this mood before. Gathering his things, he followed Enos and Doc outside into the cold. But instinct left him with an uneasy feeling about Eddie Leishman's death, and Fred was learning to trust his instincts—no matter what Enos said.

No doubt about it, Eddie Leishman was going to cause as much trouble dead as he had alive . . .

Don't miss Fred Vickery's
previous forays into murder in . . .

NO PLACE FOR SECRETS
NO PLACE LIKE HOME
NO PLACE FOR DEATH

D0851108

MORE MYSTERIES FROM THE BERKLEY PUBLISHING GROUP . . .

DEWEY JAMES MYSTERIES: America's favorite small-town sleuth! "Highly entertaining!" —Booklist

by Kate Morgan

A SLAY AT THE RACES	MYSTERY LOVES COMPANY
A MURDER MOST FOWL	DAYS OF CRIME AND ROSES
HOME SWEET HOMICIDE	THE OLD SCHOOL DIES

FORREST EVERS MYSTERIES: A former race-car driver solves the high-speed crimes of world-class racing . . . "A Dick Francis on wheels!" —Jackie Stewart

by Bob Judd

BURN	SPIN
CURVE	

THE REVEREND LUCAS HOLT MYSTERIES: They call him "The Rev," a name he earned as pastor of a Texas prison. Now he solves crimes with a group of reformed ex-cons . . .

by Charles Meyer

THE SAINTS OF GOD MURDERS	BLESSED ARE THE MERCILESS

FRED VICKERY MYSTERIES: Senior sleuth Fred Vickery has been around long enough to know where the bodies are buried in the small town of Cutler, Colorado . . .

by Sherry Lewis

NO PLACE FOR SECRETS	NO PLACE LIKE HOME
NO PLACE FOR DEATH	NO PLACE FOR TEARS

INSPECTOR BANKS MYSTERIES: Award-winning British detective fiction at its finest . . . "Robinson's novels are habit-forming!" —*West Coast Review of Books*

by Peter Robinson

THE HANGING VALLEY	FINAL ACCOUNT
WEDNESDAY'S CHILD	INNOCENT GRAVES
PAST REASON HATED	

JACK McMORROW MYSTERIES: The highly acclaimed series set in a Maine mill town and starring a newspaperman with a knack for crime solving . . . "Gerry Boyle is the genuine article." —Robert B. Parker

by Gerry Boyle

DEADLINE	BLOODLINE

SCOTLAND YARD MYSTERIES: Featuring Detective Superintendent Duncan Kincaid and his partner, Sergeant Gemma James . . . "Charming!"
—*New York Times Book Review*

by Deborah Crombie

A SHARE IN DEATH	ALL SHALL BE WELL
LEAVE THE GRAVE GREEN	

NO PLACE
FOR TEARS

SHERRY LEWIS

BERKLEY PRIME CRIME, NEW YORK

If you purchased this book without a cover, you should be aware that this book is stolen property. It was reported as "unsold and destroyed" to the publisher, and neither the author nor the publisher has received any payment for this "stripped book."

NO PLACE FOR TEARS

A Berkley Prime Crime Book / published by arrangement with the author

PRINTING HISTORY
Berkley Prime Crime edition / January 1997

All rights reserved.
Copyright © 1997 by Sherry Lewis.
This book may not be reproduced in whole or in part,
by mimeograph or any other means, without permission.
For information address: The Berkley Publishing Group,
200 Madison Avenue, New York, New York 10016.

The Putnam Berkley World Wide Web site address is
http://www.berkley.com/berkley

ISBN: 0-425-15626-5

Berkley Prime Crime Books are published by
The Berkley Publishing Group,
200 Madison Avenue, New York, New York 10016.
The name BERKLEY PRIME CRIME and the BERKLEY PRIME CRIME
design are trademarks belonging to Berkley Publishing Corporation.

PRINTED IN THE UNITED STATES OF AMERICA

10 9 8 7 6 5 4 3 2 1

For Joe Walker

thank you

one

Fred Vickery shifted in his seat at the back of the high school auditorium and struggled to keep his eyes open in the oppressive artificial heat. He scanned the nearly empty room for some sign of the school's custodian and battled irritation. True to form, Mort Lombard was nowhere to be found. Knowing Mort, he'd probably gone outside to enjoy the crisp winter air and early December snowfall while he left everyone inside suffering through a man-made heat-wave.

Pulling his checkbook from his pocket, Fred waved it in front of his face to create a breeze while his grandson, Benjamin, rehearsed a number for the upcoming Winter Extravaganza with his rock-and-roll band on the stage. The boys had already been practicing for half an hour, but they couldn't seem to get the piece right. Carl Fadel, the school's new music teacher, wouldn't let them leave until they did.

On stage, Benjamin struck a chord and the boys started again—a piece so slow and heavy it sounded more like a funeral march than a celebration of the holidays. Fred didn't mind coming to pick up Benjamin, but he hoped the boys got the piece right this time so they could all go home.

Since his youngest son, Douglas, had moved to Cheyenne a few weeks ago, chasing another rainbow and looking for a pot of gold, Fred had found himself at loose ends. He'd enjoyed the return of his privacy, but he'd also missed Douglas's company and the faster pace of having another person around. Helping his daughter, Margaret, gave him something to do.

Besides, he'd been looking for an excuse to spend time

alone with Benjamin. As the grandkids grew older and got caught up in their own lives, he had to manufacture excuses to spend time alone with each one.

Fred knew Margaret felt guilty about asking him to come out with the weather so unpredictable, but she'd been putting off Christmas shopping for weeks, and she'd been planning to drive into Denver for days. He didn't see any reason for Carl Fadel's last-minute practice to throw her off schedule.

Fred didn't feel so charitable toward Margaret's husband. Webb claimed he couldn't pick up Benjamin because he had to work late, but Fred didn't believe that excuse for a minute. He'd bet a month's retirement check that if he walked into the Copper Penny Lounge right that minute, he'd find Webb there, drinking too much, as usual.

As always, thinking of his son-in-law soured Fred's mood, so he tried to put Webb out of his mind and concentrate on his grandson. Benjamin had grown tall over the past couple of years, but at sixteen and in the middle of his junior year of high school, he was still just a stick of a boy with a sheaf of blond hair, an unquenchable spirit, and eyes that danced with the joy of life.

Fred fanned his checkbook a little faster and scanned the room one more time. If he'd still been buildings and grounds supervisor for the school district, he could have done something about the discomfort. And if he had to sit here much longer, he wouldn't let a little thing like retirement stop him from finding Mort and speaking his mind.

At that moment, Benjamin struck a loud chord on his guitar and shifted into a song so loud and fast Fred snapped his attention back to the stage. On the drums, Joshua Leishman quickly followed Benjamin's lead, but it took the other two boys a few beats to catch up. This new song didn't sound any more Christmasy to Fred than the funeral march had, but at least this one would keep an audience awake.

Almost immediately, Carl Fadel burst out from behind the curtain, waving his hands for the boys to stop. His curly brown hair looked tousled, as if he'd repeatedly raked his fingers through it. "All right, you guys. Knock it off."

One by one, the other boys stopped playing but Benjamin finished his riff first, then grinned at his teacher. "So, what did you think? Great, huh?"

"No, not great. I want you to stick to what the committee's approved, Ben. Don't get any wild ideas."

Benjamin's smile faded. "Oh come on, Mr. Fadel. This thing you want us to play sounds like somebody died."

"No shit," a man's voice called from one side of the auditorium. "Why don't you make the school orchestra play that piece of crap and let these guys play something decent. Hell, you're putting *me* to sleep."

While Carl moved closer to the edge of the stage and shielded his eyes against the spotlights, Fred again searched the darkened room, but he couldn't see anyone.

"Excuse me?" Carl shouted. "Who's out there?"

A figure moved out of the shadows at the back of the auditorium and down the aisle until it neared the front rows where the light finally revealed Eddie Leishman, the father of the drummer on stage. Wearing worn jeans, a dirty T-shirt, and heavy black boots, he made quite a contrast to Carl's more conservative Dockers, loafers, and turtleneck sweater.

Wire-thin, with a headful of longish blond hair and a chinful of brown whiskers, Eddie grinned at the boys and leapt onto the stage without apparent effort. Fred didn't know Eddie well, but he certainly knew of him. Everyone did.

As far as Fred knew, Eddie'd never held down a steady daytime job, but with his band he'd played the bars and taverns around the area for several years. Joshua had obviously inherited Eddie's musical talent, but if the talk about Eddie was accurate, Fred hoped the boy hadn't inherited some of his other traits.

Carl took a step backward, then braced himself to stand up to Eddie. "I'm sorry, Mr. Leishman, but our rehearsal time is limited. I'm going to have to ask you to wait outside for Josh to finish."

Eddie laughed, but the sound held no humor. He patted Carl's slightly rounded stomach and shot an amused glance around. "I didn't come to see Josh—it's *you* I want to talk to. Got a minute?"

"No, I don't. We're in the middle of rehearsal."

Eddie ran a hand over the hair on his chin and leaned a little closer. "It'll just take a minute. Besides, if you'd let these guys play some decent shit, you'd save yourself a hell of a lot of time."

Carl crossed his arms on his chest and shook his head, but Fred sensed some hesitation in his actions. "I'll have to ask you to watch your language in front of the boys."

"Oh, yeah. Sure. Wouldn't want to corrupt them." Eddie laughed again and looked at the boys as if he expected them to join in. Benjamin smiled, Nathan rolled his eyes, and Tyler sent an uneasy glance in Carl's direction.

Working up a little more courage, Carl planted his fists on his hips. "If this concerns Josh, why don't you make an appointment to meet with me during regular hours?"

Eddie's laughter faded. "Well, see, I need to talk. Right now." He threw an arm around Carl's shoulders and said something else too softly for Fred to hear.

Whatever it was, it made Carl's attitude change immediately. He unfolded his arms and pulled away from Eddie stiffly. "All right," he snapped. "Fine. Come into my office." Eddie laughed again and tossed what looked like a pack of cigarettes to Joshua, then followed Carl across the stage. When they reached the curtains, Carl looked back at the boys. "I guess that's enough for today. We'll practice again tomorrow right after seventh period. Don't be late." Without waiting for a response, he led Eddie offstage.

As soon as they disappeared, Fred pushed himself out of his chair and started toward the stage, almost grateful for the interruption so he wouldn't have to sit in this overheated room any longer, and relieved that he could drive home before the roads froze over again.

Onstage, Benjamin unplugged his guitar from the amplifier and wound the cord around his hand. "I don't get it— What's the committee got against us playing *our* music for the program?"

Carrying his bass guitar to the back of the stage, Nathan Grimes spoke over his shoulder. "Who *is* the committee, anyway?"

Tyler O'Neal grunted. "I wish your dad was on the committee, Josh. He'd let us play what we want."

That was probably true, but Fred didn't like seeing the boys hold up someone like Eddie as a role model.

"Do you think that's why he's here?" Nathan asked.

Joshua focused on stuffing his drum sticks into a pouch. "Who knows?"

"Maybe he's going to take over the program," Nathan said. "That'd be cool. Is that what he's doing?"

Joshua's mouth tightened and he glared at his friend. "How should I know what he wants? This is the first time I've even seen him in a month." Joshua picked up the cigarettes from his drum set and lobbed them into the auditorium.

Benjamin closed his guitar case and rocked back on his haunches. "Hey, Josh. It's no big deal. Nobody's trying to piss you off."

"Yeah. Sure." Joshua snapped shut his pouch and slung it over his shoulder. Wearing that sullen expression, he looked more like Eddie than usual.

Fred's heart went out to the boy. He knew—as did everyone for miles around—about the odd relationship between Eddie and his wife, Ricki. Eddie had never been an exemplary husband or father, but he'd stepped over the line of acceptable behavior by leaving home a few months ago and moving in with Sharon Bollinger after her divorce. That Eddie apparently had no plans to divorce his wife did little to endear him to Cutler's residents. That Ricki hadn't sought divorce herself set tongues to wagging. But that Sharon was the daughter of Doc and Velma Huggins, both pillars of the community, made the talk much worse—and that made life rougher for Joshua.

As if he knew he'd overreacted, Joshua made a visible

effort to pull himself together. "Look, I'm gonna head— I'll just see you guys tomorrow."

Stepping into the light, Fred spoke up for the first time. "If you want a ride home, Joshua, we're heading your way."

"No thanks, Mr. V. My mom's *supposed* to pick me up."

Fred tried to look as if that reassured him, but he knew how distracted and forgetful people could get when they were going through emotional times. "Well, good. But if she's not there, we'll be glad to drive you. It's snowing again."

When Joshua smiled, his resemblance to Eddie all but disappeared. "Thanks, but you don't have to do that. I've walked home before. I'll be okay, I promise." Without waiting for a response, he slipped out of sight between the curtains.

The other boys worked in relative silence for another minute or two until Nathan pronounced himself finished and pulled a set of keys from his pocket. "Anybody need a ride?"

Tyler dropped a cloth over his electronic keyboard. "I do. Hold on a second, let me grab my books."

Benjamin stared wistfully at Nathan's keys, but he carried his guitar case to the edge of the stage near Fred. "Not me. I'm going with Grandpa."

"If you want to go with your friends—" Fred began halfheartedly.

Benjamin shook his head and smiled. "No, it's okay. I need to talk to you, anyway."

Relieved that Benjamin didn't want to head into bad weather with an inexperienced driver, Fred waved to the other boys. "Drive carefully, the roads are slick."

Nathan looked faintly irritated by the advice, but he had the good sense not to argue. But he didn't wait around for more, either. The instant Tyler picked up his books, Nathan ducked between the curtains with Tyler hot on his heels.

Benjamin jumped from the stage and pulled his guitar case and coat after him. "Are you ready, Grandpa?"

Fred nodded. "If you are."

"How long have you been waiting?"

"Not long," Fred lied.

Benjamin started up the aisle toward the auditorium's doors. "You didn't need to waste all this time. I could have gone with Ty and Nate."

"I don't mind. It gave me a chance to catch a sneak preview of your performance. What did you want to talk to me about?"

Benjamin studied him for a second. "If I told you a secret, would you promise not to tell?"

"Of course I would. Christmas is a time for secrets."

Benjamin stopped walking and faced him. His blue eyes glittered and his face radiated excitement. "I heard today that Joshua's mom has this truck for sale—it's old, but it runs good." He squared his shoulders and added, "I'm going to buy it."

Fred could only stare at him. After Webb's younger brother died in an automobile accident shortly after Webb's marriage to Margaret, he'd harbored strong views about teenagers with cars. He'd used every argument against his daughter Sarah driving much when she got her driver's license two years ago, and Fred couldn't imagine that he'd changed his mind since then. "Does your dad know about this?"

"Not yet," Benjamin admitted. "That's what I need your help with."

"Telling your dad?" Fred laughed a little. If Benjamin wanted an ally in an argument with Webb, he ought to choose someone else. "Sounds like a pretty sure way to cause trouble, if you ask me."

"I'm not telling my dad. At least, not until I talk Mom into it. That's where you come in."

Fred's smile faded. "Telling your mother?"

"Sure. You always get your own way with her."

"I lose every argument I have with your mother, and you know it."

"No, you don't."

"If I got my own way, she'd stop babysitting me."

"She *has* stopped."

Fred shook his head. "You must be thinking of someone else."

"She's stopped making you pot roast on Sundays."

"But she's started making casseroles out of who knows what. And she *still* raids my cupboards." Fred held open the door for Benjamin to step out into the corridor. "I have to watch her like a hawk to keep her from tossing out everything I buy."

"She only gets rid of the stuff Doc told you not to eat."

Fred had suffered a tiny bit of heart trouble a year or so back, after which Doc had ordered him to cut caffeine, cholesterol, and sodium from his diet. The old coot had enlisted Margaret's help to keep Fred on the straight and narrow, and together they'd pulled the rest of the town into the conspiracy. To tell the truth, Fred had been a little unhappy with Doc ever since.

"That's everything I like," he groused and shook his head again. "No, you're asking the wrong person. I'm not going to sneak around behind your mother's back, or tell her what to do."

"Oh, come on, Grandpa. I've got enough in my savings for the down payment, and with what I make at the Good Sport I can make payments—"

"I thought you were saving for your education."

Benjamin made a face. "They want me to go to college, but I don't want to go—you know that."

"Then go to a trade school." Fred stopped just inside the school's front doors and held out his hand for Benjamin's guitar case. "Put your coat on, it's cold out."

"Trade school?" Benjamin curled his nose at the suggestion. "*That's* not what I want, either. I want to play music, Grandpa. And someday, I'm going to make it big. Recording contracts, concert tours . . . Josh's dad says we're good enough to make it."

Benjamin had talent, no doubt about it. And the boys sounded good together. They probably did have enough talent combined to become at least a moderate success like Eddie. But the idea of Benjamin following the same path as a man like Eddie Leishman soured Fred's stomach. And knowing how Webb would react to the idea left Fred cold. "Put on your coat," he repeated, and pushed open the door.

Though not yet six o'clock, the sun had long since disappeared behind the western mountain peaks. Thick white flakes fell through the night sky, softening the darkness and muffling the sounds of civilization under a blanket of sparkling powder.

Benjamin tugged on his coat and followed Fred outside. "So, are you saying you're not going to help me?"

"I'm saying I can't." Fred didn't elaborate on his reasons. No matter how great the provocation, he wouldn't speak ill of Webb in front of his children.

"I thought I could count on you."

Fred hated letting the boy down, but he didn't respond.

Benjamin pouted for a second or two, then brightened. "If you could see this truck, you'd change your mind, I know you would."

"There'll be other trucks for you to buy when you're older."

"Not like this one. It's in *great* shape, and I'm never gonna find such a good deal again. Next time I find something I can afford, it'll probably be run down—even dangerous."

That argument didn't even sway Fred and it would never move Webb. He handed the guitar case back to Benjamin and pulled on his gloves as they walked. "Listen, son, I don't think this is a good idea for a number of reasons. I know you're disappointed, but believe me, you've got plenty of time to do everything."

Benjamin frowned and kicked at a chunk of ice. "This isn't fair."

Only by showing magnificent restraint did Fred keep from mentioning that he'd never known life to be fair.

Turning away, Benjamin started to slide down the sidewalk, then stopped short at the sight of two figures near the parking lot. One wore dirty jeans and heavy black boots, the other wore a thick fur coat and a matching hat. Obviously, Joshua's mother had arrived, after all. Unfortunately, it looked as if Joshua had missed her; Fred couldn't see the boy anywhere.

Benjamin hurried back to Fred's side and nodded toward

the couple. "That's Josh's mom over there. How about if I ask her if we can come over tomorrow so you can see the truck?"

Looking at the Leishmans together, Fred thought only a fool would consider interrupting them now. Both Eddie and Ricki gestured with broad, jerky movements as they spoke. They leaned close to emphasize points, and the anger in their voices carried through the hush of snowfall across the sidewalk.

But Benjamin had apparently lost all common sense, and before Fred could even open his mouth to respond, the boy darted toward them. Fred hurried as quickly as he could across the slippery sidewalk, but Benjamin managed to reach the Leishmans before Fred could stop him.

Eddie must not have seen them at first. He leaned close to his wife and shouted, "I said, not tonight for hell's sake. Now leave me alone. I have to work."

"How long do you expect me to wait?" Ricki demanded.

"You don't get it, do you? I don't give a damn whether you wait or not." Eddie shoved at the air between them. "Do whatever the hell you want." He turned away from Ricki and seemed to notice Benjamin for the first time. His frown deepened and his eyes narrowed. "What the hell do *you* want?"

And Benjamin, in his naivete, looked only slightly uncomfortable. "I just wondered whether my grandpa and I could come and look at the truck tomorrow."

Beneath her layers of fur and in spite of her obvious anger, Ricki managed a thin smile. "I guess . . ."

But Eddie whipped back around to glare at her. "What truck? *My* truck? What the hell are you doing? Selling my truck?"

Fred had never liked being in the middle of family squabbles. The best course of action, under the circumstances, would be to leave and take Benjamin with him. He reached for Benjamin's arm and tried not to look conspicuous.

Benjamin shook him off and moved a step closer. "It's okay, isn't it?"

Neither Eddie nor Ricki seemed to hear him. "You *told* me to sell it," Ricki cried.

"When? When did I say that?"

"Before you left home. You said you wanted to sell the truck. Or was that another one of your lies? Are you going to claim you don't remember *that*, either?"

"I said I was thinking about it," Eddie roared. "*Thinking*. Do you even know what that word means?" He glared at Fred and shoved a hand toward Benjamin. "Get the hell out of here, man. Nobody's buying nothing—got that?"

Fred certainly didn't intend to argue. And this time when he tugged Benjamin away, the boy didn't fight him. Fred didn't look back until he stepped off the curb. Luckily, Ricki and Eddie seemed to have forgotten them.

"Well," he said without even trying to hide his relief. "I guess that's that. Looks like you'll have to forget about that truck, after all."

Benjamin didn't look concerned. "Why? Because of Eddie? Don't worry. He'll change his mind."

"I don't know if I'd count on that," Fred warned. But when he glanced back again, he wondered if maybe Benjamin was right.

Ricki huddled into her coat and seemed to be crying. Eddie turned away from her and stomped around for a few seconds. He stopped and closed the distance between them a split second before Ricki threw herself into his arms. Fred didn't know why the scene disturbed him. After all, they were married. They ought to be able to hug if they wanted.

But he'd known one or two men, like Eddie, whose very presence seemed to spell deep trouble. Fred had learned to avoid troublemakers during his seventy-three years, and he didn't want Benjamin involved with this one. He just didn't know how to convince Benjamin to stay away from them and the truck.

two

Fred followed the Main Street boardwalk toward the Bluebird Café, eager for breakfast and looking forward to a cup or two of real coffee. Sometime during the night, the snow had stopped but the temperature had dropped at the same time, and now a thin layer of ice covered everything.

Cutler sat in the bottom of a narrow valley surrounded by forest. It nestled on the shores of Spirit Lake, high in the Colorado Rockies. Lodgepole pines towered over most of the buildings, and bare aspen trees swayed in the high mountain breezes. Even in its most densely populated section it felt more like a notch in the timber than a town.

Most of the walks had been cleared after last night's storm, but Fred still tested each step carefully before fully trusting his weight. Before he'd gone halfway across town, his knees began to ache from the effort of holding himself upright on the slick spots.

Between concern for Benjamin and his normal preholiday blues over Phoebe, he hadn't slept well last night. He'd gone to bed after the news as usual, but as he lay there in the dark beside Phoebe's empty side of the bed he'd started missing his late wife more than usual.

Pulling his collar around his neck, he shoved his free hand into his pocket and tried to warm his stiff fingers. Not only did he want a coffee and a good breakfast—not some low-fat, low-cholesterol concoction of which Margaret would approve—he wanted a friend to share them with. If he hurried, he could find all three at the Bluebird.

At last, he reached the intersection with Estes Street and noted with a smile that Enos Asay's truck was still there. He must be inside finishing the free coffee Lizzie Hatch had provided the sheriff's department since her son Grady joined the force as one of Enos's deputies. Other than Fred's own sons, he didn't know a man alive he cared more about then Enos. Or one he trusted more.

The Bluebird had been a fixture in Cutler almost as long as Fred could remember. He'd brought Phoebe here and courted her in the privacy of a corner booth—back in the days when the booths allowed privacy. But since Lizzie had taken over a few years back, the place had changed considerably.

She'd ripped down the ivy-twined paper that had covered the walls since the beginning of time, replaced it with wood paneling and dozens of posters of Elvis Presley, and stocked the jukebox with every one of the King's songs she'd been able to find. And she fixed the kind of meals people could sink their teeth into. Meals made the way God intended people to eat.

Fred still loved the Bluebird. It felt like home.

Hoping to slip inside without letting in much cold air, he pushed open the door and closed it again almost immediately. But half a dozen pairs of eyes turned to glare at him, anyway. On the jukebox, Elvis came to life crooning "Blue Christmas." Lizzie's latest acquisition, a soulful-looking Elvis painted on a square of black velvet, looked at Fred with such understanding his mood dropped another few degrees.

He waved to the regulars at the counter, then hurried into the dining area and away from Elvis's velvet eyes. Enos sat at his usual table, staring out the window. Shoulders slumped and face drawn, he didn't even look up as Fred approached. A half cup of coffee and a pack of Wrigley's Doublemint gum sat on the table in front of him beside his battered old cowboy hat. Not a good sign.

Last year, Enos's wife, Jessica, had insisted he quit smoking or spend his nights on the couch. He'd chewed gum for months to combat the nicotine withdrawal. The pack on the table and his dejected posture convinced Fred he was craving cigarettes again. And that probably meant trouble at home.

Fred slid onto the chair facing Enos, pulled off his gloves and coat, and worked his fingers to force the stiffness out. "Morning."

Enos looked up and almost managed a smile. "I'm surprised to see you here this early."

"I wanted to catch you before you headed off somewhere."

"Is something wrong? You look a little haggard."

Now *there* was a case of the pot calling the kettle black. "I didn't sleep much last night. Benjamin's decided to buy a truck, and somehow I've promised to keep it a secret from Webb."

Enos drained his cup and grimaced. "That ought to make the holidays interesting around your place. How did you manage that?"

From across the room, Lizzie lifted the coffeepot in silent question. Fred nodded eagerly and turned his cup over in its saucer. "To tell you the truth, I'm not sure how it happened. And the worst part is, you're never going to believe whose truck he wants to buy." He leaned back a little while Lizzie poured, then wrapped his fingers around the cup and let its warmth seep into his joints.

Enos didn't even bother to guess. "Whose?"

"Eddie Leishman's."

Enos shot him a concerned look. "No kidding?"

"I couldn't have found a quicker way to get on Webb's bad side if I'd tried."

Enos's lips twitched. "I thought you were already there."

"Very funny." Fred sipped and felt the hot coffee tracing a pattern all the way down. "Margaret's got her heart set on Benjamin going to college, you know. She's terrified Benjamin will turn out like Webb."

Lizzie refilled Enos's cup, then rested the coffeepot on the table. "Maggie said that?"

"She didn't have to."

Enos smiled up at Lizzie. "I think it's *Fred's* greatest fear, not Maggie's."

"Well, if it isn't hers, it ought to be," Fred groused, and opened his mouth to list the other trouble spots that had kept him awake all night.

But Lizzie cut him off. "How is Maggie, anyway? I haven't seen her for a while."

Fred tried not to show his concern. Lately, Webb had been spending even less time at home and more time at the Copper Penny, if that were possible. Unfortunately, Margaret's mood reflected the number of hours she spent alone. But since he didn't like to discuss Margaret behind her back, he said, "Fine. Busy. The holidays are coming, you know, and there's always so much more to do. She drove down to Denver yesterday, which is how I happened to get caught in the middle of this truck business."

Lizzie didn't look at all sorry for him. "Seems to me, Benjamin needs somebody to hear his side." She turned away to pour coffee at other tables before Fred even had a chance to respond.

"I hear it," Fred explained to her retreating back. "I just can't do anything about it."

Enos rubbed a hand over his face. "Webb's not going to like Benjamin going behind his back. And after what happened to Whit—" He broke off, remembering. Whit's tragic death had affected everyone—still did, even after thirty years.

"All I know is, if I let myself get dragged into the middle of this, I could land in a heap of trouble."

Enos lifted an eyebrow. "That's never stopped you before." He picked up his pack of gum and studied it absently. "You're not worried about Maggie's reaction, are you?" He obviously thought he'd managed a casual question, but his face colored slightly and his expression softened the way it always did when Margaret's name came up. They'd dated through high school, and they'd remained friends since, but neither had ever quite gotten over the other. You only had to be with one when the other entered a room to notice.

Fred shook his head, though he did worry a little about Margaret's reaction.

"So what's really troubling you?" Enos asked. "Webb?"
Enos's opinion of Webb just about equaled Fred's.

Fred had never understood what prompted Margaret to
break up with Enos and marry Webb Templeton, but he'd
seen right through Enos's marriage to Jessica Rich less than
six months later. Fred tried not to think about what might
have happened if Enos had just waited a while longer. It was
hard enough watching them moon over each other from a
distance. Hard enough to watch them both suffer unhappy
marriages in silence.

Fred lowered his cup. "The truth? I don't care beans if
Webb's mad at *me*, but I don't want him to take it out on
Margaret or the kids. Trouble is, I can't say anything to
Margaret. Not without upsetting everybody. I tell you, these
are the times I seem to miss Phoebe the most." He looked at
his coffee cup for a long moment, then glanced back at
Enos.

The younger man's lips curved in a gentle smile. "She
was one special lady."

"I don't know how she managed to fix everything without
seeming to get involved. Nobody ever got upset with her for
making suggestions or offering advice."

Enos's smile widened into an outright grin. "I thought *you*
were the one who wanted to fix everything."

Fred waved his words away. "That's what I'm talking
about. When *I* get involved, everybody knows it. But
Phoebe—"

Before he could finish his thought, the front door banged
open again and Doc Huggins blew inside on a blast of
frozen air.

Fred thought Enos looked bad, but Doc's haggard appearance put the younger man to shame. His fringe of hair
looked as if it hadn't been brushed in days, his cheeks and
chin sported at least a day's growth, and his eyes looked lost
in the dark circles beneath them.

He spotted Fred and Enos immediately and headed
straight for their table, flipping over his coffee cup as he slid
into an empty chair. Fred tensed and waited for Doc to

launch into an inquisition about the contents of his coffee
cup. Doc didn't seem to notice.

Enos unwrapped a fresh piece of Doublemint and stuffed
it into his mouth while Doc settled himself. "Good billy
hell, Doc, what happened to you?"

Doc rolled his eyes as if to say *don't ask*, then proceeded
to tell. "I've been up all night. At Sharon's."

Enos's eyes narrowed in concern. "What's wrong? Is she
sick?"

"It's not her. It's Eddie." Doc spoke the name as if it left
a bad aftertaste. And it probably did.

Enos flicked a glance at Fred. They both knew what was
coming next. They'd heard Doc spout off about Eddie more
than once since Sharon took him in.

"Sharon called just as we were *finally* drifting off," Doc
complained.

"What was wrong with Eddie?" Fred asked.

Doc sighed heavily. "Nothing serious. He had an insulin
reaction."

Enos looked surprised. "I didn't know he was diabetic."

Doc nodded, but he looked disgusted. "And with his
lifestyle, I'm not surprised he has trouble. He brings it on
himself the way he drinks and carries on. Anyway, Sharon
was beside herself, and Velma wouldn't let me rest until I
went over there."

"But everything's all right now?" Enos asked.

Doc nodded and smiled up at Lizzie while she filled his
cup with decaf. "Yes, thank God. But I'm telling you,
nursing that piece of filth was the hardest thing I've ever
done. Sharon lives less than two miles from home, but do
you know the last time she invited us over? Not since *he*
moved in." Doc said it as if he *wanted* to socialize with
Eddie Leishman. "And you should see that house. It's
terrible. Filthy. She's working all the time while that jerk
lays around making a mess for her. I'm telling you—"

Enos managed a stiff laugh. "You know, Doc, I wish
you'd just say how you really feel."

Doc didn't even acknowledge the joke. He shook his head
slowly and stared at his fingers. "He's a bloodsucker, that's

what he is. You *know* how vulnerable Sharon was after her divorce. That's another story in itself."

Which they'd all heard a number of times before. Fred hated to air Margaret's problems in public, but Doc flapped Sharon's about to anyone who'd listen.

"Maybe it won't last," Enos suggested.

Doc's eyes clouded. "It had better not. It *can't*. It's killing Velma." He paused just long enough for his mind to jump to another track and for fresh anger to blaze across his face. "What kind of woman is that wife of his, that's what I want to know."

Fred had no answer. He felt uncomfortable knowing about the Leishmans' argument of the night before, slightly guilty for having witnessed their embrace.

Doc didn't seem to really want a response. "Doesn't it seem to you that she'd make him come home? Or at least divorce him as soon as she could? What would *you* do, Enos, if Jessica suddenly moved out and started living with some other man? You'd divorce her, that's what." Nodding vigorously, Doc lifted his coffee cup, changed his mind, and banged it back to the table. "Maybe I should be grateful she *hasn't*, or Sharon would marry the scum. And Vance— Have you seen Vance lately?"

Fred figured Doc's grandson must be about twenty by now, give or take a year, and he'd seen him buying a soda at Jefferson's One-Stop a few weeks ago, but he didn't figure that's what Doc meant.

"He's so miserable with Eddie there, he's ready to move out. But where's he going to go? And why should Vance leave his own home so Eddie Leishman can have a place to stay? He's got a place. And a *wife*."

Enos managed to look outraged and sympathetic at the same time. Fred just tried not to show any expression.

"I tell you," Doc plowed on. "Velma and I are at our wits' end. We've done our best with that girl. Brought her up exactly the same way as the other kids. What she sees in that— That—" He broke off as if he couldn't manage to say more.

"Well, at least he has a job," Enos said.

Doc rolled his eyes. "If you count playing music in some seedy bar half the night a job."

"It brings money home—"

"If it does, Sharon never sees a penny of it." Doc took a mouthful of coffee and swallowed it slowly. "I can't tell you how many times last night I wanted to walk out that door and let him suffer."

Fred didn't believe that for an instant. No matter what his other faults, Doc would never let anyone suffer. "Well, you're smart to stick by Sharon," he said. "You'll be there when she needs you, and she *is* going to need you."

Enos managed an understanding nod.

Lizzie came up behind them so quietly Fred didn't think any of them heard her until she spoke. "Phone call for you, Doc. You can take it in the kitchen."

Looking weary and long-suffering, Doc hurried away with Lizzie a step behind. Fred watched them disappear, then pulled in a steadying breath.

Enos had been watching, too. He looked back at Fred and worked up a thin smile. "Poor Doc. This whole business with Sharon is rough on him."

"Letting himself get so worked up over it makes it rougher."

Enos considered that, then grinned. "I'll let *you* tell him that."

"He wouldn't listen if I did."

Before Enos could respond, Doc rushed out of the kitchen. Weariness and anger had given way to genuine concern. He nearly ran to the table and yanked his coat off the back of his chair.

"Who was it?" Fred asked.

"Sharon." Doc shoved his arms into his coat and stuffed his hands back into his gloves. "She thinks Eddie's dead."

Enos shot to his feet and jammed his hat on his head. "What was it, another insulin reaction?"

Doc answered with a brisk nod. "Has to be. He could be in a coma, I guess, though I don't understand how. He was sleeping when I left."

"You're going over there now?" Fred asked.

"I'll drive you," Enos said. "Where's your medical bag?
Do we need to stop by your house?"

Doc shook his head and quick-stepped to the door. "It's in
my car."

Without waiting to be invited, Fred tugged on his own
coat as he followed them outside to Enos's truck. When
Enos looked as if he might protest, Fred held up a hand to
stop him. "I need to do something. At least let me sit with
Sharon and Vance while Doc's working on Eddie."

Enos hesitated less than a second, then shrugged. "All
right. Get in." Two cars away, Doc grabbed his medical bag
from his trunk while Enos attached the emergency lights to
the truck's cab. When Doc climbed in beside Fred, Enos
pulled away from the curb before Doc could even shut the
door.

With siren blaring, they careened down Main Street, slid
around the corners of Ash and Oak streets, narrowly missed
clipping a jogger by the school grounds, and finally came to
rest in the driveway of Sharon's small split-level house.

Doc hit the icy pavement at a run—or what passed for
one at his age. Enos leapt from the truck and crossed the ice
and snow as if they didn't exist. He reached the door first,
yanked it open for Doc, then followed him inside.

Fred approached the house a minute later, but he paused
with his hand on the knob and glanced around the neighborhood, a little worried their arrival might have made the
neighbors curious. Because Janice and Bill Lacey lived
across the street and two houses down, Fred checked their
house for signs of life, and thanked everyone's lucky stars
Janice was on duty at Lacey's General Store this time of
day. Sharon had enough on her plate, she didn't need a
serving of gossip from Janice, as well.

Inside the house, he closed the door behind him and stood
on the narrow landing, savoring the warmth and contem-
plating the split stairway. He couldn't see a soul in either
direction, but he could hear Sharon crying softly. Gripping
the handrail, he followed the sound up the stairs which
deposited him in the living room.

Shabby furniture in a variety of styles and upholstery

patterns lined the walls. Half a dozen beer cans, a coffee cup, several outdated television guides, and a clutter of papers rested on a cheap-looking coffee table. True to Doc's word, the room looked the worse for someone's presence— probably Eddie's.

Behind Fred, a sound caught his attention and he turned just as Vance Bollinger emerged from the kitchen. From a scruffy little boy with freckles and buckteeth, he'd turned into a handsome young man with broad shoulders and muscles bulging under his T-shirt. His dark hair, shaved in the back and longer on top, fell into his face as he bent over a soda can and used the tail of his shirt to wipe its rim.

"Vance?"

The boy looked up, obviously startled. "What? Oh, Mr. V. I didn't know you were here. What'd they do, bring the whole town with them?"

"I was with your grandpa and Enos when your mother called. How's Eddie?"

Vance shrugged and sent a venomous glance down the hallway. "Who cares?"

Obviously Vance didn't. He walked into the living room, kicked angrily at a couple of shoes on the floor, shoved a pair of Levis from a chair, and dropped onto the seat.

Fred perched on the edge of the couch near a blanket and a couple of pillows. "Do you know what happened?"

Vance took a long swig of soda. "My mom came home on a break from work and found him passed out in the bedroom. That's all I know."

"Passed out? Had he been drinking?"

Vance pushed a handful of dark hair from his face. "Maybe. Probably." He looked at the beer cans on the coffee table and made a bitter face. "Obviously."

"You weren't here?"

"Well, yeah, I was. But I was downstairs in my room." He drank again and slid down on his tailbone.

Fred pulled off his gloves and stuffed them in his coat pocket. "Does he have trouble like this often?"

Vance shrugged again as if to show supreme indifference. "Yeah, I guess. Not this bad though." He leaned forward, rummaged through a stack of papers on the coffee table, and held up the remote control like a trophy. "You want to watch TV?"

Fred shook his head. Vance pressed a button anyway and a talk show popped onto the screen. One of the guests was in tears, another sat so far down in her chair it looked painful to Fred, and the third eyed the camera and the television audience with a hostile, challenging expression and said something so vulgar it had to be censored.

Fred leaned forward to recapture Vance's attention. "Where's your mother?"

Vance jerked his head toward the hallway. "With him."

"Oh." Vance obviously didn't want or need comfort, and Fred felt useless and a little silly sitting here as if he did.

Thankfully, he heard Enos's quick, heavy footsteps coming down the hallway just a few seconds later. Relieved, he stood and headed out to meet him, but the expression on Enos's face stopped him in his tracks.

Grim-faced, Enos jerked his head for Fred to follow him back into the living room. "Can we turn the TV off for a few minutes, Vance? I need to talk to you."

Vance flicked the remote and met Enos's gaze. "Yeah?"

"Have you been here all morning?"

The boy nodded slowly. "In my room downstairs."

"When did you see Eddie last?"

"Yesterday sometime, I guess."

"Didn't you come up here at all this morning?"

Vance's expression turned wary, and two red splotches flamed on his cheeks. "No. Why?"

"Is Eddie all right?" Fred asked.

Enos met his gaze and held it so long it left Fred cold. "Not by a long shot," Enos said at last. "He was dead before we got here."

three

Fred heard Vance pull in a sharp breath, but the boy quickly reset his features into an expression of indifference. "Was he murdered?" Fred asked softly.

Enos dropped onto a clean portion of the couch and unwrapped a piece of gum. "Doc says he died of an insulin overdose." Stuffing the gum into his mouth, he started to say something to Vance, but immediately glared back at Fred. "Please don't start trying to make this something it's not."

Having spent the past two days running into people who didn't like Eddie Leishman much, it seemed to Fred a perfectly logical conclusion to draw. "It was an innocent question."

"Yeah, I know." Enos nodded and shoved his fingers through his thinning hair. "That's what you always say."

"That's because it's always true. Don't accuse me of something I didn't do, for Pete's sake. I asked you a simple question, that's all."

Enos looked only slightly appeased. "Well, he wasn't murdered. Are you satisfied?"

Fred held up his hands in a gesture of surrender. "Perfectly. Thank you."

But Enos snorted in disbelief before he turned back to Vance. "You going to be all right, son? Anything I can do for you?"

The boy shook his head and looked a little surprised. "Me? No, I'm fine. But where's Mom?"

"With your grandpa in the other room. They'll be out in a minute." Enos rested his elbows on his knees and leaned forward with a kind expression on his broad face. "I need to make a few phone calls to get things moving at the coroner's office and all. But Fred'll stay here with you until I'm done."

Vance glanced at Fred and shrugged. "Okay. Fine. Whatever."

"I'll call your grandma and let her know. Your mother wants to stay there tonight."

Vance didn't speak.

Enos waited a second or two and looked as if he were a million miles away. Abruptly pulling himself back, he slapped his knees as if he'd just settled something with himself and pushed to his feet again. "Is there a phone in the kitchen?"

Vance nodded. "Against the far wall."

After Enos disappeared around the corner, Fred turned back to Vance. "I guess you'll want to get a few things together if you're spending the night at your grandparents' house."

Vance looked at him from under thick dark eyebrows. "I'm not going anywhere."

"You're planning to stay here?"

"Why wouldn't I?"

Fred didn't know how to respond to the challenge in Vance's tone. "Your mother doesn't want to stay here tonight. Maybe by tomorrow—"

"Hey, if she wants to go, she can. But I didn't let Eddie drive me out when he was alive, and I'm sure as hell not going to let him do it now." Vance fell back against his chair again and stared sullenly at the television.

Fred supposed he should let the comment lie there, but curiosity got the better of him. "Eddie tried to drive you out? Why?"

Vance pushed out a disbelieving laugh on a burst of air. "Because I hated him, and he knew it. I saw through him, and he knew that, too. He didn't want me anywhere around."

If Vance felt that way, no wonder he didn't seem

overcome with grief. "What do you mean, you saw through him?"

A shadow crossed Vance's features. "Eddie Leishman was a no-good son of a bitch who was using my mom for sex and money and a place to stay. She's probably the only person in town who believed he loved her."

Fred could only blink in response.

Vance kicked his feet up on the coffee table and linked his hands behind his head. "I'll tell you what— She ought to be happy he's gone. *I* am."

Fred didn't hear the footsteps behind him until a split second before Sharon entered the room with Doc behind her. Sharon had to be a little over forty by Fred's calculation, and she looked just like her mother had at the same age. Thick auburn hair hung in waves to just below her shoulders. She had her mother's nose and chin, with a feature or two from her paternal grandmother that softened the edges just a little and made her truly beautiful. Her dark eyes, usually soulful and warm, were red-rimmed and puffy from crying, and she looked pale.

The glare she sent Vance left Fred with no doubt she'd heard every word. "I can't believe you're saying those things."

At the sound of her voice, Vance jerked upright and shot to his feet, but his legs and arms flew in all directions like a newborn calf trying to stand. "Mom. Are you okay?"

She shook her head. "Not with you talking about Eddie like that. Can't you lay off for a little while? Can't you even let him *die* in peace?"

For a second, Fred thought Vance might respond. But he apparently thought better of it, and dropped back into his chair. "Whatever."

Almost immediately, Sharon's anger evaporated and grief replaced it. "Oh, Vance. What am I going to do?" She buried her face in shaking hands and began to sob again.

Doc stepped out around her, making a noise of disgust as he did.

Vance's hostility immediately evaporated and remorse took its place. "Hey, Mom, I'm sorry." He stood again, crossed the room, and put an arm around her shoulders. "It's just that . . . well, you know." When Sharon melted against him with a sob, Vance let her cry against his chest. He touched her hair gently as one might a child.

After a few seconds, Sharon regained composure and pulled slightly away. She pressed her fingertips to Vance's cheek. "I know you and Eddie had your differences, sweetheart. But can't we just forget that now? He's gone. Please don't make this any harder than it already is."

Doc nodded in his grandson's direction. "Your mother's right. This could turn ugly when word gets out, and it's going to be rough enough without you saying things you shouldn't."

Vance looked sullen. "It's nobody else's business."

"There's going to be talk," Doc insisted in a voice that sounded as if he were explaining to a small child. "You know your mother wasn't married to Eddie, and Eddie was still legally married to Ricki. But he died here . . ." He broke off and left Vance to put two and two together on his own.

With a tiny moan, Sharon dropped into Vance's chair.

Vance's jaw tightened, but Fred couldn't tell whether it was because of Doc's attitude, Sharon's distress, or the reminder of details he'd rather forget.

Fred couldn't help but agree with Doc—at least in part. "I'd say there's a good chance Mrs. Leishman will set up a fuss, and your mother's going to be right in the middle of it. Between that and the gossips—"

Sharon shot back to her feet and held a hand to her breast. "*She* won't do anything, will she?"

Fred tried to look reassuring. "I wouldn't worry too much, but I happened to run into Eddie and his wife last night outside of the school. They were . . . arguing."

Sharon managed to grow even paler. "She was bothering him again? Poor Eddie." Tears kept her from speaking for several more seconds while Fred watched helplessly and decided not to mention the embrace he'd witnessed. He couldn't see what earthly good it would do to bring it up now.

Sharon paced a few steps away and leaned her head against the wall. "I can't do this. I don't want to stay in this town any longer. Not now."

Vance seemed to perk up at the thought. "Good. Let's go to Colorado Springs."

Doc rested one hand on Sharon's shoulder. "You can't run away now. That'd be the worst thing you could do."

"Why? Because people might talk? In case you haven't noticed, they've already been talking, and they'll talk even more now. There's nothing I can do to stop it."

Fred had to admit she had a point. There'd be talk no matter what. But in all his years, he'd never seen a bad situation made better by running from it.

Doc flushed an angry red. "Now listen, Sharon. You've got to realize you're in this position now because of the choices you made."

She stepped away from him. "Oh, Dad— *Please*." Her voice had the weary sound of someone who'd heard it all before.

Doc didn't seem to care. "*I* didn't let Eddie move in here. In fact, I tried to convince you to kick the bum out—"

Sharon's face twisted in a spasm of grief and anger, and Fred didn't know which was greater. But he did know if Doc kept going, he'd upset Sharon even more, and right now didn't seem like the best time to press home that particular point.

Fred tried to steer Doc to a safer topic. "Maybe you should help Sharon get some things together if she's going to your place tonight."

As usual, Doc's mind only seemed to want to follow one track. He shook a finger in Sharon's direction. "Your mother and I will do everything we can to help you, but we can't protect you from the consequences of your actions."

Exercising tact had never been one of Doc's strong points. Fred opened his mouth again, but Sharon beat him to the punch. "Not now, Dad."

"I just want to make sure you understand."

Sharon's eyes flashed with anger. "I *understand* you're going to start telling me how I've screwed up my life again, and I don't want to hear it. I just want a little peace and quiet and a chance to mourn."

Vance made a noise that could have been agreement or disgust. Doc pushed his chin forward and creased his forehead. "Mourn? For heaven's sake, Sharon."

"*Please*," Sharon shouted. Her eyes looked a little wild and her lips quivered. "Just do what you have to do for Eddie, and then leave." She dragged in a calming breath. "I'll talk to you tomorrow."

Doc looked as if she'd hit him. "Aren't you staying with your mother and me tonight?"

"No. I've changed my mind. I'd rather be here."

"I don't think that's a good idea," Doc argued. "You'd better come home with me so we can talk about this. Decide what we're going to say."

"To *say*?" Sharon shouted. "What about the truth?"

Doc obviously didn't like that. His face puckered into a frown. "Now, listen, Sharon. I'll admit this was an unfortunate way for things to turn out—"

"You don't even care that he's dead, do you?"

"Well, of course I do," Doc insisted, but he didn't look particularly heartbroken.

Sharon whirled to face Fred, but she pointed behind her at her father. "Will you please get him out of here?"

Fred only took one step toward Doc, but that was enough to set him off. He reared back, colored deeply, and bellowed, "You stay away from me, Fred. What in the Sam Hill are you doing here anyway?"

Fred didn't bother to answer. He'd been in similar situations with his own family, and he could empathize with Doc's confusion and embarrassment. When emotions started running that close to the surface, nothing made sense.

Apparently satisfied that he had Fred under control, Doc turned back to Sharon. "You aren't being logical."

Sharon didn't answer him, but Fred didn't think logic figured anywhere in her list of priorities.

"Sharon, your relationship with Eddie was wrong from the very beginning—"

"Go away."

"You're acting like a child," Doc insisted. "You never should have taken up with him."

Sharon refused to look at her father.

"All things considered, this is probably a blessing—"

Sharon's face froze and her eyes grew cold. She took a step away. "Get out of here, Dad. I mean it. I'm not going to talk to you about this."

Slowly, Doc seemed to realize that Sharon didn't want to hear what he had to say, but he didn't seem to understand why. Looking betrayed and hurt, he pivoted away and started back to the bedroom. He stopped at the door and sent one last look back at Sharon. "At least call your mother. Explain to her why you've changed your mind."

The instant he disappeared into the bedroom, Sharon's hard-won confidence evaporated and she dissolved into tears again. This time, Fred offered his own shirt front. He'd known her all her life. He'd bounced her on his knee during Sunday services and pushed her higher than her dad thought she should go on the school's swingset. And if now she needed a place to cry, he could provide one.

Knowing he was filling Doc's place, he felt a pang of guilt. But Doc was too interested in making his point to offer Sharon what she needed.

Fred reminded himself that the old fool had been up all night and that he tended to be a bit ornery when he went without sleep. He'd just lost a patient, and that always upset him—even if he hadn't liked the patient. But denying Sharon's right to grieve for Eddie wouldn't draw them closer. And expecting her to share his opinion when she had obviously loved Eddie would only drive her away.

With Enos's voice rumbling at them from the kitchen and Vance's talk show blaring from the television, Fred patted Sharon's shoulder and murmured soothing words of understanding. He told himself that Doc would soon calm down and come to his senses. That Sharon would somehow recognize the concern under her father's anger. And he tried not to worry. Somehow, they'd find a way to put things right.

* * *

Fred reached the intersection with Main Street just as the sunlight faded from the late afternoon sky and the horizon turned the same deep, cold blue as the lake. He hadn't been able to get Eddie's death out of his mind for even a minute since he'd left Sharon's house that morning. He'd spent the afternoon thinking about Doc, worrying about Sharon, and stewing about Vance. He'd finally decided to stop stewing and do something.

Across the street, Enos's truck sat in its usual parking spot in front of the sheriff's office. Its windows were clear of snow, which probably meant it hadn't been sitting there long. Fred hesitated on the corner, wondering whether Enos knew anything more about Eddie's death.

Fred knew he shouldn't disturb Enos; breaking the news to Ricki would have been difficult enough, and Enos probably needed peace and quiet more than anything. But Fred wouldn't rest until he heard how Ricki and Joshua took the news and whether Sharon had calmed down enough to forgive her father.

No matter how many times he reminded himself of Enos's reassurance that Eddie hadn't been murdered, Fred couldn't shake the uneasy feeling that had plagued him all afternoon. So, while pretending to be on his way to Lacey's General Store, Fred would peek in long enough to ask one or two questions and be out of Enos's hair again within five minutes. Even Enos couldn't find fault with that.

Crossing the street, he climbed the boardwalk and stepped inside. The aroma of fresh coffee filled the air, and the coffeemaker gurgled sporadically as it finished brewing. Enos struggled to smile, but he looked as weary as Fred felt. "What are you doing out this time of night?"

Fred crossed to one of the battered old chairs in front of Enos's desk. "It's not even six o'clock. Saw your truck outside on my way to Lacey's, so I thought I'd stop by and see how you're doing." He tugged off his gloves and tucked them into his coat pocket, then glanced at the coffeepot to see how soon coffee would be ready.

Enos followed his gaze and smiled, more easily this time.

"You know, I'm beginning to think Doc's right. You must be able to smell that stuff from a mile away. I guess you want a cup."

"I wouldn't turn one down," Fred admitted.

"Just don't tell Maggie who gave it to you." Enos stood, spent a few seconds figuring out which mugs were clean, and filled two. "I just got back a few minutes ago myself. It's been a long day." He handed a mug to Fred and perched on the corner of his desk, sipping noisily.

Fred sat for a minute, letting the warmth from the cup work into his fingers. "You got everything taken care of, then?"

Enos nodded. "I guess so. I *hope* so."

"Have you heard from Doc?"

"Not since we left Sharon's. Have you?"

Fred shook his head. "No. I sure hope they work things out soon. I hate to see bad feelings in a family."

"Yeah. So do I." The glare of headlights from the street swept across the room and Enos glanced out the window. "Speaking of the devil, I'll bet that's Doc now. Looks like his car."

Fred took two quick sips of coffee while Doc's footsteps echoed on the boardwalk outside. A second later, Doc barged inside. He wiped his feet on the mat, then pulled off his coat and hat. He slapped his hands on his arms, moaned a bit, and blew air out between his lips to show how cold he was. Then, in case Fred and Enos had trouble understanding, he growled and jerked his head toward the door. "It's cold out there."

Enos nodded. "The temperature's probably dropped twenty degrees in the past hour."

Just thinking about it made Fred cold again. "Shut the door—the temperature in here's dropped thirty degrees in the past minute."

Doc slammed the door and started toward the unoccupied chair by Enos's desk. Partway there, he focused on the mug in Fred's hands and scowled. "Coffee, Fred? It had better be decaf."

Fred sipped again. "That's all you allow me to drink, isn't it?"

For some reason, Doc didn't look convinced. He tossed his medical bag to the floor in front of Enos's desk and reached for a mug of his own. "If it's not, don't come running to me when your heart gives out."

This time Fred smiled. "If my heart gives out, I won't go running anywhere."

Enos filled Doc's mug, stretched with a groan, and perched back on the corner of his desk. "I'm worn out. Just don't let there be another crisis tonight."

Doc shook his head. "I'm with you. I was up all night, and then Eddie died before I could even get a nap—" He sounded as if he suspected Eddie of dying on purpose to spite him.

"Have you had a chance to talk with Sharon again?"

Doc laughed scornfully. "I just came from there, but I wouldn't say we'd talked. I called once earlier, but Vance said she was lying down and couldn't come to the phone. This time, she stayed in the bedroom and sent a message out with Velma. If I didn't know better, I'd think she was avoiding me."

Fred glanced up, almost certain Doc was joking, but Doc looked honestly puzzled.

Enos sat in his chair and moved a stack of files out of his way. "Why don't I stop by and check on her later this evening? If there's any trouble, I'll call you."

Doc slanted forward, his eyes dark with concern. "Why? Do you expect trouble?"

"No." Enos smiled gently. "Calm down. I'm just offering to look in on her if it'll set your mind at ease."

This time, Doc looked a little embarrassed at having overreacted. "I guess I'm worried about that wife of his. There's no telling what she'll do, and I'd like Sharon home where she belongs if anything does happen."

"Well, you can stop worrying about Ricki," Enos said. "I've already talked to her, and she's all right."

"How'd she take it?" Fred tried not to look overly

interested so Enos wouldn't read more into the question than Fred intended.

Enos shrugged. "She was upset, of course, but I think she took the news fairly well—all things considered. To tell you the truth, I think she's still numb from Eddie walking out on her the way he did. I'm not sure she's over that yet."

Doc made a noise in his throat, but he didn't speak.

"What about their boy?" Fred asked. "Did you see him?"

"Joshua?" Enos nodded. "Yep, he was home. But he's hard to read. At that age . . ." He shrugged as if sixteen-year-old boys defied explanation, then cocked an eyebrow at Fred. "Why?"

"He's a friend of Benjamin's. I'm worried about him."

"He was pretty shook up," Enos admitted. "We had a couple of rough minutes, but they both calmed down pretty quick."

Doc furrowed his brow and looked puzzled. "So, the wife was really all right? She didn't fly off the handle because Eddie died at Sharon's?"

"Well, she wasn't real happy about it," Enos admitted. "But she didn't threaten to hunt Sharon down, if that's what you're worried about."

It must have been. Relief washed over Doc's face as he shifted position. "Well, good. I don't mind telling you, that's a load off my mind."

Enos settled back in his chair again. "By the way, I told the coroner's office we'd send Eddie's insulin supplies to the lab so they can determine whether there was something wrong with the batch or just how on earth he managed to give himself an overdose."

Doc looked up quickly. "What do you mean, an over-dose?"

"That's what you said at Sharon's," Enos reminded him. "You listed the cause of death as an insulin overdose."

"I said that's what it *looked* like, but it couldn't possibly be."

Fred lowered his mug to the desk. "You really don't think so?"

Doc shook his head. "No, I don't."

"Why not?"

"Because there's absolutely no way it could have been," Doc insisted. "Absolutely none."

Enos didn't look concerned. "Fine. They're doing an autopsy—if it wasn't an overdose, they'll let us know. In the meantime, they want all of Eddie's insulin sent to the lab."

"Waste of time," Doc predicted.

Enos knit his brows together. "Why do you say that?"

Doc pushed his coffee away. "Eddie couldn't have died from an insulin overdose because *I* gave Eddie his last injection before I left the house this morning. If insulin killed him, then *I'm* the one who gave it to him."

four

Fred glanced from Enos to Doc and back again, and wondered whether anyone else felt the same sense of foreboding.

Enos looked worried. His thoughts must have been running along the same line as Fred's. "Maybe Eddie woke up after you left and injected himself—"

Doc sighed heavily. "I *told* you I gave Eddie a glucagon injection at about six this morning. That stuff is a hormone that triggers a reaction in the liver to give the patient's body what it needs to stay alive. But it's pretty drastic, and it wipes the patient out for hours. I expected him to sleep at least until noon—maybe longer. I planned to have him eat a little and *then* have an insulin injection."

"Are you sure about this?" Enos asked.

Doc blinked rapidly, as if he had to struggle to understand. "Am I sure I didn't give him an overdose?"

"Are you sure you gave him his last injection?" Enos said patiently.

"You bet I am. Besides, even if Eddie did make a mistake, his usual dose wouldn't have been enough to kill him—and certainly not as quickly as he died. Besides, there weren't any needles or syringes in the garbage. I looked."

"No chance you accidentally gave him insulin instead of the other stuff?" Enos asked.

"Instead of the glucagon? No chance." Doc jerked his medical bag back up onto his lap and fished out a narrow syringe. "Take a look at this. This is what you'd use to give an insulin injection. Now, look at this . . ." He delved back into the bag and pulled out a small white box. He broke the seal and pulled out a much wider syringe than the first one. Holding the tube in front of Fred's face, he demanded, "See the difference? This one could hold at least twenty times as much."

Fred nodded.

Looking mollified, Doc faced Enos. "Do you think you could tell the difference?"

Enos had the good grace to look sheepish. "Well, yes."

"And this is the first time you've ever seen them. Let me assure you, *I'd* never make that kind of mistake."

"Then what are you saying?" Fred mused aloud. "That Eddie was murdered?"

Enos shook his head, slowly at first, then more quickly. "That's not what he's saying, so don't start."

"Then what *are* you saying, Doc?"

"Nothing," Enos insisted. "Don't start."

"I'm not starting anything," Fred said. "I'm asking a simple question."

Enos glared at him. "There's no evidence that Eddie Leishman was murdered."

"Well, he wasn't killed by a sloppy doctor, either," Doc insisted.

"Then where does that leave us?" Fred asked.

Enos's face darkened. "It doesn't leave *us* anywhere. No matter what happened over there, you're not involved. And if Doc didn't make a mistake—"

"And Doc *didn't*," Doc chimed in.

"—then Eddie probably gave himself the injection that killed him." Enos nodded stiffly to underscore his point.

But it didn't persuade Doc. "Impossible."

Enos's nostrils flared slightly. "What do you mean, impossible?"

Doc ticked reasons off on his fingers. "Eddie must have died shortly after Sharon and I left this morning. He obviously didn't get out of bed all morning, because he was in exactly the same position as when I left him. In fact, after that reaction he had last night, it wouldn't have been unusual for him to sleep round the clock. The magazine Sharon left for him to read if he woke up was still on the pillow beside him. Nothing had been disturbed, and the house was still locked up tight when Sharon came back and found him."

"Maybe he put everything back the way it was," Enos argued, unwrapping a piece of gum and folding it into his mouth.

Doc didn't answer. He didn't have to. The look on his face said it all.

Fred leaned back in his chair and pondered, but the more he thought, the worse the situation looked. Eddie, dead, inside Sharon's locked house, with only Vance for company. "I suppose the autopsy results will tell us whether there's anything to worry about," he said slowly. "In the meantime, Doc, maybe you ought to be careful about saying you gave Eddie his last injection."

Doc snorted his response. "What is this? You think I did something wrong?"

Fred shook his head. "I just think you should be careful. I know how easy it is for things to get turned around in a situation like this."

Enos nodded reluctantly. "Fred's right. There's probably nothing to worry about. Most likely, Fred's imagination is running away with him, but you should be careful about saying anything that will feed gossip."

Doc put on his most stubborn expression. "Well, for heaven's sake. You're both paranoid."

Fred leaned forward a little. "What if the autopsy shows that Eddie died of an insulin overdose? Who will people think gave it to him?"

Doc murmured something, then flicked an uneasy glance in Fred's direction. "You really believe people will think *I* killed him?"

"I think it's a good possibility," Fred said.

"It's probably not going to be an issue," Enos said.

"I *didn't* kill him," Doc insisted.

"I know that," Fred said. "But the other possibilities aren't much better. Even if people believe you're innocent, you know who they'll accuse next."

Doc's face paled. "Sharon?"

"Or Vance."

Enos creaked back in his chair and rubbed his face with an open palm. "I don't like this. Look, we're getting riled up over nothing. Let's not jump to conclusions—"

"All I want," Fred insisted, "is for Doc to keep his mouth shut about that last insulin injection until we learn the official cause of death. If it wasn't insulin, there's nothing to worry about. But if it was—" He broke off with an elaborate shrug.

Doc looked as if he might be sick. He slumped down in his chair and rubbed his forehead with a shaky hand. "This is unbelievable."

Fred could certainly understand his reaction. He'd felt that way himself when Enos arrested Douglas for murder a few months ago. Even proving Douglas innocent hadn't completely erased the horrible memory. He put a hand on Doc's shoulder and tried to look reassuring. "Look, maybe it'll be all right. Maybe everything will work out. Just be careful what you say."

Enos nodded, but he looked tired. "Everything will work out fine. Let's not go overboard."

"I hope you're right," Fred said. "But I'm having a hard time believing a man like Eddie Leishman would just keel over dead when I saw him last night looking healthier than any of us in this room."

Enos let out a heavy sigh. "The man *was* a diabetic."

"The man was a scumbag," Doc said.

"The man was alive twenty-four hours ago and arguing with his wife in front of the high school."

The room fell silent. Enos flicked a glance at Doc, then turned back to stare at Fred. "That doesn't mean anything."

"I didn't say she murdered him," Fred pointed out. "But he didn't have the kinds of symptoms that convince me he died as a result of his diabetes."

Enos held out both hands in a gesture of helpless confusion. "What's this? You're a doctor now?"

"The least you could do is ask Doc."

Doc opened his mouth as if he intended to say something, but Enos didn't want to listen. "I'm not doing anything but waiting for the autopsy report to come back. And I'm keeping *my* imagination under control."

"All I want to know is—" Fred began.

"It's useless to speculate until we know something," Enos argued. He checked his watch and flipped off the light on his desk. "I'm tired and hungry. It's been a long day for all of us. I'm heading home. Doc, go get some rest. You need it. You, too, Fred."

Fred didn't want to rest. He wanted to get to the bottom of this. But it wouldn't do him any good to argue—he'd seen Enos in this mood before. Gathering his things, he followed Enos and Doc outside into the cold. But instinct left him with an uneasy feeling about Eddie Leishman's death, and Fred was learning to trust his instincts—no matter what Enos said.

No doubt about it, Eddie Leishman was going to cause as much trouble dead as he had alive.

Fred dug through the containers in his refrigerator, looking for something to eat. He found a dry chicken breast with no skin, half a container of wilting salad, and a bowl of cardboard-tasting rice—nothing that looked even slightly appetizing.

Sighing in frustration, he straightened and scowled at the leftovers. Some of Phoebe's homemade clam chowder would have tasted just right, but he'd never bothered learning how to make it himself, and Margaret wouldn't make it for him anymore—too much cholesterol.

Just as he started rooting through containers again, the sound of a car in the driveway pulled him upright. A door closed and rapid footsteps clicked toward the back door. Margaret. He'd been expecting her. She'd have heard about Eddie by now, and she'd be worried about Fred getting involved. As a matter of fact, he was a little surprised that she hadn't arrived before now.

She smiled when she saw him standing there, hung her coat on a hook beside his, and tugged the hem of her sweatshirt over her hips. She stood a head taller than Phoebe had and she'd grown into a striking woman. With her dark hair and usually serene face, she often made Fred think of Olivia de Havilland—until she got angry. Surprisingly, she didn't look angry now.

Crossing the room, she brushed a kiss onto his cheek. "What are you doing, Dad? Haven't you had dinner yet?"

"Not yet. I'm trying to figure out what sounds good."

Margaret worked her way between him and the refrigerator, stuck her nose inside and began poking around among the containers. "How about that vegetarian casserole I made the other night?"

Fred stepped back to give her room, but he had a hard time suppressing a groan at the thought of her latest concoction. "Actually, I was thinking about bread and milk."

She glanced up, curled her nose to show what she thought of that idea, and went on digging. "You need something more substantial than that. Well, where on earth—? Did you eat it already?"

"Eat what?"

"The vegetarian casserole."

"Probably."

She looked at him again, this time with a scowl. "No, you didn't. I'll bet you threw it out." She straightened and leaned an arm on the door. "I don't know why you have to be so closed-minded. No matter what you think, it was good."

"I'm sure it was."

"Next time, I wish you'd try what I make before you throw it out."

Fred didn't say a word. He didn't like making promises he might not keep.

She rolled her eyes at him and closed the refrigerator. "I suppose you've already heard about Eddie Leishman."

"As a matter of fact, I have," Fred admitted, and braced himself for the assault.

"Yes, of course you have." She pulled out a chair and sat at the table. "So, what do you think?"

The question surprised him. Scratching his chin, he lowered himself into a seat beside hers. "What do I think about Eddie?"

She nodded.

He took his time answering. He'd expected her to confront him, to accuse him of getting involved where he had no business, and to demand that he leave well enough alone. Instead, she was approaching the argument from a direction that left him off balance. "I don't know what to think."

"I've been thinking about Sharon ever since I heard. Wishing I could do something to help." She leaned her chin on a fist and stared out over the kitchen. "This is going to tear her apart, and her family isn't going to be any help. You know how they felt about him."

Fred certainly did. "Doc's not having an easy time."

Margaret ticked her tongue against the roof of her mouth. "Doc hasn't had an easy time since Sharon started seeing Eddie."

"No, he hasn't." Fred traced the rim of an empty coffee cup with his finger. "It's been hard for him to keep his mouth shut and watch her make a mistake."

"He hasn't kept his mouth shut for a minute." She glared at Fred as if he were somehow responsible. "Have you talked to him today?"

"I saw him for a minute."

"And—?"

"And what?"

"Does he understand how Sharon feels? Does he even *care*? Is he offering her any support at all, or is he just trying to get her to admit he was right all along?" Her voice sounded bitter.

"Well, I don't—"

"That's what I figured." She shot to her feet and paced to the window. "Poor Sharon. Velma hated Eddie. Doc hated him. Even Vance hated him. She's got nobody to turn to, Dad."

"Maybe you should call her."

"I've tried. No answer."

"Really? I thought Velma was staying with her tonight. Maybe she's gone over to stay with her folks, after all."

She looked back over her shoulder at him. "I'm not sure whether that's good or bad."

Fred studied her, surprised by her reaction, more surprised that she still hadn't accused him of anything. "Is something bothering you, sweetheart?"

"Of course something's bothering me. Didn't you hear a word I just said?"

"Something else?"

She shook her head and returned to the table. "I'm fine. Really. Just worried about Sharon." She pulled in a breath and released it slowly. "So, do you know what happened? Did Eddie give himself an overdose?"

"Nobody knows. They've sent the body in for an autopsy."

"An autopsy? Why? Enos doesn't think there's anything suspicious about this, does he?"

"I don't think it's that," Fred said carefully. "I think it's a pretty routine step. After all, Eddie was a young man who died unexpectedly."

Margaret looked slightly mollified. "Have you talked to Enos?"

"For a minute."

"And you didn't discuss it?"

"For a minute."

"But you don't know what he's thinking." She sounded skeptical.

"No."

She narrowed her eyes. "Why do I get the feeling you're not telling me the truth?"

"I don't have any idea." He pushed to his feet and busied himself with the refrigerator again. "Maybe you ought to try to reach Sharon again in the morning. In the meantime, don't worry about it too much. There's only so much you can do."

Margaret nodded slowly, but she didn't say anything.

Strange. Fred studied her face. She looked drawn. Tired. Worried. "I guess Webb's heard about Eddie—"

Her gaze shifted away the way it always did when she wanted to avoid discussing something. "Yes."

"What did he have to say about it?"

"Not much."

Fred didn't believe that for a second, but at least he thought he understood her mood better. Webb must have said something that disturbed her; she'd come to Fred to clear her mind, not to attack him.

He worked up a warm smile and closed the refrigerator again. He patted her shoulder and tried to change the subject to one more comforting to both of them. "I guess you didn't bring the kids with you."

She followed his lead as if they were dancing. "No. Deborah has homework and Ben . . . who knows what he's up to?"

"Isn't he home?"

"Home? *Ben*? No. He had practice again this afternoon."

Fred checked the wall clock. "It's after seven. Shouldn't he be home by this time?"

She pushed her fingers through her hair and shook her head at the table. "Last thing I heard, he was going to ride home with Joshua Leishman. When I heard about Eddie, I didn't think Josh would be giving anybody a ride anywhere, so I drove over to the school to bring Ben home." She reached for Fred's stack of mail almost absently, sorted through the envelopes, then handed the stack to Fred. "They were gone when I got there, and Carl said they'd all left together."

"He can't still be with Joshua. Enos said he talked to Joshua at home this afternoon."

"He's somewhere with Nate and Ty. I've already called their mothers, and none of them have come home yet. I'll be honest with you, Dad. I don't know what's gotten into Ben lately."

Fred wanted nothing more than to set her mind at ease, but he skirted the subject with a time-honored response. "He's at the age where he thinks nothing's more important than friends."

"He's mad at me all the time. Last week it was over shoveling snow. This week—" She broke off with a shrug and a thin laugh. "Who knows?"

"What about Sarah?" Fred asked. "Has she called lately?"

Margaret nodded and her expression lightened. "She called the other night. She'll be home next week for the holidays. This week, she's studying for finals."

"That must be keeping her busy."

"She's nervous," Margaret admitted. "But she'll do fine. You know how bright she is."

"She's still getting along with her roommates?" Fred pulled two slices of bread from a loaf and began tearing pieces into a glass.

"Of course. You know Sarah. The kids—with the notable exception of Benjamin—are fine. That's not what's bothering me."

Fred poured milk over the bread and added a dollop of honey. "Benjamin will be fine, too. He's just kicking up his heels."

"He's sixteen, not twenty-one. It's a school night, and he's probably got homework. And his dad—" She broke off and looked away.

Fred tried to keep his face expressionless and to concentrate on his dinner. "Webb's upset with him again?"

Margaret nodded and slid down in her seat a little, and Fred knew he'd touched a nerve. "Benjamin's been acting so different," she said. "*I* can't even reach him anymore, and Webb's absolutely convinced he's getting into trouble."

"What sort of trouble?"

She threw her arms up in a gesture of futility. "I don't know. It's just that they argue all the time. About money. About school. About a car. About Benjamin's music. I can't stand listening to the way Webb talks to Benjamin, but I don't like the way Benjamin talks to Webb, either."

Fred waited for several seconds to respond. He couldn't say any of the things that came immediately to mind, not without breaking a promise or overstepping his bounds. Margaret already knew how he felt about Webb, he didn't need to remind her. It wouldn't help. "Benjamin *is* sixteen," he reminded her gently.

But obviously not gently enough. She lurched to her feet and paced to the window. "Yes, I know. And Webb's never been good with teenagers. You remember what a hard time he and Sarah had when she started high school."

Fred remembered. Unfortunately. He took a mouthful of bread and milk and nodded without speaking.

Margaret paced back to the table. "Has Benjamin talked to you? Did he say anything when you drove him home the other night? Do you have *any* idea what's wrong with him?"

Fred scooped up another mouthful to give himself a second to decide what to say. He didn't want to actually *lie*.

Thankfully, Margaret must not have expected an answer. She dropped back onto her chair and buried her face in her hands for a moment. When she looked at him again, her eyes glittered with unshed tears. "You know what, Dad? I feel as if my family's falling apart, and I don't know what I'm doing wrong."

"You're not doing anything wrong."

"I always thought if Webb and I just stayed together, we wouldn't have this kind of problem with our kids. But now, Ben's talking to Webb the way Sharon says Vance used to talk to Eddie, and I'm worried."

If that were true, she ought to be concerned. Fred had seen firsthand how Vance felt about Eddie. "You think Benjamin resents Webb?"

A bitter laugh exploded from her. "Resents? At the very least."

"Why?"

"I don't know," she said, but Fred knew she did. He could see it in her eyes. But he'd gotten too close to the truth for comfort, and he could see her closing down again, shutting everything away from the light. After a few seconds, she smiled and kissed his cheek again. "You're tired. I'm keeping you up."

"I'm fine. I'm not even sleepy. We need to resolve this."

She retrieved her coat and started working her fingers into her gloves. "We can't. It's something Webb and Ben and I have to work out. I'd better get home, anyway. Webb will be wondering where I am." She crossed to the door, then looked back at him. "You're still coming for Webb's birthday dinner on Thursday, aren't you?"

Fred nodded and tried to look happy about it. "Of course."

Margaret smiled with relief. "Good. Get some sleep, Dad. I'll talk to you tomorrow." She pulled open the door and turned back once more before she stepped through. "I love you."

"I love you, too. More than you'll ever know."

She closed the door softly behind her, and Fred stayed at the table, listening to her footsteps as she retraced her route to the car and drove away. Only then did he turn out the lights and walk down the hall to his bedroom. He undressed slowly and climbed into bed, pulling the quilts up under his chin. And he lay there, staring at the ceiling and trying to sleep.

After a long time, he turned on a light and tried reading to clear his mind. But when he'd gone over the same page three times and still couldn't make sense of the words, he gave up and flipped off the light again.

Worry danced through his mind, and he lay there and watched the minutes tick by on his clock, listening to the rising wind, with nothing but the night between him and his thoughts.

five

Fred pulled the collar of his coat tighter around his neck as he rounded the corner from Lake Front onto Main Street. A brisk wind had blown into the valley overnight, and now it gusted from the mouth of the canyon and picked up bits of powdery snow to fling against buildings, windows, and Fred's exposed face.

Today, even his warmest clothes did little to keep the cold from his fingers or the ache of arthritis from his knees. By the light of day, some of his worries seemed to shrink, and he'd started to think maybe he had let his imagination run away with him. A few bad feelings between Vance Bollinger and Eddie Leishman didn't necessarily set up a scenario for murder, and no matter how much Doc disliked the man, that alone didn't guarantee a problem. So Fred had decided to stop borrowing trouble.

Hurrying past Video Ventures, the latest addition to Cutler's business district, he waved to Hettie Jeppson as she rushed down the boardwalk across the street toward the *Cutler Crier's* office. When another nasty blast of cold air whipped around him, he ducked his head and increased his pace still more.

"Fred?" Doc's voice managed to cut through the layers around Fred's ears and pull him up short.

He turned around, checking his watch as he did. "What in blazes are you doing out this time of morning? Don't you have appointments?"

"I did, but my first appointment canceled so I thought I'd treat myself to breakfast out." Doc closed the distance between them and clapped one hand on Fred's shoulder. "Figured I might join you."

Wonderful. Just what Fred wanted. Doc would insist that Fred eat something healthy. He'd ruin breakfast with lectures about cholesterol and caffeine. He'd complain about Eddie and moan about Sharon. Fred could feel his appetite start to fade. "Won't Velma mind?"

"She's still at Sharon's, so I'm on my own."

"What did she do, spend the night?"

Doc nodded and looked put out. "*She's* welcome there, but I'm not."

"You still haven't talked to Sharon, then?"

"I tried again last night. She won't talk to me."

Fred started toward the Bluebird again, more slowly this time. "She's going to take Eddie's death hard, Doc. Can't get around that. No matter how you felt about him, she loved him."

Doc snorted. "Now you sound like Velma. Sharon wasn't in love with him. She just needed somebody around to get her over the rough spots after Alex left."

Debating the issue when Doc had obviously made up his mind would be a waste of time. Fred drew in a deep breath and tried to think of something else to talk about. Behind him, a four-wheel drive vehicle whined across the intersection and somebody's snowshovel scraped in steady rhythm on a sidewalk.

They passed a couple of buildings in silence before he spoke again. "Have you talked to Enos today?"

Doc nodded. "Just came from there."

"How's he doing?"

Doc looked surprised by the question. "He's fine. Why?"

With everything else going on yesterday, Doc must not have noticed that Enos seemed troubled, and Fred decided not to bring it up now. He tried for an easy smile. "Making small talk, I guess."

Doc skirted an icy patch in front of the Kwik Kleen, then slowed to study the window display at the Good Sport. He turned to Fred as if he intended to speak, then snapped his mouth shut and glared at something on the boardwalk ahead.

Fred followed his gaze. Ricki Leishman stood on the boardwalk a few feet away with Tom Sandusky, a friend of Eddie's and fellow musician known to most folks as "Bear." He stood an inch or two shorter than Fred, a distinctly unbearish man with a round face framed by pale blond hair. He wore a pair of baggy sweatpants slung low on his hips and a light flannel jacket over a thin white T-shirt.

Fred could think of at least a dozen people he'd rather run into in Doc's company than Eddie Leishman's widow, but before he could suggest turning at the corner, Ricki noticed them. She took a step away from Bear and folded her arms on her chest. Wrapped in layers of fur—coat, hat, and boots—she looked fragile, and Fred's heart went out to her. She managed a thin smile at Fred, but she didn't look directly at Doc.

Fred tried to think of an appropriate way to offer condolences that wouldn't offend Ricki or start Doc complaining again once they were alone. But everything he could think of sounded inappropriate. He settled for, "I'm sorry about your husband, Mrs. Leishman."

She stared at him, wide-eyed, as if the words had to process through the haze of her grief. "Thank you."

"Are you all right? Is there anything you need?" Standard questions, under the circumstances.

"No. I'm fine." Again that thin smile flashed across her face, only to disappear immediately.

Bear's face reddened. He sent both Fred and Doc an unreadable look. "She's *not* all right, she's in shock. Hell, *I'm* in shock. It blows me away to think of Eddie gone."

Fred nodded as if he'd been blown away by the news himself. Doc remained stubbornly mute, but Fred figured silence might be preferable to anything Doc might have to say.

Bear studied Doc for several seconds. "So, you're the one who was with Eddie?"

"I treated him for an insulin reaction the night before, but I wasn't there when he died."

Bear raised his eyebrows at Ricki, and Fred couldn't fight the uneasy suspicion they'd been discussing Doc.

Whatever point Bear hoped to make with Ricki must have escaped her. She turned her dark eyes on Doc, acknowledging him for the first time. Fred could only see the side of her face, but he didn't think she looked particularly friendly. "Since I've run into you, Dr. Huggins, I wonder if you'd deliver a message to your daughter for me."

The look on his face said there were at least a hundred things he'd rather do, but he tried not to show it. "Of course."

"Please tell her I'd like my husband's things. I'll come by this afternoon to get them. I'd like her to have everything ready so I don't have to wait. I'm sure you understand, I don't want to be in her house any longer than I have to."

"I'll tell her," Doc said, but Fred could tell he had to work to keep his voice even.

Bear's expression went through a couple of changes, as if he had to argue something with himself. "Why don't I go, Rick?" he said at last. "You don't need to put yourself through that. This whole thing'll be hard enough without having to see Sharon."

Ricki touched his arm gently and shook her head. "I'll be fine. Besides, there are one or two things I'd like to say to her. Alone."

Fred didn't like the sound of that, and he didn't like setting Sharon up for a confrontation. "Maybe it would be best to wait a few days," he suggested. "Until everybody's calmed down a little."

"Calmed down?" Ricki stared at him as if he'd spoken a foreign language, but something in her expression hardened. "That slut stole my husband, and now he's dead. I don't intend to calm down."

"Eddie's death had nothing to do with Sharon," Doc said. "He had an insulin reaction in the middle of the night, and she called me. I gave him a glucagon injection—which is what anybody with half a brain would have done—and he gave every appearance of a full recovery before I left."

Ricki didn't look impressed. "Obviously, you were wrong."

Doc's mouth tightened into a thin line, but he managed to keep his voice level. "Sharon went home that morning to wake him and get him eating again. Eddie was dead before she got there. I'm sure you've been through the drill yourself. He died, Mrs. Leishman, because of the kind of life he led, not because of anything my daughter did."

"It isn't your daughter I'm worried about. Even *I* know she thought she loved him. But you hated him. Everybody in town knows that. I want to know what *you* did."

Doc took a step backward as if he'd been punched.

All Fred's hard-won optimism evaporated. He put a hand on Doc's arm. "If you're thinking there was something odd about the way Eddie died, I can tell you—"

Ricki's wide mouth twisted into an ugly frown. "You? Please, Mr. Vickery, spare me. Of course you'll assure me your friend did nothing wrong—just like the sheriff did. You'll stick together, a bunch of good old boys protecting each other." Tears filled her eyes and she turned to Bear for solace.

Looking decidedly ill at ease, Bear threw an arm around her shoulder and glowered over the top of her head at Doc and Fred.

Doc glowered back, seemingly untouched by Ricki's distress. "Everything humanly possible was done for your husband. You have no reason to think otherwise."

She tilted her face out of Bear's flannel jacket into the frigid air again. "Don't I?"

"When the results of the autopsy come back, you'll see." Doc's words came out clipped and angry, and his face looked several shades too red for comfort.

Blinking away her tears, Ricki turned the rest of her face away from Bear's chest. "I suppose it *will* tell us what happened, won't it?"

"That's what we're expecting it to do," Doc said stiffly.

Bear glanced at the top of Ricki's head. "If there *was* anything suspicious about Eddie's death, we'll know then. How long do we have to wait?"

Doc shrugged. "A few days. A week. It depends on how many tests they have to run to determine what happened."

Ricki made a visible effort to pull herself together. "I don't want to wait that long."

Though he'd seemed initially reluctant to comfort her, now Bear seemed equally reluctant to relinquish his hold. "Then we'll find a way to speed things up."

Doc shook his head. "Don't push. Let Lydel take his time to do the job right."

"Even if there is some way to speed things up, Doc isn't going to tell me about it," Ricki said, and turned to leave.

Doc's slim hold on his temper seemed to slip. "Don't be ridiculous."

Ricki drew back and stared. "*Ridiculous?* I'll tell you what's ridiculous, Dr. Huggins. And that's you and Sharon trying to cover up what happened to my husband."

Fred hadn't expected her to be happy about Eddie's death but he hadn't anticipated this. "We're all trying to find out the truth," he said in his most soothing voice.

Bear made a face. "Sure you are."

Doc's expression grew so cold, his face might have been carved in ice. "Mrs. Leishman—"

She held up a hand and took a quick step away almost as if she thought Doc might hit her. "No. I don't want to hear any excuses or explanations."

"You're not thinking clearly," Fred began, then stopped when he realized how offensive that sounded.

She glared at both of them in turn. "I'm warning you not to try a cover-up just because Dr. Huggins and his daughter are involved, because if you do, I'll make sure everyone knows the truth about what happened from the minute Sharon got her hooks into Eddie until the minute he died." Ricki pivoted away and managed to drag a surprised Bear after her.

A muscle in Doc's cheek jumped, and Fred could see how much it cost to keep from going after her. "It was a sad day when people like that started moving into Cutler."

The town was changing, Fred wouldn't debate that. And he decided not to point out how few women would enjoy their husband dying in another woman's bed. Instead, he dropped a hand to Doc's shoulder and smiled. "Once the autopsy comes in, she'll calm down. You'll see. It'll clear everything up."

Doc didn't look convinced. "That woman worries me."

"She's upset," Fred said with a shiver. They'd been outside too long.

"She's going to make trouble for Sharon. Mark my words."

"She may try," Fred agreed, and led Doc a few steps toward the Bluebird.

Doc followed reluctantly. His shoulders slumped and he looked as if he'd aged ten years in the past ten minutes. "Sharon should never have gotten involved with that animal. That's the only word for him—an animal."

"Well, it's too late to change that now." Fred urged him forward again. "Come on. Let's forget it. Breakfast's on me."

Doc shook his head. "I don't have much of an appetite left."

"Coffee, then. You look at least as cold as I am."

Doc made a face, but a gust of wind whipped around them and helped him make up his mind. "I guess coffee sounds good."

"It'll be the best thing for you," Fred promised. "Once you're inside the Bluebird, surrounded by friends, you'll feel better."

Doc still didn't look convinced, but he allowed Fred to lead him over the remaining distance quickly. By the time they reached the Bluebird, Doc seemed almost as eager as Fred to get out of the cold.

Inside, the aromas of fresh coffee and a hearty breakfast lifted Fred's spirits a little. Every stool at the counter had someone on it. Every head in the place looked up as he and Doc entered. Even the jukebox came to life with Elvis singing "Moody Blue" as if he'd been waiting for them to arrive.

Fred waved a greeting to the room in general, and everyone returned his hello in some way. Doc did his best to look as if he had nothing on his mind, but he didn't convince anyone. George Newman chewed solemnly and watched

Doc pass into the dining area. Bill Lacey pretended a sudden interest in a magazine on the counter. Alan Lombard stirred extra sugar into his coffee and tried to pretend he hadn't seen them arrive.

Fred trailed Doc to the table beneath the "Love Me Tender" poster and turned to sit, only to find himself face-to-face with George. George worked his suspenders and rocked back on his heels. "Mornin', Doc. Fred."

"Morning, George." Fred dropped onto his chair and flipped over his coffee cup. "Cold out today, isn't it? It must have put down twelve inches of snow yesterday."

George ignored the weather report and claimed the chair beside Fred's. He rested an arm on the table and leaned toward Doc as if he had a secret to share. "Heard about the excitement over to your daughter's place."

Doc scowled. "I don't think someone's untimely death qualifies as *excitement*."

"Bill was tellin' me about it this morning." George nodded toward Bill Lacey's innocently averted back, completely oblivious to Doc's foul mood. "Terrible thing, that's what we were saying. And we were wondering what, exactly, happened."

"We don't know what, exactly, happened," Fred said.

Doc leaned back in his seat while Lizzie poured his coffee. "We're waiting for the autopsy, George. That's all I can tell you. Now, if you don't mind, I'd rather not discuss it."

Fred ordered his favorite breakfast—eggs over easy, white toast with jam, bacon, and hash browns. He waited for Doc to argue, but to Fred's surprise, Doc did nothing more than shake his head when Lizzie asked for his order. Nothing. No lectures on cholesterol. No dire warnings. Nothing. He must have been feeling worse than Fred thought.

The instant Lizzie moved away again, George took up where he'd left off. "Well, I guess that's good. The autopsy, I mean. It'll be the best way to stop the talk—"

Doc lifted an eyebrow. "What talk?" He could have drilled a hole through metal with his voice.

George paused, looked at Fred for support, then went on anyway, deliberately ignoring the warning Fred tried to send with his eyes. "Well, there's bound to be talk. After everything Eddie put you and your family through." He nodded at Doc for a second or two, then leaned a little closer. "'Course it's too late now, and this is just between you and me and the fence post," he sent a nod in Fred's direction, "but it might have been better if you'd let somebody else take care of him. Why only last week, my boy David—you remember David, don't you? The attorney? He was telling me how careful he has to be—"

Fred glanced over at Doc and prayed he'd hold onto his temper a few minutes longer. "How is David?" he asked. "We don't see much of him these days."

George smiled slowly. He never tired of talking about his boring son and his son's dubious contributions to society. "He's fine. Doing well."

"An attorney you said?" Fred looked innocent and interested, though he already knew far more about David Newman than he wanted to know.

"And a darned good one, too." George leaned back in his chair and beamed with pride. "See, that's my point. According to David, you have to avoid even the *appearance* of evil. Not that David would do anything evil, it's a figure of speech is all—"

"He lives in Boulder now, doesn't he?" Fred asked.

"Aurora," George said without taking his eyes off Doc's face. "It's not that any of your friends will believe the rumors, Doc. But it's probably best not to put yourself in a position like that. The thing is, you've got to look at everything you do backwards, that's what David tells me. If somebody really hated you, how could they use it against you—see what I mean?"

Doc lifted his cup and met George's gaze squarely. "What's your point, George?"

George leaned back and managed, somehow, to look surprised at Doc's tone and the expression on his face. "My *point* is, some people are saying you wasn't as careful as you should have been."

"You can tell *some damned people* I did everything by the book. One hundred percent." Doc slammed down his cup and sent coffee sloshing over the sides. "And I'll stand by my actions any day of the week. Now, you can spare me your lecture on ethics, George. I don't need it."

"Well, excuse me. See what a body gets for trying to help?" George spoke to the room in general, but only a few people acted as if they'd heard him.

"I can't see why this is anybody's business." Doc raised his voice and let the cold expression in his eyes say the rest.

George lurched to his feet and glared down at them. "You know, that's your trouble, Doc. Your temper. That's exactly why people are talking in the first place." He pulled back his shoulders and started away, then turned around to send Doc one last word of warning. "Well, I hope for your sake, you're right. I hope everything was on the up-and-up between you and Eddie."

At that moment, Elvis finished his song on the jukebox, and an unnatural quiet fell over the small crowd. At a corner table near the restrooms, Sterling Jeppson dunked a doughnut and pretended to be engrossed in a copy of the *Cutler Crier*, even though he'd written every boring word himself. Bill Lacey looked over his shoulder. Alan Lombard added another spoonful of sugar to his cup. But Wayne Openshaw and Geneva Hart sat together at a nearby table and stared, making no attempt to hide their interest.

Lizzie slid Fred's plate in front of him, but Doc didn't seem to notice; he was too busy glaring around the room as if daring someone to make the next comment. Luckily, nobody said a word.

George beat an injured retreat back to the counter, and Wayne finally, slowly, turned his attention back to Geneva. Sterling slopped coffee and doughnut crumbs along his bow tie and down the front of his shirt, and somebody popped a quarter into the jukebox so Elvis would erase the silence.

Fred wolfed down a slice of bacon and pushed the plate to an inconspicuous place on the table. He spread grape jelly on one piece of toast. Doc still didn't notice.

Fred waited through two songs on the jukebox for Doc to

calm down and lecture him on his meal, but when the third song began and Doc still hadn't spoken, Fred began to worry. Sitting here at the Bluebird and glaring at everyone in town wouldn't do Doc a bit of good. Doc needed to hold his head up and meet every eye squarely—without looking as if he'd like to blacken the eye when he did.

Hoping to ease the tension by changing the subject, Fred nudged Doc's knee with his own and rolled his eyes at Wayne and Geneva. "Look at those two over there. I didn't know they were seeing each other."

Doc didn't even look. "Wayne and Geneva? Neither did I."

"I'd have never pictured them together, would you?"

Doc shook his head. "Surprises me."

"Do you think they're serious?"

Doc lifted his eyes to meet Fred's. He looked more than a little perturbed. "What in the hell do you think you're doing?"

"I'm trying to have a conversation."

"I don't want to have a conversation."

"I'm trying to help."

Doc's frown deepened. "I don't need help."

"Well, then, I'm curious. Wayne and Geneva are nice kids, and they make a nice-looking couple. How old do you think they are now?"

Doc sighed in resignation. "I know she's twenty-four. I don't know about him. Maybe a year or two older." He tried valiantly not to look, but curiosity eventually got the better of him and made him glance over his shoulder. "I hope for her sake they *are* serious."

Fred raised an eyebrow. "Why?"

Doc didn't say a word, but he glanced at his shirtfront the way he always did when he spoke about women and pregnancy.

Fred leaned a little closer and dropped his voice. "She's pregnant?"

Doc's frown deepened. "I didn't say that."

He didn't have to. Fred looked at the youngsters again. But Doc had obviously reached the end of his rope. He raised his voice a notch. "Can we just act normal here? Pretend like nothing's wrong?"

"That's exactly what I've been trying to do," Fred said. "But it's a little difficult with you in that mood."

Doc tossed down his napkin and stood to glower down at Fred. "What mood? I'm fine, dammit."

Sterling Jeppson lowered his paper. Bill Lacey closed his magazine and glanced over his shoulder again. Fred tried to silently point out the renewed interest in their conversation, but Doc's patience had apparently run out.

He made a noise of impatience and turned on his heel. "I'm getting out of here." He took three steps away, halted by Geneva Hart's table, and tried to pin a smile on his sour face. "Don't forget your appointment, young lady. I'll see you at three o'clock in my office."

Geneva's bland features colored with embarrassment. She lowered her eyes, then lifted them slowly and shook her head. "I can't, Doc. My dad told me to cancel my appointment this morning. After what happened . . . well, he doesn't want me coming to you anymore."

"After *what* happened?" Doc demanded.

Geneva looked at Wayne, then over at Fred as if he'd tell her what to say. "My dad thinks maybe you should retire. He wants me going to a younger doctor."

six

Somebody at the counter drew in a sharp breath. Somebody else's chair groaned. Fred's heart dropped.

Gathering the remnants of his dignity about him, Doc pivoted away and walked out the front door. Silence rang off the walls as Fred folded a piece of bacon into his mouth, tossed off the rest of his coffee, and left the rest of his breakfast on the table.

He hurried outside while the room stood silent, but he could almost feel the conversation buzz the second the door closed behind him.

Doc plowed along the boardwalk nearly a block ahead. Fred watched, heartsick to know how he must be feeling. Doc slipped once and almost lost his footing on a patch of ice. When his foot slid a second time, Fred hurried after him.

He managed to avoid both of the icy patches that caused Doc trouble and caught up with him in front of Lacey's General Store. "Slow down, for Pete's sake. Everybody with half a brain knows you didn't do anything wrong."

Doc shook his head. "Seems to me, everybody thinks I'm an incompetent old fool."

"You're letting a few people bother you."

Doc came to a sudden halt and faced him. "A few people? You know as well as I do if Bill Lacey's talking, Janice must have spoonfed the story to most of the county by now. Half of my appointments for today have canceled. I've been advised to retire and practically accused of murder. And you say not to let it bother me?"

"It'll blow over."

"I don't think so, Fred. Seems to me, they're all giving me the same message, and maybe they're right. Maybe it is time for me to call it quits."

"You can't be serious."

Doc laughed, a harsh, bitter sound. "Can't I? I don't see why not. Velma and I have been talking about traveling for years. Her sister's constantly gadding about somewhere, and Velma's always after me to slow down. Well, maybe now's our chance." He started walking again, but slower this time.

"Is that what *you* want?"

Doc kicked a chunk of ice from the boardwalk. "Maybe I've reached the time of life when what I want doesn't matter so much anymore."

"There isn't any such time," Fred argued.

Doc didn't answer.

Fred stuffed his hands in his pockets and tried to match his pace. "Look, if that's what you really want to do, then do it. But not because you're feeling sorry for yourself—"

Doc reared back and shouted, "Sorry for myself?"

"Just make sure it's your own idea."

"It *is* my idea, you damned fool. Didn't you just hear me say it?"

"I heard."

"All right, then."

Fred held back all the things he could have said and let Doc hang onto his wounded pride. They walked the rest of the way to Lake Front Drive in silence. "If Velma's still with Sharon," Fred said at last, "why don't you come by the house and we'll finish breakfast there?"

Doc shook his head and nodded toward his car parked in front of the volunteer fire department. "No. Thanks. I've lost my appetite." He looked out over the lake, then glanced at Fred. "Maybe I'll drop by Sharon's and see if I can patch things up with her."

That sounded like a great idea to Fred. He patted Doc's shoulder and made sure he put as much warmth as he could into the contact. "Good luck."

"Thanks." Doc managed a wounded smile. "I'll probably need it." He started toward his car, and Fred watched him go. Doc looked different to him today. Older. Hopeless. And he hoped Doc would receive a warmer reception at Sharon's than he had yesterday.

Turning toward home, Fred readjusted his collar and shivered as he stepped into the shadows of the trees. Snow mounded along the edge of the road where the snowplow had cleared a spot wide enough for a single lane of traffic.

He kept to the edge of the snow and trudged past the Kirkhams' big ugly cabin, waving to Loralee in the window. He tried to ignore the cold, but it crept through his outer layer of clothing and worked its way into his bones. His joints began to ache, and the blasted arthritis that plagued him even in the best of times suddenly tried to make his knees seize up. His hands already burned from the cold, and his nose and mouth felt numb.

Glancing at the sky, overcast with clouds the color of metal, he shivered. He wondered how long Doc would talk about retiring. The old goat might be annoying sometimes, but Fred knew exactly how far he could push him, and he didn't like the idea of some young, new, overeager doctor in town. Or, worse yet, of Cutler losing local medical care altogether.

Until now, he'd never seriously considered life in Cutler without Doc. He was a few years older than Doc, but they'd been friends for well over half a century. They'd been through hell and back again. Their wives had been friends. Their children had grown up together. Doc and Velma had mourned Phoebe's passing almost as deeply as Fred had. If Doc retired, it would leave a hole in Fred's world. Well, it simply couldn't happen. Not over Eddie Leishman's death, anyway.

But the more he thought, the worse he felt. And by the time he reached the northern edge of his property, he'd convinced himself he wanted nothing more than to get inside, make a pot of coffee, start that new Deloy Barnes Western novel he'd picked up last week, and put things he couldn't fix out of his mind.

He watched for his house to appear through the trunks of the trees—almost impossible to do in spring and summer, but easier after the leaves fell from the aspen trees. He caught a glimpse of the lake beyond, slate gray to match the clouds, and a patch of red where nothing red should have been.

When the red patch moved a second later, Fred realized he had a visitor, and when he rounded the corner onto his driveway, he could make out Benjamin waiting on the porch.

Digging his keys from his pocket, he signaled the boy to walk with him to the back door. "It's freezing out. How long have you been waiting?" Before Margaret started raiding his cupboards and Fred started locking his doors in self-protection, Benjamin could have waited inside.

Benjamin lifted a shoulder and jumped from the porch. "Not long."

Fred didn't believe him. His nose and chin were red from the cold, and he sniffed every few seconds. He'd been waiting a while. "If I'd known you were here, I'd have hurried home."

"That's okay. I just came over to find out if my mom came over here last night."

"As a matter of fact, she did."

Benjamin matched his stride and looked over at him. "You didn't tell her anything, did you?"

"No, but it wasn't easy. She's worried about you." Fred unlocked the back door and stepped inside, grateful for the sudden rush of heat. He tugged off his gloves and hung his coat over a hook on the back door.

Benjamin shrugged out of his coat and pulled something from the pocket before dropping the coat to a chair. "Look at this." He shoved a stack of brochures at Fred. "This is what she gave me today."

Fred needed only a glance to see what had raised Benjamin's hackles. "College brochures?"

"Get this," Benjamin said as he dropped into a seat by the table and kicked his feet onto another chair. "Now my dad's decided I should try to get into the Air Force Academy in Colorado Springs."

What on earth was Webb thinking? Even Fred knew

Benjamin would hate it there. He handed the brochures back and started trying to separate a coffee filter from the stack. "Maybe you can work out a compromise."

"With *my* dad?"

The boy had a point. "What does your mother say about all this?"

Benjamin averted his gaze. "You know Mom. She takes his side." Propping both elbows on the table, he wedged his chin between his hands. "You're sure you didn't say anything to her?"

Pulling out the decaf can where Fred hid his regular coffee, he scooped coffee into the filter. "I'm sure, but I don't like keeping this a secret from your mom. Besides, I thought the Leishman truck would be out of the picture— especially now, with Eddie gone and everything."

Benjamin's eyes widened as if he hadn't connected Eddie's death with the truck before, and he groaned aloud.

Fred pulled out a chair for himself. "Look on the bright side, it might work to your advantage."

"No, Grandpa, you don't understand. I need the truck now."

"You need it? Or you want it?"

One corner of Benjamin's lip curled and he rolled his eyes in disgust. "I'm serious, Grandpa. I need it."

"Why?"

Benjamin looked down at his fingernails for several seconds, as if he had to decide how much to tell. Finally, he lifted his eyes to meet Fred's. "We have this great chance to get the band in front of people, but without a truck to move our equipment, we're going to lose it."

"What chance?"

"There's this guy Josh's dad knows . . . knew. Anyway, he said he could maybe get us some weekend jobs around."

"Jobs? Where, in bars? Your mom and dad will never agree to that." At least, Fred hoped they wouldn't.

Benjamin leaned forward and smiled sadly. "No kidding. But it wouldn't be in bars, Grandpa. It'd be for dances and stuff. Real jobs, Grandpa. They'd pay us *money* to play."

Fred had the uneasy feeling he'd just learned more about

Benjamin's plans than he wanted to know. "I take it this is part of the secret, too?"

Benjamin nodded. "I can't tell Mom and Dad, they wouldn't understand. Dad hates my music. In fact, I think he'd be happy if I never played another note."

The coffeemaker gurgled happily in the background, almost mocking Fred while he tried desperately to think of an acceptable solution—both for Benjamin and for himself. He sighed heavily and rubbed the bridge of his nose. "I thought you were paying for the truck from your wages at the Good Sport. Now you're saying you want to take your college fund to pay for this truck, is that right?"

Benjamin nodded hopefully.

"Well, let me tell you what my concerns are—and I'll bet these are the same reasons your mom wouldn't want you to buy the truck." He ticked arguments off on his fingers. "If you get the truck and you start playing at dances and what-not, chances are you'll forget about your homework—"

"No, I won't. I promise." Benjamin spoke with all the optimism of youth.

Fred didn't argue the point. He just kept listing. "You'll spend your weekends playing with the band. You'll get in late. You'll sleep in the next day. You won't get the lawn mowed in the summer or the walks shoveled in winter. Your grades will start to slip—"

"No, they won't." Benjamin sounded positive. Full of high ideals. Optimistic and confident. But studying had never come very high on his list of priorities.

"Your dad must be thinking about his brother—"

Benjamin rolled his eyes. "I'm not Uncle Whit."

"And on top of everything else, with Eddie Leishman fresh on everybody's mind right now, you think you're going to convince your parents to let you do this?"

"What was wrong with Eddie?"

Fred stared at the boy for a long minute, half convinced the question was some sort of joke. But when Benjamin stared back at him, wide-eyed and serious, Fred had to answer. "Well, he was morally irresponsible, for one thing."

Benjamin looked genuinely puzzled for a second, then his

expression cleared. "Oh. You mean because of Ricki and Sharon? That wasn't Eddie's fault. Besides, Grandpa, these are the '90s. Things are different now than they were in your day."

"In *my* day? You're making it sound like I'm already gone. Seems to me, I'm still very much alive." Fred crossed to the cupboard, pulled down a mug, and scowled over his shoulder. "Doesn't matter what year it is, it's never right to hurt people. Eddie hurt a lot of them—Ricki, Sharon, Joshua, Vance, Doc, Velma . . ." Fred probably could have gone on, but he filled his cup and leaned against the counter. "You're going to have a hard time convincing your mother to let you follow in Eddie's footsteps."

Benjamin straightened his shoulders. "Yeah. Well, they're not going to make me be what they want, either. It's my life, I ought to be able to choose what I want to do."

"They just want you to have every advantage—"

Benjamin snorted in response. "They want me to do something they approve of. They don't even care what I want." He jerked to his feet and paced to the other side of the room. "Besides, who says I'd turn out like Eddie, anyway? It's like they don't trust me."

"I don't think it's a matter of trust."

But Benjamin was far too worked up to listen. "Okay, you're right. I'm going to use the money from my college fund to buy the truck. But I'm going to pay it back from the money I make playing in the band. I figure I could have it all put back by the time I graduate from high school."

The argument sounded good, but it didn't seem very likely to Fred. "So, you'd go to college, after all?"

Benjamin didn't even miss a beat. "Maybe. Probably. I mean, who knows? With the experience I get, I could even get a scholarship."

"Not unless you keep your grades up."

"I *will.* I told you that."

Yes, he had. But deciding something didn't always make it so.

Benjamin sighed and turned away again, as if dealing with Fred at this moment required all his patience. "I thought you'd be different, Grandpa. You and Grandma used to tell us all the time that we could be anything we wanted."

"It's true."

"Yeah? Well, I believed you. But now I find out that what you meant was, I could be anything on Mom and Dad's list of what's respectable."

Fred left his coffee on the counter and crossed to Benjamin. "You're arguing with the wrong person, son. You can be anything you want—as long as you're willing to pay the price. But first, you've got to understand what the price is. Have you seriously thought about what you'd have to give up and weighed it against what you'd gain?"

Benjamin's lips curled. "Okay, what about the other way around? If I gave up my music, what would I get? A job like my dad's? *That's* something to look forward to."

"Nobody says you have to give up music," Fred argued. "But maybe there's some other way to pursue it. Have you ever talked to Mr. Fadel about being a music teacher?"

Benjamin's expression froze. "No. That'd be selling out, too. I want to play my music, Grandpa, but I guess nobody wants to understand that—not even you." Pushing past Fred, he snatched his coat from the back of the chair.

Fred cursed silently and started after him. "Don't go, Benjamin. Let's talk this over."

But Benjamin wrenched open the door. "What's the use? You've already made up your mind, and I know what you're going to say." He slammed the door behind him and almost ran down the driveway.

Hoping to head Benjamin off, Fred hurried through the living room to the front door. In sixteen years, he couldn't remember Benjamin ever being angry with him before, and he didn't like it. He wanted to set things right, but he had no idea what he should do other than keep Benjamin from leaving when he was so upset.

Through the open curtains, he could see Benjamin's jacket moving toward the street and he tried to walk faster, but his knees had grown stiff from the time spent outdoors, and he moved too slowly.

When he finally reached the door and yanked it open, he stepped out onto the porch and searched for some sign of his angry grandson. "Benjamin? Wait."

No answer.

Fred stepped off the porch and into the snow again. "Benjamin?"

But only silence floated back to him. Reluctantly, Fred turned back to the house. He stood on the porch and watched until his hopes died and he was forced to admit Benjamin was gone.

seven

Fred made a few minor adjustments to his Christmas list, leaned back and studied it for a minute, then pushed it to the corner of the table and cleared his lunch dishes away. He'd been working on the blasted list off and on for the past three days as a way to keep his mind occupied, but it hadn't helped much.

More than anything, he wanted to spend some time with Benjamin and to find out how things were going with Doc. Instead, he planned Christmas, shoveled snow, and knocked wicked-looking icicles from the eaves of the house.

He had a hard time believing this would be his fourth Christmas without Phoebe. The first year, after her death in August, he'd let Christmas slide past without notice. By the second, he'd known he should do something, but he hadn't known exactly what. Last year, he'd tried his hand at making a list—just like Phoebe always had. This year, he thought he finally had the hang of it.

Sighing to himself, he pulled the calendar from the wall by the phone and chose a date at random for putting up the tree. He'd invite Margaret's kids and Douglas's daughter Alison to join him. They'd make an evening of it with cocoa and brownies—instant and store-bought instead of Phoebe's homemade varieties. Maybe he could patch things up with Benjamin then.

He returned the calendar to the wall and poured another cup of coffee, then crossed to the kitchen window and looked outside. The view from this window was one of his favorites. He could see clear across the lake from here in the winter. Straight through the bare trees to Doc and Velma Huggins' place.

Sipping carefully, he wondered again how Doc was getting along. Since Eddie Leishman's death, Fred had gone out a couple of times. Each time he'd hoped to casually run into Doc, but Doc hadn't been out much since his last disastrous visit to the Bluebird. Fred had tried calling, but Doc had sent word back with Velma that he didn't want to talk. Fred had even toyed with the idea of making an appointment to see the old fool, but once before he'd tried sneaking in a few questions during a checkup and Doc had seen through his efforts. Fred knew he wouldn't get away with it this time, either.

He felt helpless, at the mercy of the worries that crept up on him. And no matter what else he found to occupy his time, he couldn't rid himself of the dreadful certainty that disaster was looming out there nearby, just biding its time.

Well, there was no sense standing here worrying about it. He wouldn't accomplish anything that way. The past three days had shown him that. No, Fred needed to do something. To take some sort of positive action.

He *could* go to Lacey's and catch up on the gossip about Doc there. He felt reasonably certain that Janice would have the whole story, plus a few fictional details for spice. But Fred didn't like to encourage Janice to gossip. Besides, he told himself, she'd probably worn herself out spreading stories this week—she'd need a break. He didn't really want to hear gossip, anyway. He wanted to know the facts, and there was only one place he could turn for those.

Dumping the rest of his coffee down the drain, he rinsed his cup, lifted his coat from its hook on the back door, and trudged through the living room on his way out. He needed to deposit his retirement check, so he'd use a trip to the bank as an excuse to pay Enos a short visit. And he'd let Enos volunteer whatever information there was to be had.

He pocketed the check, put on his hat and gloves, and hurried up Lake Front Drive toward town. Luckily, much of the snow had melted from the sides of the streets, which made the walk a little wetter but easier, and he reached Main Street after only a few minutes.

Enos's truck stood in its usual spot, and both Grady's truck and Ivan's car were gone. Good. That meant they'd have a few minutes alone. Fred couldn't ask for more.

He clomped up the steps and along the boardwalk, and pushed open the door to the sheriff's office, wearing his friendliest smile. But Enos wasn't alone. Doc sat across the desk from him.

Fred tried not to smile at his luck as he stepped inside and closed the door behind him. The aroma of stale coffee filled the air and an empty doughnut box lay on the desk—obviously Doc had been there a while.

Enos creaked back in his chair and linked his fingers over the front of his duty belt. "Well, well, well. Look what the cat dragged in."

"Good morning to you, too." Fred pulled off his coat and gloves and claimed the other chair in front of the desk with a nod at Doc. "Good to see you, Doc. You haven't been around much for a day or two."

Doc shook his head, but the movement seemed forced and stiff. "I've been busy."

"So have I. Been making my Christmas list."

That put an expression of surprise on both faces. Enos rocked back a little further and toyed with a half-empty pack of Doublemint gum. "Really? Well, now, I'm impressed."

Doc managed to smile a little. "Velma takes care of all that at our house."

"So did Phoebe," Fred admitted. "But I'm getting better every year."

Doc ran the palm of his hand over his fringe of hair, but he didn't say anything.

Enos creaked forward a little. "I guess we'll be spending the holidays with Jessica's parents this year." He didn't sound excited about the prospect.

"Really?" Fred tried to look honestly interested in everyone's Christmas plans. But he didn't want them to stop discussing anything far more interesting. "That's a switch, isn't it?"

Enos shrugged. "Well, they're getting up there, and Jessica wants to spend time with them this year . . ."

Doc flicked a glance at Enos, then looked away again. "Nothing like having family around," Fred agreed and cocked an ankle across his knee. "What about you, Doc?"

"Hell, I don't know. The way things are going, we might not even have a Christmas."

"I was hoping things were looking up."

Doc shook his head. "Not really. My practice is all but gone. Velma's over at Sharon's most of the time, Sharon's still not speaking to me, and Vance is—" He broke off and shook his head, obviously at his wits' end. "You know, there was a time when I'd have thought getting rid of Eddie would be the best thing that could have happened. Now, I'm not sure."

Enos leaned all the way up in his chair and his sandy brows knit together. "You're going to have to watch what you say, Doc. It'd be easy to misunderstand that last comment."

Doc flushed a deep red. "Well, I know. But it's hard enough listening to people make unfounded accusations when there's something to question. We don't even have the autopsy results, for hell's sake, and half the county's trying to make me guilty of something shady."

Enos lifted both hands to ward off the attack. "I know that, but you still ought to be careful."

"I refuse to spend the rest of my life watching every little thing I say." Doc squared his shoulders and rested his arms on those of the chair. "I did my job the way it was supposed to be done."

Enos left one hand up as if he thought that alone might keep Doc in line. "I just meant—"

"I know exactly what you meant," Doc said with a sniff.

"What happened the other day?" Fred asked. "Did Ricki Leishman ever come after Eddie's things?"

Doc rolled his eyes and gritted his teeth. "Oh, yes. She stopped by that afternoon, just like she said. I wasn't there, of course, but Velma was. It wasn't a pretty scene."

Fred had never expected it would be one. "What about Sharon? How's she coping with all this?"

"Not as well as I'd hoped. Velma says the talk is getting to her, and she's still moping around . . ."

Enos nodded and looked understanding. "Hopefully it'll die down soon. It's been four days already. Something else is bound to come along and take people's minds off Sharon and Eddie."

"That's right," Fred said. "And once the talk slows down, things tend to get a little better."

Doc tilted his head back and groaned as if he carried the weight of the world on his shoulders. "I hope so, but I'll be honest. It's not the gossip that bothers me as much as the way Sharon's acting. She's well rid of that loser, but she absolutely refuses to see it."

And Doc probably insisted on pointing it out to her. No wonder Sharon still didn't want to talk to him.

Enos looked as if he wanted to say something, but the telephone rang and cut him off midthought. He held up a finger to mark his place in the conversation and picked up the receiver. "Sheriff Asay." Immediately, his expression sobered and he flicked a glance at Doc. "You've got it, then?"

The autopsy. It had to be. Fred put both feet flat on the floor and leaned forward. Doc didn't move.

"Right." Enos flicked another glance, first at Doc, then at Fred. "Right. Right." A deep sigh. "Good hell."

That didn't sound encouraging.

Enos wiped his face with an open palm and nodded at the receiver as if his caller could see him. "All right. Got it. You'll send me the full report? Okay, Lydel, thanks." He replaced the receiver slowly, but he didn't lift his gaze.

Definitely not good news.

Finally, slowly, Enos looked at Doc. "Well, you were right. It was an insulin overdose. A massive one."

Doc huffed in protest. "Impossible."

"What does that mean," Fred asked. "He was murdered?"

Enos wiped his face again, pushed the hand through his thinning hair, and wagged his head back and forth as if he didn't know what to say. "Or someone made a dreadful mistake."

Doc's face lost all its color. "Are you implying that I made a mistake?"

Enos didn't respond.

Doc's eyes widened. "Dammit, I've already told you what I did."

Enos pushed to his feet and paced to the back of the room.

Fred watched his progress and tried to make himself breathe normally, but the disaster he'd been anticipating had struck and now his lungs only wanted to pull in shallow gasps. "Look," he said to Enos's back, "you and I both know Doc didn't make a mistake like that."

Enos glanced over his shoulder. His face looked hard, his eyes almost cold. "We've found two empty insulin bottles in Sharon's refrigerator."

"I didn't miscalculate," Doc insisted.

Fred raised his voice a notch to force Enos to listen. "Somebody killed Eddie, and for some reason they're trying to make it look as if Doc did something wrong. It's obvious what we need to do."

Enos raised one eyebrow. "*We?*" He shook his head. "I'll tell you what you need to do. Go home. Me and the boys'll do the investigating."

Fred wanted to argue, but he knew exactly how far doing so would get him. "All right. Then hurry and find out what happened so you can stop all this silly gossip."

"I know how to do my job," Enos snarled. He turned to look at Doc for the first time in several minutes. "I intend to look into this, but I'm going to need you to tell me exactly how you measured the insulin—"

"I didn't give him any insulin," Doc shouted.

"Dammit, Enos. This is *Doc* we're talking about." Fred pointed at the other man as if Enos might need a visual reminder.

"I know. But I can't cut corners on this investigation just because a friend is involved. You know people will be watching me like a hawk. Ricki Leishman will be watching every blasted step I take."

"Then we have to prove that somebody else gave Eddie that overdose."

Enos scowled. "You are *not* getting in the middle of this, Fred."

"Too late. I'm already involved."

Enos met his gaze and held it. He didn't look happy. "If I catch you interfering with official department business, you know what I'll have to do."

Fred didn't even blink.

"Check the syringe I used on him," Doc insisted. "You won't find any insulin in it."

Something flickered across Enos's expression. "What syringe?"

"The syringe I used when I was there that night." Doc waved his arms as he spoke.

"There wasn't any syringe," Enos said softly. "You said so yourself, and there wasn't one listed among the contents of the house after we gathered evidence."

"Somebody *took* the syringe?" Fred asked, more to himself than to anyone else. "Then that's how they did it. They got the insulin from Sharon's fridge and gave it to Eddie all in one whack."

Enos shot him a look. "Fred, keep quiet or you'll have to leave. Doc, start at the beginning and tell me exactly what happened."

"For Pete's sake—" Fred began.

Enos slapped his palm on the desktop and color flooded his face. "I mean it, Fred. This is fair warning. Stay out of this."

Fred took an involuntary step back at Enos's unexpected reaction. "How can I when you're already treating Doc as if he's guilty?"

Doc dropped back into his seat. "I've already told you everything, Enos. What earthly good will it do to go over it again?"

With visible effort, Enos dragged his eyes away from Fred and pulled his temper back under control. "Well, tell me again, Doc. We'll go over every detail with a fine-toothed comb—*after* Fred leaves."

Common sense and Enos's expression convinced Fred
not to refuse. But, for the life of him, he couldn't understand
Enos's reaction to his few innocent comments. He pulled on
his coat and settled his hat on his head, then frowned at Enos
for a few seconds. The younger man's expression didn't
waver. "All right," Fred conceded. "I'll leave. For now."

Enos didn't move a muscle. Doc didn't even look up.

Fred crossed the office slowly, giving Enos plenty of time
to realize how he'd overreacted and to call Fred back. He
didn't. Fred pulled open the door and stepped outside,
letting the door swing shut behind him. He could hear Enos
start up where he'd left off. "Now, tell me about that night.
Sharon called you . . ."

Fred walked slowly away and tried to reassure himself
that everything would work out. But he'd seen this side of
Enos before. If Enos thought Doc was guilty, Doc would
end up in jail.

Fred wasn't willing to let that happen, but short of
looking for Eddie's killer himself, he didn't know what to
do. He put another few feet behind him and argued with
himself with each step. If he started asking questions, Enos
would blow a fuse. He'd probably break his neck telling
Margaret about it, and she'd get upset and angry. Fred had
been through it all before, and he felt no particular hurry to
repeat the experience.

But the alternative left him cold. He knew he'd never be
able to face himself in the mirror if he sat back and did
nothing while Doc suffered.

Slightly winded from his walk, Fred pushed open the
door to the Silver City Bank and stepped into the warm
lobby. Only two other customers were inside. Good. He
could get in and out quickly, then figure out a plan of attack
to clear Doc's name.

He endorsed his check and filled out a deposit slip, then
stepped to the end of the line without looking at the other
customers. When he recognized Summer Dey at Faith
Arnesson's teller window, he had to fight to hold back a
groan.

Summer wore all black, as usual. Today's garb included a pair of pants made of a material too thin for the weather, a thick sweater, and heavy-soled army boots. An oversized black leather pouch slid from her shoulder, tugged the sweater down an extra inch or two at the neck, and threatened to spill its contents onto the floor.

Fred had heard a rumor a few years back that Summer thought she couldn't paint a thing unless she was depressed. Fred had seen what she called her artwork; privately, he thought a change of wardrobe might do her abilities some good.

For a split second, he considered leaving and coming back later, but now that he'd endorsed his check he certainly didn't want to carry it all over town and run the risk of losing it.

Behind Summer, Carl Fadel tapped an envelope against one leg and waited impatiently for his turn. It was a little too early for school to be out, so he must have been sneaking in a visit during his free period.

Carl acknowledged Fred with a nod toward Summer and an impatient smile. "She's been there for ten minutes. Wouldn't you think they'd open the other window?"

Fred glanced around the lobby. "It looks like Faith's the only one here."

Carl jerked his head toward the president's office at the back of the building where Kirby Manning sat behind the desk he'd inherited after the bank's previous president landed in prison for embezzlement.

Kirby kept his attention on his computer screen. Thin-shouldered, narrow-chested, and gaunt-faced, he hunched over his keyboard and typed furiously. Carl clicked his tongue impatiently and made a show of checking his watch.

Nobody seemed to care.

Summer shook her head at something Faith said, and her straight blond hair caught on the sweater and weaved a net across her back. Leaning a bit further onto the counter, she pointed at something. "Not that account. The Cosmic Tradition account," she said, and rattled off a set of numbers.

Faith scrunched up her face and stared at her computer screen, hopelessly confused.

Fred could feel Carl's impatience climb a notch and his own took a matching upswing. His encounter with Enos had left him a little edgy. A little short on patience.

When the bank's door swished open again and Janice Lacey slipped inside, Fred nearly groaned aloud. She made her way across the lobby in a coat that had seen several seasons and seemed to shrink with each one. A pair of black stretch pants molded around her legs and her gray curls bobbed limply in the fluorescent lighting. She carried her purse across one arm and clutched its top with the other hand as if she were in imminent danger of losing it.

Her eyes lit up when she saw Fred standing there, as if she'd been hoping to run into him. He could only imagine the kinds of discussions she'd been having about Eddie and Sharon, and about Doc. Living across the street from Sharon would give her stories an added zest.

Fred started to turn away, then stopped and looked back at Janice with interest. He hadn't thought of it before, but Janice *might* actually know something useful. Odds were, she'd been at the store when Eddie died. But if there was any possibility she knew something about Eddie's death, Fred supposed he ought to at least ask.

He worked up a warm smile. "Hello, Janice."

"Well, Fred. I don't suppose you've had this dreadful cold hit you yet?" She took her place in line behind him, sent a pained smile at Carl, and dabbed a tissue to the end of her nose.

"Not yet," Fred admitted.

"Between the sniffles and everything else that's been happening around here, I haven't slept well for days," Janice complained, and readjusted her hold on the purse. "It's gotten so it's like living in New York City. I suppose you're right in the middle of this *latest* nasty business."

"I wouldn't say I'm in the middle," Fred said slowly.

Janice heaved a tremendous sigh. "Poor Doc. It's all I've heard about. I don't think there's a soul left in town who'll really trust him again. Not after this."

"I don't know why not," Fred argued.

Janice rolled her eyes at him. "Oh, for heaven's sake, Fred. I know how you feel about Doc, but really. And I'm not for one minute saying I wouldn't have felt exactly the same way if one of my girls had done something like that." But her tone said she didn't believe one of her girls ever would.

"I suppose you knew Eddie," Fred suggested. "Living across the street the way you did."

"I certainly knew *of* him." Janice patted the back of her hair. "He wasn't really the sort Bill and I socialized with."

"No, of course not. But you know Sharon."

"Of course. And I feel so awful for Doc and Velma, I really do. The things that girl has put them through. And now this!"

"Children can be a trial," Fred admitted.

Janice leaned a little closer, as if she had a great secret to share. "Everybody knows Eddie wasn't a nice person—the way he treated his wife and the kinds of things he did—" She broke off and looked at Carl as if she'd noticed him for the first time.

Carl lifted one shoulder in a vague response and checked Summer's progress at the counter. "I wouldn't know," he said when he turned back. "I don't think I ever met any of them."

"I thought the Leishman boy was in one of your classes," Fred said.

Carl looked embarrassed. "He is. I meant the parents."

"Didn't I see you and Eddie together at the school a few nights ago?"

"At the school?" Carl tried to look confused, but Fred thought he caught a flash of alarm in his eye. "Oh. Yes. Of course. I forgot. I did meet him once." Carl managed a stiff laugh in Fred's general direction and tapped his bank transaction against his leg a little faster.

"Well, I used to tell Bill there was something wrong with that man. I could feel it."

Fred could only imagine.

Carl nodded. "His death certainly was a tragic accident."

"Tragic," Janice repeated, then bowed her head for a moment.

"Dr. Huggins probably shouldn't have tried treating him for something so serious," Carl said. "He should have let another doctor do it. I'd like to give him the benefit of the doubt, he's a nice old guy, but he *is* old and he messed up."

"Doc did not mess up," Fred insisted.

"Hey, I'm not saying anything bad," Carl protested. "He was probably a good enough doctor in his day. And, hell—nobody *wants* to get old, do they?"

Janice shook her head in dismay. "You know I hear a lot in my position at the store. People tend to confide in me." She flicked a glance at Fred as if daring him to contradict her.

Fred wouldn't have dreamed of it.

"There are quite a few people who say they're going to look for a younger doctor. I hate to even think about it, but you can't be too careful where your health is concerned."

Fred struggled to keep his voice steady so he wouldn't betray his temper. "You know, I'm getting awfully tired of this whole silly business. Has anyone even considered that Doc might not have made a mistake?"

Carl snapped his mouth shut and glanced uneasily at Janice. "Well, yes," he said at last. But the expression on his face didn't make Fred feel any better. "Actually, I think a lot of people believe Dr. Huggins killed Eddie on purpose."

eight

Fred stared at Carl for a few seconds, trying to find the right words to argue against such a foolish notion. Imagine Doc committing murder. Even if the victim *was* Eddie Leishman. The idea was too ridiculous for words.

But Carl went on, oblivious to Fred's growing anger. "I mean, Doc was right there with Eddie, and he certainly had everything he needed to kill him."

Fred didn't even try to keep his voice low this time. "Doc wasn't the only one who saw Eddie that night. As a matter of fact, wasn't that the night Eddie visited you?"

The rush of color to Carl's face made Fred feel a little better. "I only met Eddie once," Carl reminded him.

Fred didn't believe that, and he had every intention of saying so, but Summer Dey chose that moment to step away from the teller window. Carl slipped into her place so quickly Fred couldn't even frame his next response.

Janice moved a little closer to Fred's ear. "Well, imagine that—"

Fred struggled to work his temper back under control. He wouldn't do Doc any favors by arguing about the case in public. And he wouldn't earn any points with Enos that way, either.

He turned away from Janice, subtly so as not to offend her, and noticed Summer Dey still watching him from near the counter. When he met her gaze, a slow smile curved her lips and she veered toward him. "I knew I'd see you today." She paused and cocked her head toward the ceiling, as if the ceiling tiles had something to say. "You're working again, aren't you?"

Fred reasoned that if there was one jot of truth to this psychic business, she ought to be able to read his thoughts and keep her mouth shut. "I don't work," he reminded her. "I'm retired."

Her brows knit and she looked at the ceiling. "But I— No, you must help. You have no choice."

Even under the best of circumstances, Fred didn't like someone pushing him. He certainly didn't classify Summer's psychic mumbo jumbo as the best of circumstances.

Never one to stay out of a conversation that didn't concern her, Janice bulldozed her way between them. "Who are you talking about? Doc? Are you helping Doc?"

Fred shook his head, but he found it more difficult by the moment to maintain his usual friendly attitude. "I'm not doing a thing."

Summer tugged her bag back onto her shoulder. "Maybe you should come in for a reading. I have the strongest feeling you need the guidance of the spirits."

The only guidance Fred needed from Summer's spirits was for them to guide *her* away. "I'm not interested."

Janice tugged at his sleeve. "Oh, but you should. Really. If you're going to help Doc, you really should see Summer. Every single thing she's ever told me has come true. Oh, her timing's been a little off." She flashed Summer an apologetic smile. "But it's all happened."

Thankfully, Carl Fadel finished at the teller window and hurried away. Without giving Summer or Janice another chance to speak, Fred took his place at the counter and slapped his check and deposit slip in front of Faith with a hearty smile. "Got a little business this afternoon."

To his dismay, Summer moved up with him. "This will be a difficult time for you," she whispered.

Fred glanced at her from the corner of his eye. She didn't need to be a psychic to figure that out.

"The truth is hidden too well. Nothing around you is as it seems."

That wasn't unusual, either.

Summer smiled softly and her eyes grew soft and dreamy. Unfocused. She seemed to ponder for a few seconds, then her smile faded. "But even knowing that, we often fail to see clearly. And that will be your trouble this time. There's too much anger in the air. Too much hatred. And too many lies."

Fred slipped his receipt into his pocket and moved away from the counter. Janice maneuvered past him, removed a small stack of checks from her purse, and waved them at Faith. "I need to get these in the bank. I've felt like a moving target all day, carrying these around."

Faith sounded so sympathetic, Janice practically leaned across the counter. Hoping he could slip outside before Summer realized he was on the move, Fred headed for the front door. But she trailed him outside.

"You must not ignore the energy around you. It's coming at you from every direction."

"If you mean trouble, you're absolutely right," Fred admitted grudgingly.

Summer smiled softly. "Trouble? Yes. If you want to call it that. Troubled spirits. Karmic debt. You can't alter destiny, and perhaps this is Doc's. He, too, must pay for his mistakes."

Fred scowled at her. "What mistakes?"

"Those committed in other lives." Summer tilted her head again and smiled slowly. "Maybe Doc accused someone unjustly in a previous incarnation and now he has a chance to pay off the debt. I wonder how great a sacrifice the universe will demand from him. I wonder whether you can truly help him, or whether he'll need to work through karma alone." With that, she turned away, leaving Fred alone and confused.

He stared after her for a minute, then yanked up the zipper on his coat and tried to remember what he'd been thinking before Summer started in on him with all her foolishness.

He'd been thinking about finding Eddie Leishman's killer—that much he knew. But he didn't know where to begin. He didn't know Eddie well enough. Didn't know where he'd spent his days. Or his nights. Didn't know his likes and dislikes. In fact, almost everything he knew of Eddie came from Doc. Considering the source, Fred figured there might be one or two slight inaccuracies in his perception. If he wanted to help Doc, he needed to know more about Eddie. And he fully intended to help Doc—no matter *what* Summer said.

Fred supposed he could pay a condolence call on Ricki Leishman, but after their brief encounter the other day, he didn't think she'd be eager to talk with him. So, maybe he ought to check on Sharon, offer his sympathy, and see what she could tell him about Eddie.

Crossing the street, he hurried past Lacey's General Store to the corner. He skirted Tito Romero's auto repair shop so he wouldn't have to run into Webb, and turned the corner onto Oak Street a few minutes later.

Sharon's place stood a few houses from the corner. It looked lifeless in the pale sunlight; the curtains were closed, her car still had snow on its windshield, and long, dangerous icicles hung from the rain gutter. Fred didn't see Velma's car anywhere, and that pleased him. Sharon would probably talk more openly without her mother there.

Sharon opened the door when he knocked, but she didn't look like herself at all. She took a moment to focus, as if she were just waking from a nap. "Fred? What are you doing here?"

"I came to see how you're doing. I've been worried."

"About me?" She blinked rapidly. "I'm all right."

He waited for her to ask him inside.

She didn't.

He patted his arms briskly and shifted from foot to foot, looking cold. "Do you mind if I come in?"

She nodded slowly and moved away from the door. "Of course. I'm sorry. I'm not thinking straight, I guess." She led the way up the stairway to the living room and Fred immediately saw evidence of her mother's stay. The furniture was still old and mismatched, but now every piece of wood gleamed from recent polishing. With the clutter removed from the floor, the coffee table empty, and the cushions plumped, it looked like a new room.

Sharon stood in front of a shabby wingback chair for a

second, then folded herself into it, drawing her knees up and tucking her feet beneath her.

Fred chose the same spot on the couch he'd occupied on his last visit. Sharon stared at him, waiting, but he didn't want to sound heartless by asking personal questions right off the bat. "Is your mother still here with you?"

She shook her head. "She went back home a few hours ago. I needed time alone."

"What about Vance? Is he around?"

Another headshake. "No."

"Are you really all right? Is there anything I can do?"

Sharon pushed the fingers of one hand into her hair. "I have to be all right. I'm supposed to go back to work tomorrow."

"That soon?"

She glanced away. "I wasn't his wife. I don't need time to mourn—at least that's what everyone seems to think."

"What about the funeral? When will that be?"

She lifted a shoulder listlessly. "None of my business. You'll have to ask Ricki."

"I see." He unzipped his coat and readjusted his position on the couch. "I understand she paid you a visit the other day."

"Yes." Sharon's face clouded, but she didn't elaborate.

"Everything went all right, then?"

With an acid laugh, she looked away. "That woman is a bitch."

"It must have been uncomfortable for both of you."

Sharon widened her eyes in surprise. "Ricki uncomfortable? You've got to be kidding. She'd never allow it."

Her bitterness didn't surprise Fred. He couldn't imagine Sharon taking up with Eddie if she'd felt anything more for Ricki. He waited for her to go on, but she folded her hands into her lap and stared at her fingers.

"Has Enos told you about the autopsy results?"

She jerked her gaze up to meet his and the pain he saw there broke his heart. "No. Did they get them?"

"A little while ago. Eddie died from a massive insulin overdose."

Tears filled her eyes and she looked away again, blinking rapidly. She spoke, a mere whisper of a sound, far too soft for Fred to hear.

"I'm sure Enos will contact you himself, so it might be best not to mention that I've told you already."

She shook her head and lifted her eyes again. "He's not going to tell me anything. As far as the law's concerned, I was nothing to Eddie."

"I'm sure Enos doesn't feel that way."

Sharon didn't argue, but she didn't look convinced. "I can't help plan his funeral. I can't do anything."

"That's not entirely true. You can help catch the person who killed him."

It seemed to take forever for his words to reach her. When they did, she narrowed her eyes and frowned. "Is that why you're here?"

He nodded. "Would it be all right for me to ask you a couple of questions?"

"Like what?"

"First, I need to know whether you think it's possible Eddie gave himself the injection that killed him?"

Sharon gripped both arms of the chair and shook her head. "You mean suicide? No way."

"It might have been an accident."

"No. Eddie was diabetic all his life. He knew how his body responded to even the slightest variation in his blood-sugar or insulin levels. He'd never have given himself that much insulin. Never."

"Maybe somebody substituted a larger dose," Fred suggested.

"No. Impossible. Eddie would have recognized such a massive dose the minute he looked at it, not to mention the feel of the syringe. Why? What are you thinking?"

Fred tried to keep his voice steady. He didn't want to upset her more, but she needed to know the truth. "Enos seems to think your dad made a mistake. I don't agree."

"Dad?" She laughed once, then stared at him for several long seconds. She tried to make herself laugh again, but nothing came out. "That's ridiculous."

"I know that."

"So, you're helping Dad?"

"In a way," Fred admitted.

She almost smiled. "Does Enos know?"

"No. And neither does Margaret."

She touched her fingers to her lips and considered his answer. "All right. I'll help you. What do you want to know?"

"Did Eddie have any enemies?"

She closed her eyes and leaned back in the chair. "Ricki, of course. I don't think she ever forgave him for leaving her."

Fred pictured Ricki Leishman swathed in fur and wondered whether she could have killed him. Not impossible, he supposed. He'd been surprised before. "Was she here that day?"

"*Here*? No. Nobody came here that day."

"How can you be so sure?"

"After a reaction like Eddie had, he could have slept thirty-six hours without moving. Even if someone came by the house, he wouldn't have gotten up. I've seen him sleep like that before. Besides, when I came home, the house was still locked."

"Maybe he let someone in and then locked it after they left."

She smiled sadly. "I always locked the door—habit, I guess. Eddie never did. He would have let the world parade through my house if I'd let him. If he'd gotten up to let someone in, he'd have left the door unlocked."

"Did anybody else have a key?"

"Besides Vance, Eddie, and me? No."

"What about Ricki? Did she come here often?"

Sharon flushed. "She *never* came here. I wouldn't let that woman in my house."

"Are you sure Eddie didn't let her in?"

Sharon stared at him as if he'd suggested something vile. "Eddie didn't want anything to do with her. Besides, he knew how I felt. It was bad enough living in the same town, seeing her when we went to the store or passing her when she was jogging . . . No. She never came here."

"All right. Was there anyone else you'd consider Eddie's enemy?"

"No. Eddie was friends with everybody."

Fred glanced at her quickly. She must be speaking of a different Eddie. "You never saw him argue with anyone except his wife?"

For the first time since he'd arrived, Sharon's face showed some color. Heaving a sigh, she leaned her head against the chair and closed her eyes again. "Yes, of course I saw him argue. *We* argued. But not about anything major."

Fred tried not to let exasperation creep into his voice, but this conversation wasn't getting them anywhere. "All right, we've got you and we've got Ricki. Anybody else?"

She shrugged. "He and Bear argued sometimes."

"Sandusky?" Fred leaned forward eagerly. "What did they argue about?"

"Eddie never told me."

Fred pondered that for a moment and pictured Bear comforting Ricki outside the Kwik Kleen. "Is there any possibility that Bear and Ricki might have been seeing each other?"

The idea seemed to catch Sharon off guard. "Bear and Ricki? I don't think so." She paused, then shook her head. "No."

"You're sure?"

"Not with *Bear*."

"Could there have been another man?"

Sharon shook her head. "Eddie told me Ricki wasn't interested in sex. Not really. That's one of the reasons he left."

Sounded like a convenient excuse to Fred, but he let it pass. "Can you think of anyone else who might have been upset with Eddie? Anyone I should talk to?"

"No."

"What about Vance? How did he get along with Eddie?"

Sharon unfolded her legs and straightened her spine. "You're accusing my son?"

"I'm not accusing anyone," Fred said. "I'm just wondering whether he'd know anything that might help."

"I don't think so. They didn't really get along that well."

"What about at the clubs Eddie played? Any trouble there?"

"Not that he mentioned."

"How about his son?"

"Josh?" She sounded appalled. "No. He adored Eddie."

For one brief moment, Fred thought she might be using sarcasm, but her expression remained serious and he realized she believed it. Obviously, she hadn't seen Joshua and Eddie together recently. "And you can't think of anyone else?"

"No. I wish I could. I don't want to see my dad in trouble over this."

Fred held back a sigh. It seemed the only people who'd had trouble with Eddie were the people Fred least wanted to suspect. "Let's try this from another angle. Did anything unusual happen in the last few days before he died?"

"No."

"No strange phone calls or unusual visitors?"

She didn't even think about it. "No."

Fred tried not to sound exasperated. "Where was Eddie working?"

"Tex's Tavern in Snowville. Why?"

"We need to find someone besides your dad who disliked Eddie enough to kill him."

She looked away for a few seconds. "If you want to know about the band, talk to Bear. He's been around a couple of years—he knew Eddie better than the others did."

"Do you know where I can find him?"

"Somewhere on the way to Snowville. In an apartment, I think. I've never been there, but I think Eddie had the address." She stood slowly, walked into the kitchen, and returned a minute later with a beat-up address book in one hand. She flipped through it for a few seconds, then pointed to something on one of the pages. "Here it is. The Clarion Apartments outside of Snowville. Number eight."

Fred pulled his checkbook from his pocket and jotted the

address on the back of a deposit slip. He touched her shoulder lightly. "You're tired. I've overstayed my welcome."

She smiled, but it seemed to take great effort.

"If you need anything, I want you to call me or Margaret. She's concerned about you."

Another nod.

"Promise?"

Her lips trembled into a half smile. "I promise."

"Good. And try not to worry. We'll get to the bottom of this." He did his best to sound reassuring in spite of his own misgivings.

Sharon didn't say anything to that, and Fred knew she didn't believe him. But he refused to let anything discourage him. He had to believe he'd find the answers. He couldn't even let himself think about the alternative.

nine

Fred walked home quickly, fired up the Buick, and set out again toward Snowville without even setting foot inside the house. But it still took over an hour to find the Clarion Apartments. Finally, after checking a number of side roads, he located a small, white brick building a quarter mile off the highway, not far from the Snowville junction.

After parking on the edge of the lot, he spied number eight on the second floor—all the way on the other end of the building. Stepping cautiously, he crossed the muddy parking lot and climbed the stairs. There, he picked up the beat of a rock-and-roll song and followed it to the end of the balcony. He knocked once and waited, but with the music blaring loud enough to shake the door, Fred wasn't surprised Bear didn't hear him.

He knocked again, louder and longer this time. Almost immediately, the music dimmed by a hair and the front door flew open. Bear's eyes narrowed in surprise when he saw Fred standing there. He swigged from an open beer can and belched under his breath. "Yeah?"

"I need to talk to you for a minute," Fred shouted over the music.

Bear turned away from the door, but he left it standing wide open as if he expected Fred to follow him.

Fred wiped his feet on the mat and trailed Bear inside, closing the door behind him. He'd expected clutter, dust, and general chaos. Instead, he found a well-cleaned room, fairly new-looking furniture, and half a dozen flourishing houseplants around the room.

Bear draped himself in a corner of the couch beside an

open paperback novel and nodded toward a flimsy-looking chair across the room for Fred. "What can I do for you?"

Fred perched carefully on the edge of his seat. "You could turn down the music, for one thing."

Bear smiled and complied by flicking a remote control at the stereo system on the opposite wall. Immediately, the music died away and left Fred's ears ringing. Bear sat back again and smiled. "Next?"

"I'd like to ask you a few questions about Eddie Leishman."

"Oh, really? Why?"

"I'm a friend of the family's. I understand you knew Eddie well."

"Yeah, I guess I did. We'd been together long enough."

"I imagine his death came as quite a surprise to you."

Bear took another drink and held out the can as if he'd just remembered his manners. "Beer?"

"No. Thank you."

Another swallow. "Did Eddie's death surprise me? Yeah. Why wouldn't it?"

Fred could think of one reason, but he didn't suggest it. "Do you think he gave the injection to himself?"

Bear gave himself a moment to speculate, then shook his head. "Naw. Not Eddie."

"Why not?"

"Because Eddie always took care of Eddie. No way he'd ever mess himself up like that."

"You're sure?"

"Positive. Anyway, I thought Dr. Huggins screwed up somehow."

"There's some question as to whether Doc made a mistake." Fred crossed an ankle over his knee and tried to look like someone Bear might want to confide in. "The other day, you told Doc and me that you saw Eddie the night before he died."

Bear shrugged. "That's right."

"That was the last time you saw him?"

"Yeah."

"Then, you didn't see him Friday?"

"That was the day he died?" Bear started to shake his head, stopped, and eyed Fred curiously. "Why? What are you, a private investigator or something?" The last words came out on a sneer.

Fred didn't let himself react. "No."

"Then why should I tell you anything?"

"You don't have to if there's some reason you don't want to talk about it."

Bear glanced away, swigged more beer, then laughed as if he found the entire conversation amusing. "Well, I don't, so I guess I'll tell you. We were supposed to practice Friday, but he died before I saw him again."

"I see. Where was this practice supposed to be?"

"At Eddie's."

Now they were getting somewhere. "What time?"

Bear shrugged, but the fingers of his free hand drummed on his thigh. "I don't remember. Three. Four. Something like that."

"Where were you when Eddie died?"

Bear didn't even pretend to like that question. His fingers stopped drumming and started fanning the pages of his novel. "Here. Asleep. Alone."

"What kind of relationship do you and Ricki have?"

"With Ricki? The ice maiden? I don't have any relationship with her."

Fred tried to keep his voice innocent. "I was under the impression you were friends."

Bear took a few seconds to ponder that question, then let his expression thaw piece by piece. "I've known her for a while, but we're not exactly close. I knew she and Eddie'd been having problems, and I felt kinda sorry for her when Eddie finally decided to leave her."

"What kinds of problems did they have?"

Bear looked a little disturbed by the question, so Fred did his best to look only mildly curious. "The usual stuff," Bear said at last. "Money. Sex. Kids." He hesitated again. "Look, I'm not sure I should tell you all this—"

Fred didn't want Bear to shut him out, so he agreed. "All

right. Tell me about the band. Did you always practice at Sharon's house?"

Bear seemed to relax slightly. He nodded. "Ever since Eddie moved in."

"And how often did you go there?"

A hesitant shrug. "Once, twice a week."

"Did any of you have a key to get in?"

"To Sharon's house? Hell, no. She would *never* have let anyone else have one. She's too paranoid."

"Cautious, maybe. Is there any way in without a key?"

Bear shook his head and stopped fanning the book, more sure of his ground now. "No way. Eddie lost his keys once, and even *he* couldn't get inside. Gave him a good excuse to stay out all night."

"Eddie lost his keys? When?"

"I don't remember. A while ago."

"Did he ever find them?"

"Yeah." Bear laughed a little. "Right on the coffee table where he left them. Did you ever see that house, man? You could lose an elephant for a week in there. I don't know how they could live that way."

Fred supposed the explanation could be that simple, but a lost set of keys might explain a lot. "Besides the band, who else was at Eddie's house on a regular basis?"

Bear looked amused. "Eddie's woman of the moment."

"Who was that?"

Bear leaned back and draped an arm across the back of the couch. "What moment are we talking about?"

Fred thought about Sharon and pushed away the sick feeling that accompanied Bear's words. "Let's get back to the night before Eddie died."

"What about it?"

"How was Eddie that night?"

Another shrug, this one lazy and nonchalant. "He seemed pretty normal, I guess. He started out mad because he'd been fighting with Sharon again, and he got worse as the night wore on."

"That was normal?"

Bear nodded, narrowed his eyes, and asked. "You're a nosy old man, aren't you?"

"Concerned. Do you know what the argument was about?"

"No. And I didn't want to know. He came in complaining, but I told you, that wasn't unusual. And since he didn't stick around and have a beer after the last set like he usually did, I figured he'd gone home to settle things."

Fred tried not let his dismay show. "You figured he left to finish his argument with Sharon?"

"Either that or he hit it off with some girl."

Fred liked that explanation better. "Did you see him leaving with anyone that night?"

Bear tipped up his beer, shook the last few drops into his mouth, and swallowed. "No," he admitted. "In fact, the only person I remember him talking to was that guy—what's his name? Wayne something."

This time, Fred couldn't hide his reaction. "Wayne Openshaw?"

"Yeah." Bear stood, stretched, and muffled another belch. "You sure you don't want a beer?"

"I'm sure. What about Wayne Openshaw?"

Bear crossed to the kitchen door and disappeared through it without answering. When he returned a second later, he held another can. Popping the top, he swigged a mouthful as he settled back into place.

"You were telling me about Wayne Openshaw," Fred prompted. "I didn't realize he and Eddie were friends."

"Friends?" Bear snorted a laugh. "I don't think so. I never got the impression Wayne liked Eddie too much and Eddie pretty much ignored Wayne, but that night they got into an argument over by the jukebox after the first set." He held up a hand to stop Fred from speaking. "Don't ask me what it was about, because I don't know. All I know is Eddie was snapping at everybody when he came back onstage after the break. To tell the truth, we were glad he *didn't* stick around afterward."

Fred pictured Wayne sitting in the Bluebird with Geneva Hart a few days earlier and, with great reluctance, added

Wayne to the growing list of people he wanted to talk with. "What about you? Did you and Eddie get along?"

Only the fleeting unsettled expression in Bear's eyes gave him away. "As well as anybody could get along with Eddie, I guess."

"What do you mean by that?"

"Eddie wasn't an easy person to get along with. I didn't always like the way he treated other people—including his wife and son. But he was one hell of a musician, and we had a good sound together."

"You never argued with him?"

"Maybe once or twice," Bear admitted casually. "Creative differences. Nothing big." He glanced at his watch, made a face, and stood. Obviously, the interview was over. "Well, look, it's been real, but we're trying out a new lead guitar player tonight and I've still got to shower and shave before I meet the guy, so if you don't mind—"

Fred did mind, but he stood and followed Bear to the door anyway. There, he stopped to ask one last question. "Can you think of anyone else who might have had something against Eddie?"

Bear's face tightened. "Eddie grated on people."

"Even you?"

To Fred's surprise, Bear tipped back his head and brayed a laugh. "Old man, you are naive." He clapped a hand on Fred's shoulder and used it to propel him through the door. "Finding somebody who hated Eddie isn't going to be your problem. The trouble's going to be finding someone who didn't." And without giving Fred a chance to respond, he slammed the door between them.

Fred quickly rinsed his breakfast dishes to remove the evidence of egg yolk in case Margaret stopped by, and stacked them beside the sink to wash later. He carried his coffee cup back to the kitchen table where he pulled out the telephone book and began searching the Os for Openshaw.

He scanned quickly, missed the only Openshaw in the book, and had to come back to it. He couldn't find a listing for Wayne, but he did find Wayne's parents listed in

Mountain Home. He'd just have to stop by Glen and Beth's and hope Glen would be at work. Glen would ask too many questions, but Fred could probably finagle Wayne's address from Beth.

He wrote the address inside his checkbook next to Bear's and made a mental note to buy himself a pocket-sized notebook next time he was at Lacey's. When he heard a car approaching the house, he closed the telephone book quickly and stuffed the checkbook into his pocket in case it was Margaret coming to check on him.

To his relief, the car drove past without stopping. He locked the door behind him and hurried into the garage, anxious now to get away. He drove the back roads through Cutler until he couldn't go any further, then turned onto Main just long enough to speed past the Bluebird and out of town.

Though his joints ached from the approach of another storm, it hadn't started snowing yet and the roads stayed clear all the way up the mountain. Fred pulled off the road in front of the Openshaws' tiny white frame house a little after ten and followed a narrow path through the ice and snow to the front porch.

Fixing a friendly smile on his face, he waited for someone to answer his knock. Wayne's mother, Beth, peeked out of the lace-curtained front window a minute later and scurried to meet him.

She couldn't have been more than a year or two older than Margaret, but she looked much older. Strands of gray shot through her limp hair. Her face, once mildly pretty, looked puffy and pale and her eyes a little watery. She wore a full-length apron over sweatpants that looked as if they'd seen better days and a T-shirt that looked too small.

"Mr. Vickery? For heaven's sake, I haven't seen you in years. What are you doing here?" Without giving him a chance to answer, she pushed open the storm door with one arm and backed out of his way. "You'd better come in, before you catch your death of cold. It's freezing out there."

Fred stepped eagerly into the warm house and took a moment to phrase his opening remarks exactly right.

She didn't wait for him to speak, but closed the door on the frigid air and asked, "Are you here to see Glen?"

"Actually, I'm looking for Wayne."

"For Wayne? He's at work right now." She looked confused, but she glanced over her shoulder anyway, as if her son might surprise her and appear without warning.

Fred checked his watch and pretended surprise. "For Pete's sake, it's already after ten. The morning's gotten away from me. Maybe I should see him there. Where's he working now?"

"He's still at Summit Auto, working for LaMont Tingey. Why?"

"It's nothing important," Fred said casually. "I want to ask him a question or two." He paused half a beat, then quickly added, "About a car."

Beth fluttered her hand over her chest and gave an embarrassed laugh. "Oh. Well. *I* certainly can't help you with that. But I'm sure you could stop by the dealership. LaMont won't mind. He's so pleased with Wayne, he's always telling me how grateful he is to have him there."

Wayne must have changed a great deal from the boy Fred remembered for that to be true. He'd always been a troublemaker in school, backed by a mother who refused to believe her child could be involved in anything questionable.

She bobbed her head toward the door. "You know where Summit Auto is, don't you? Just north of town a mile or two?"

Fred nodded. "I'm sure I've passed it before. Thanks." He swung open the door and stepped back onto the porch. The temperature must have dropped in the short time he'd been inside.

"By the way," Beth called before he reached the first step. "How's Maggie?"

"She's fine. Busy getting ready for Christmas."

"Like the rest of us, I guess. Between family and the Winter Extravaganza, I'm practically beside myself. I'm on the committee this year, did you know that?"

Fred knew some people considered serving on the committee a mark of prestige. Phoebe'd often complained about the members who'd signed up just for show.

Beth beamed at him, obviously pleased with herself. "Poor Glen's had to pick up the slack around the house, and he's not pleased. I hear about it every night."

Fred couldn't remember Phoebe leaving any slack. Or maybe he hadn't been bothered by doing his share around the house. He lifted his hand in a wave and tried to leave the porch again.

"You'll tell Maggie hello for me?" Beth asked. "And we'll see all of you on Saturday, won't we?"

Fred smiled. "I wouldn't miss it." He'd been to the Extravaganza every year, and he wasn't about to skip one now—even if they weren't the same with Phoebe gone.

Beth screwed up her face, and seemed to pull another question from the clouds. "I saw Enos Asay the other day when I was dropping off some things for the Extravaganza. He seemed . . . distracted, I guess. Is he okay?"

Fred refused to voice his own worries about Enos and his marriage. He widened his smile and tried to look unconcerned. "As far as I know."

"Are you sure? He almost acted as if he didn't know me. And you know how close we all were in school. I couldn't help but wonder whether everything's all right with him."

"I'm sure he's fine."

Beth sighed and leaned against the doorjamb. "I suppose it's all that funny business with that Leishman fellow dying the way he did. And, of course, with Enos and Doc being such good friends, I'm sure it's hard for Enos to even think about putting Doc in jail."

Fred's smile slipped. "What makes you think he'll need to?"

"I heard Doc gave the wrong medication or something."

"Hogwash," he said in a tone he intended to be the final word on the subject.

But Beth seemed to think he'd left the matter open for discussion. "It's frightening, isn't it? I can't imagine Doc doing a thing like that, and yet . . ."

"Doc didn't do anything wrong."

Beth's mouth thinned. "I don't know how you can sound so certain. From what I hear, Doc might not have been as careful as he should have been—what with his daughter, and all. You know, I thank the good Lord every day that Wayne didn't turn out like that."

"Sharon is a fine young woman. No reason to be ashamed of having her for a daughter."

"Well, I know," Beth said. "But some of the things she's done." Her voice dropped as if she'd given explicit details. "As far as I'm concerned, Eddie Leishman belonged at home with his wife. Sharon had no business taking up with him, and it's tragic that Doc has to pay for her mistakes."

Fred glared at her. "How many years have you been a patient of Doc's?"

"All my life that I can remember."

"Have you ever questioned anything he's done before now?"

"Well . . . No. But there's all that business with Sharon, and Doc *is* getting up there." At least she had the grace to look embarrassed at saying something so stupid.

"Doc's age has nothing to do with Eddie Leishman's death. Nothing. *Doc* had nothing to do with it, for hell's sake, and I'm tired of listening to people insinuate that he did."

Beth's nostrils flared and she pulled back slightly. "How do you know?"

"I know Doc."

"I don't think you're facing facts, Mr. Vickery."

"And I think you're listening to too much gossip."

"*Gossip*?" Beth jerked her chin up in indignation. The tiny lines around her mouth turned white. She gripped the door with one hand and pulled her shoulders back. "If you don't know the difference between idle gossip and honest concern, I feel sorry for you." She shut the door hard enough to rattle the front window.

Fred glared at it for a few more seconds, then pivoted away. He'd had enough of that brand of concern to last a lifetime. He stormed back to the Buick, dropped onto his seat, and ground the ignition too far while he slammed the door. He turned the heater on high and let the car warm up while he tried to cool down.

He'd been the topic of conversation often enough to know how the grapevine worked. Nobody gossiped, yet everybody knew everything. "Must be a modern-day miracle," he groused, and jerked the gearshift into drive.

His tires spun uselessly for a second, then caught suddenly and the Buick shot onto the road. He took the corner a little too fast, and followed the highway the rest of the way through town a few miles over the speed limit.

The sky seemed to darken by the second, and the wind stiffened noticeably. Fred could feel the storm in his bones, and it didn't help his already sour disposition. He snorted to himself and glared at his windshield. From the sound of things, Fred and Summer were the only folks around who didn't believe Doc had killed Eddie. And to tell the truth, Fred didn't know whether having Summer on his side made him feel better or worse.

With every passing mile, he grew more determined to learn the truth and to clear Doc's name and restore his reputation. Then he'd watch all these *concerned* friends rally round Doc and claim they'd never lost faith in him.

ten

Fred found Summit Auto about three miles outside the city limits in a small trailer on the edge of a narrow parking lot. He parked in an empty space near the highway and started toward the office, but he didn't make it past the first row of cars before the trailer door opened and Wayne Openshaw bounded down the metal steps.

Wayne pulled on his coat as he walked, and every breath turned into a thick cloud around his face. With his brown hair and eyes and the light dusting of freckles across his nose, he had his mother's coloring—at least the coloring she'd had once—but the stocky legs, the barrel chest, and thick neck had come straight from his father.

Wayne flashed a gap-toothed smile when he recognized Fred. "Mr. V? What are you doing so far out of your way? Looking for a good deal in a used car?"

"Maybe," Fred said, and rocked back on his heels to study an ugly yellow Mercury Comet that had to be older than most of his grandchildren. "Actually, your mother told me I could find you here."

"My mother?" Wayne sounded surprised. "Where did you see her?"

"I went by your house to find you. I'd like to talk to you about something. Do you have a minute?"

Wayne stuffed his hands into his pockets and hunched his shoulders against the cold. He glanced back at the trailer, then shrugged. "Sure, I guess. What about?"

"Eddie Leishman."

The boy's shoulders stiffened again. "What about him?"

"You knew him?"

Wayne nodded cautiously. "Yeah. Slightly."

"He was a friend of yours?" Fred leaned against the Comet, but the metal conducted too much cold for comfort, so he straightened up again.

Wayne narrowed his eyes slightly. "Eddie? No, I barely knew him. His band played at this club I go to sometimes. Tex's in Snowville—have you ever been there?"

Fred shook his head. "I don't get out a lot."

"Too bad. It's a nice place."

"I'm sure." Fred waited for Wayne to continue.

He didn't.

"I understand you argued with him the night before he died."

Wayne flushed and flicked his glance away long enough for Fred to be sure he'd scored a hit. This boy should never play poker. He didn't have the face for it. "I don't know where you heard that," he protested. "It's not true."

"It's not?" Fred fixed him with a steady gaze. "Are you sure?"

"Why do you want to know?"

"By now, you've probably heard the rumors about Doc Huggins," Fred began.

Wayne shook his head and sighed heavily. "It's unbelievable."

"I think so, too. I've been talking to a few people, trying to help Doc by piecing together what happened during Eddie's last few hours. I can't help wondering whether Eddie gave himself that insulin."

Wayne laughed through his nose. "Eddie? You're kidding, right?"

"What makes you say that?"

"Just the way he was."

"You don't sound as if you liked him much."

Wayne flashed him an uneasy smile, then looked down at his feet and kicked at a pile of ice with the toe of his boot. After several seconds, he glanced at the ashen sky and sighed heavily. "Oh, hell, I guess I might as well admit it. Try and keep *anything* quiet in this town." He lifted his shoulders in an elaborate shrug. "No, I didn't like him, and yes, I argued with him."

"Do you mind telling me what you argued about?"

Wayne looked as if he did mind, but he answered anyway. "Nothing. Everything. He was a real jerk, you know?"

"So, what happened that night?"

"Nothing in particular. It was just the way he acted. Did you know him?"

"Not well."

"You're lucky." Wayne sagged against the Comet and stared out at the highway. "Eddie Leishman thought he was God's gift to women, and he assumed they were all dying to get into bed with him. You should have seen him come on to them, it was enough to make you sick." He shuddered at the memory and examined his feet, as if he expected Fred to sympathize with him.

Fred didn't have any sympathy to spare. "Maybe so, but that doesn't explain why you argued."

For a moment, he thought Wayne might refuse to say more. The young man pulled in a deep breath, held it for a minute, then finally seemed to quit resisting. "I don't know. Maybe I just had too much to drink."

"He must have done *something* to upset you."

"No." Wayne answered so quickly, Fred knew it had to be a lie. As if he could sense Fred's reaction, Wayne answered again, more slowly this time. "No. Nothing."

"Was anybody there with you?"

"No. I was alone." He looked out at the highway with such determined nonchalance, Fred knew it had to be another lie.

But he didn't think calling Wayne on it would get him anywhere. He pretended to ponder. "So, you argued with Eddie about nothing in particular?"

Wayne smiled sheepishly. "I know that sounds weird, but it's true."

Fred nodded slowly as if he believed him. "I take it you didn't know Eddie well enough to ever visit him at home?"

Wayne's cheeks flamed and his expression grew stony. "No. I don't even know where he lived."

A nasty gust of wind sent a blast of cold air up Fred's pant legs and worked it into his bones. He pulled his collar up and clutched it around his neck with one hand. "How often do you go to Tex's?"

"I don't know," Wayne said uneasily. "Maybe twice a month."

"I saw you with Geneva Hart the other day. Did she go with you?"

Wayne dropped his gaze and shifted from one foot to the other, but Fred couldn't tell whether he was cold or nervous. "She never went. She's pregnant."

"So I heard. Congratulations." He flicked another anxious glance toward the sky. "Well, that's too bad. I thought maybe an outside observer could offer some insight."

"Geneva can't tell you anything. She didn't even know Eddie Leishman."

"I take it you've seen the band together quite a few times?"

"Yeah, I guess."

"What can you tell me about them?"

"What do you want to know?"

"Do you know whether Eddie ever had trouble with anyone at the bar? Musicians? Customers? Bartenders?"

Wayne's shoulders relaxed visibly. He laughed. "Eddie? Always. It depended on the day of the week." He sobered almost immediately and gave it some thought. "There was Bear—his bass player. His wife—especially after they split."

"What about Bear?"

Wayne shrugged. "Bear was usually upset about something, but that's just how Bear is. He's a real hothead. The drummer and the keyboard player are a little more laid-back. Eddie didn't get to them the way he did Bear."

Interesting. "Did Bear and Eddie argue a lot?"

Wayne managed a thin smile. "I don't know what you'd call a lot, but they had some beef every time I was there. You know, like Eddie's guitar was too loud, or Bear's bass was drowning Eddie out, or one of their microphones was up louder than the other. Stupid stuff like that."

Maybe not so stupid. It might be worth checking out. The wind whipped past again and worked its icy fingers down Fred's neck. What a miserable day to stand outside questioning witnesses. "What about the night before Eddie died? Did they argue that night?"

"Thursday? What was that, the first? Not that I remember. At least nothing out of the ordinary." Wayne paused and stared hard at Fred. "This doesn't make sense. If you think Eddie gave himself that insulin, why are you asking me all these questions?"

"Trying to establish his state of mind."

Wayne shook his head and took a step backward. "I don't think so. You think he was murdered, don't you?"

"I didn't say that."

"You didn't have to. That's what you think, isn't it?"

"For the sake of argument, let's say he was. In that case, who would you guess did it?"

Everything in Wayne's expression closed down. His eyes grew more guarded, his shoulders hunched, his neck tensed. "How would I know?"

"I'm just asking for a guess. You knew Eddie. You'd have a better idea than I."

Wayne backed a step away. "I don't know. Doc, I guess. Everybody knows how much he hated Eddie."

Wrong answer. "Anybody else?"

Wayne shook his head. "Not really. I mean, Eddie was a real jerk, but I don't know who'd kill him."

"What about a jealous boyfriend? Or a woman scorned?" Fred demanded.

Wayne laughed a little. "Hell hath no fury, huh? But the problem with that is, Eddie didn't scorn women."

Fred was beginning to understand that. "Where were you Friday morning?"

The laugh died. "Right here at work." Wayne pushed his fingers through his hair and took another step away. "You don't think *I* did it, do you?"

"I'm asking these same questions of everyone." At least, he *would* when he talked to them.

Wayne didn't look as if that made him feel much better.

He glanced over his shoulder and suddenly seemed to remember where he was. "Look, I've got to get back inside before LaMont comes out to check on me. I don't want him to know about this." He broke off and his eyes widened suddenly. "You didn't tell my *mother* what you wanted, did you?"

"Don't worry. She thinks I came to look at a car."

Wayne tried to relax, but he cast another worried glance toward the trailer. "I've got to go. I don't know how I'll explain this as it is."

"Why don't you give me one of your business cards and tell LaMont I'm thinking about buying this Comet."

Wayne took a few seconds to decide that sounded reasonable, then he fumbled with his card holder and extracted one.

Fred dropped the card into his pocket and jerked his head back at the ugly yellow car. "Tell LaMont I particularly like the color."

That seemed to set Wayne at ease. His lips curved into a tight smile. "Nice, huh? We could work out a deal for you. Nothing down. Monthly payments . . ." He let his voice trail off with the inducement, but his grin wobbled a little.

"I'll give it some thought."

Wayne's smile died, and he stuffed his hands into his pockets and turned toward the trailer just as LaMont opened the door and filled the entryway with his bulk. Without so much as a backward glance, Wayne scurried toward the trailer as if he couldn't put distance between them fast enough.

Fred lifted a hand to LaMont and hurried back to his car almost as quickly. He didn't intend to stand out here in the wind for another fifteen minutes while LaMont tried to sell him that hideous car.

LaMont had to step aside while Wayne passed into the trailer. Fred took advantage of the moment to slide behind the wheel of the Buick and pull onto the highway before LaMont could get through the door.

He made a U-turn and headed for home, smiling a little as he drove. Fred wouldn't have admitted it aloud to anyone, but he enjoyed talking to people and piecing together puzzles like this one. It got his blood pumping and cleared the cobwebs out of his head. If he'd been a younger man, he might have pursued a career in law enforcement or seriously considered becoming a private investigator.

He headed back down the mountain and replayed his conversation with Wayne. He believed most of what Wayne told him, but *something* had started that argument between Wayne and Eddie, and Fred wanted to find someone who'd tell him what that something had been. Whether or not Geneva Hart knew Eddie, she did know Wayne. Chances were, Wayne had complained about Eddie a time or two. A visit to the young lady might be well worth a few moments of Fred's time.

He thought he remembered hearing that Geneva was working for her sister and brother-in-law at the new video store in Cutler. With any luck at all, that's where he'd find her.

Several miles from home, the first few lazy flakes of snow began to drift past his windshield. He flipped on his windshield wipers and squinted to see through the sudden blur they created. And he tried to force his mind off Eddie Leishman's death and onto the road long enough to get safely down the mountain in one piece.

Within minutes, the snowfall grew heavier. Thick, wet flakes splotched on his windshield and stuck to the highway, turning to ice almost immediately. He drove slowly, almost creeping down the mountain until at long last he drove into Cutler.

He breathed a sigh of relief that he'd made it home, then steeled himself for the drive through town. Even with the storm, there seemed to be a lot of traffic about.

Fred inched down Main Street, not daring to touch his brakes and send the car into a skid, especially with so many people out and about. Angus and Conan Rawley leaned from ladders across Main Street to hang a banner advertising the Winter Extravaganza. Alan Lombard looked up from supervising the stringing of lights in front of his insurance office and waved as Fred drove past. And Lacey's General

Store, with its windows painted for Christmas, seemed to be doing a booming business in spite of the weather.

Fred had to drive all the way to the end of Main Street to find a parking spot, and then he had to park between somebody's oversized Suburban and the barrier beside the lake in the only spot available.

He'd have to walk past the sheriff's office to get back to the video store, but he couldn't see Enos's truck anywhere around, so he figured he was probably safe. Still, he crossed the street to walk in front of the volunteer fire department and hoped whichever deputy Enos had left on duty wouldn't notice him.

Before he got halfway to the corner, the door to the sheriff's office opened and Grady Hatch stepped outside. He stretched to his full height, yawned loud enough for Fred to hear him across the street, and looked up at the sky as if he needed to come outside to check the weather.

Fred saw the exact moment Grady noticed him. He crossed to the boardwalk's railing and peered into the falling snow. "Fred? Is that you?"

"Morning, Grady."

Grady looked up the street, then back down to where Fred had left his car. "What are you doing?"

Nosy young whelp. "Just doing a little shopping."

Grady nodded as if that made perfect sense and almost turned away, but something stopped him and made him walk to the steps and down onto the street in his shirt-sleeves, proving once and for all that he hadn't an ounce of common sense. "Where've you been?"

"Here and there," Fred called back. "Tell Enos I said hello, would you?"

Grady shook his head and kept walking toward Fred. "Can't. He took the day off."

Fred stopped in his tracks. "A day off? With a murder investigation to conduct? That doesn't sound like Enos."

An expression Fred couldn't read flashed across Grady's face. "No, it doesn't, does it. He and Jessica drove into Denver."

"In this weather? Why?"

Grady had reached Fred's side by this time and he shrugged. "I guess to do some Christmas shopping. I don't know, he didn't tell me."

"Will he be back tomorrow?"

Grady nodded. "Far as I know."

"Well, good. I'll stop in to see him then." Fred started away again, taking care to plant his feet on the most solid looking patches of ground.

Grady tromped after him. "Where are you going, anyway?"

"I told you. Shopping."

"Then you're not going around asking questions about Eddie Leishman?"

Under the best of circumstances, Grady's habit of leaping to conclusions was annoying. Today, Fred found it downright irritating. He stopped again and faced Grady squarely. "Why on earth are you asking me that?"

Grady's lips twitched as if he found Fred's reaction amusing. "Oh, I don't know. Maybe because you're driving your car and the only time you drive your car anywhere is when you're sticking your nose in the middle of someplace it doesn't belong."

Fred glared at him. "You're jumping to a conclusion like that because I'm driving my car?"

Grady smiled. "You're snooping around again, aren't you?"

Fred humphed his answer and started away again.

"I can see right through you," Grady warned. "Why don't you tell me what you've found out? Or ask me what you want to know?"

"What makes you think I want to know anything from you?"

Grady brayed a laugh. "Oh, I don't know. You've got that look in your eye." He shivered a little and pounded his arms to keep warm. "You don't really expect me to believe you're not asking questions about Eddie Leishman, do you?"

Fred stared at him in dignified silence. "I don't expect you to believe anything."

"Doesn't matter." Grady looked at the sky again and sniffed. "We already know what you're up to."

The young whelp needed to be brought down a peg or two. Fred faced him with a thin smile on his lips. "I may ask a few questions from time to time," he said at last. "And I may have found some interesting information that helped solve a puzzle or two in the past. But I don't automatically start asking questions the minute something happens in this town."

Fred expected Grady to at least have the grace to look embarrassed, but he didn't even react. "Listen, Fred, you know how upset Enos gets when you stick your nose where it doesn't belong. He's convinced you're going to get yourself killed one of these days."

"Nonsense."

"If somebody did kill Eddie, you could get in over your head. We don't know who, we don't know why, and there's no guarantee he or she won't strike again—especially if *they* start feeling cornered. You have no business getting involved in official department business. Especially this time."

"I'll have you know, young man, that I've *never* interfered with an *official* investigation, and I resent you saying that I have." He started toward the video store again.

Grady followed him again. "Just tell me who you've been talking to. You might as well. We'll find out anyway."

Not if Fred could help it.

"Come on, Fred. Admit it."

Fred pivoted back toward him. "What on earth is bothering you, Grady? You want me to give you some pointers on questioning suspects? Is that it?"

Grady's smirk drooped. "No, that's not it." He took a step closer. "I don't want you upsetting Enos this time, that's all. I'm worried about him."

"I don't intend to upset Enos," Fred muttered, and would have started away again if Grady hadn't grabbed his coat sleeve and stepped closer.

"I'm serious, Fred. Something's been bothering him lately, haven't you noticed?"

"Of course I've noticed."

"I don't know what it is," Grady said. "Do you?"

Even with Grady, Fred didn't want to speculate. He hoped Enos's shopping trip to Denver with Jessica meant things were going better. But Grady looked so concerned, some of his exasperation evaporated and his own concern grew. "No. He hasn't said anything to you?"

Grady rolled his eyes. "Enos? You know how he is. He doesn't say anything."

That was true. Getting Enos to discuss a personal problem in anything but the most general terms was an accomplishment. Enos and Jessica had been over rough spots before, and Enos didn't usually let them show. This time, people were noticing.

"I'll talk to him next time I see him," Fred promised.

Grady didn't look particularly relieved. "Just don't tell him I said anything."

"I wouldn't dream of it, any more than you'd upset him by claiming that I'd been asking questions about Eddie Leishman."

Grady flicked an uneasy glance at him. "I can't keep that a secret."

"There's nothing to keep secret. It's all a product of your imagination."

"Right."

"Good. Now, go back inside where it's warm. You don't even have a coat on."

Grady still didn't look relieved. "Just don't do anything to upset him."

"Don't you worry about me."

Grady finally shrugged his acceptance and started to turn away, but halfway around he stopped again. "So, are you going to tell me who you've been talking to or not?"

"Believe me, Grady, if I knew anything about Eddie Leishman's death, I'd tell you." Fred smiled innocently to set the boy's mind at ease. After all, he didn't *know* anything about Eddie Leishman's death. Not really. And the few tiny pieces of information he'd managed to pick up didn't even form a complete clue.

"All right. Then where are you going now?"

Fred glanced toward the other end of town. "To the Bluebird. I'm cold and I need a cup of coffee. Want to join me?"

Grady hesitated for only half a beat, then shook his head. "No. Thanks." He took a step toward the door. "You'd better be telling the truth. Enos told me to lock you up if I caught you interfering."

"You won't," Fred promised.

He stood on the street and watched until Grady disappeared inside the office again. Saddened at the prospect of Enos having to suffer the pain of a failing marriage, Fred breathed deeply of the cold, thin air and turned his face to the sky. He watched the flakes spiral down from the slate-colored clouds the way he had as a boy, but he couldn't work up his usual pleasure in the snowfall. At last, he gave up trying and forced himself to remember why he'd stopped in town in the first place. Geneva Hart. Eddie Leishman. And murder.

eleven

After putting a block behind him, Fred checked over his shoulder to make certain Grady couldn't see him from the sheriff's office window, then ducked inside Video Ventures.

Luck must have been smiling on him because Geneva Hart sat with her elbow propped on the counter and her eyes glued on a television screen in the corner. She shivered and looked up with a vague smile as Fred entered, then returned her attention to the television screen. She obviously expected him to browse.

The television emitted a bloodcurdling scream and Geneva jerked back in fright, then managed an embarrassed laugh. "I don't know why I watch these kinds of movies. They terrify me." But she didn't even try to tear her eyes away.

Fred glanced at the television, grimaced at the scene playing there, and looked away quickly. Leaning an arm on the counter, he surveyed the room. A series of metal shelves held a collection of movie boxes, posters from movies Fred had never heard of lined the walls, and the smell of fresh popcorn filled the air. An interesting place, he supposed. Not one he'd want to spend much time in, but the grandkids would probably like it.

Geneva sent him a sideways glance from her wide brown eyes. She used one hand to gather her thin blonde hair behind her neck, then let it go again. "Do you need some help?"

Fred shook his head and scanned the room again. "Just thought I'd check out your sister's store."

She lifted her eyebrows. "Yeah? Well, here it is."

"She has a lot of movies," he said, hoping he sounded appreciative. "Everything going all right?"

"Yeah. I guess so." She peeked at the television again.

"Anything that might interest an old man like me?"

She glanced around as if she'd never really looked at the store before. "How about war movies? They're over against the west wall." She turned immediately back to the movie, leaving Fred no real choice but to follow through on what he'd started.

He walked all three steps to the west wall and scanned the titles there. To his surprise, there were movies he recognized but hadn't seen in years. He skimmed the next shelf over. "You have Westerns, too?" Maybe he'd have to reconsider buying a videocassette recorder.

"Do we?" Geneva sounded as surprised as he was. "I don't know, I just work here part time." As if that explained her complete lack of interest.

Fred pretended to study the next row of movies. Action hero stuff. Outrageously muscled young men with hair to their shoulders. Fred would pass on those. "Very interesting," he said as he returned to the counter. "By the way, I understand congratulations are in order."

She didn't bother to turn around. "That secret didn't take long to get out."

"When's the big day?"

That earned a curious glance. "May first."

"Are you and Wayne thinking of getting married?"

For the first time, she voluntarily whirled away from the television and stared at him. "Married? To *Wayne*? I don't think so."

"I thought you were a couple. That he was . . ." Suddenly embarrassed, Fred picked up a video box and gestured toward her with it.

"That Wayne is the father of my baby?" Geneva snorted a laugh. "No way."

"Oh." Her reaction left him groping for words and struggling to remember why he'd felt so certain.

"Who told you that, anyway?" she demanded. "Wayne?"

He shook his head quickly. It wouldn't do Wayne any

good to let her think that, and he didn't want to make any more trouble for Doc. Besides, he couldn't honestly remember whether either of them had actually said as much or whether he'd just assumed. "I saw you together the other day at the Bluebird, and I guess I drew the wrong conclusion."

Surprisingly, some of her anger seemed to dissipate. "Then Wayne didn't tell you?"

"No."

She seemed to relax even more, but her frown lines didn't completely disappear. "Well, that's good." She started to turn back to the television, then glanced over her shoulder one more time. "Did you find what you wanted?"

He looked at the box in his hand. A huge purple dinosaur stood behind a group of smiling children with his thick purple arms wrapped around the children's shoulders.

Geneva followed his gaze and looked back at him with a half smile. "You're not here for a movie, are you?"

"Not exactly," he admitted, and returned the box to its display rack on the counter.

"Then what do you want?"

"Actually, I was hoping you could tell me something about Eddie Leishman."

Her eyes darkened and her smile faded. "Eddie? What about him?"

"You knew him?"

"I knew him."

"Did you know him well?"

She peered at him through narrowed eyes. "Why?"

"Just trying to piece a few loose ends together."

Geneva stared up at him, expressionless, for a long time. She'd always been a difficult child to read, and adulthood obviously hadn't changed her. "What are you trying to do, help Dr. Huggins?"

"Yes."

"Why?"

"Because he didn't do anything wrong. And because he's a friend of mine. I won't let him suffer for something he didn't do."

"Maybe he did. My dad won't let me go to him anymore. He says Doc's too old to practice, anyway."

Fred looked deep into her eyes. "You know Doc didn't kill Eddie. No matter what your father's concerns are, you'd be perfectly safe with Doc caring for you."

"He's old," she repeated.

"He's still a good doctor."

She flicked a glance at him. "You really don't think he gave Eddie an overdose? Even accidentally?"

"No."

She still took an agonizingly long time to speak again, and Fred waited as patiently as he could. At long last she gave a brief nod. "Okay, I guess. But make it quick—before Donelle comes back. I don't want her to know I even *knew* Eddie."

That made a certain kind of sense. Eddie wasn't the kind of friend you'd take home to meet the family. He started again. "Did you know him well?"

She nodded slowly. "Yes."

"When did you see him last?"

"I don't know. A few days before he died, I guess."

"Not the night before?"

"No."

Surprisingly, Fred battled disappointment at having Wayne's story corroborated. He wondered briefly whether they'd coordinated their stories, but he didn't think so. "How did Eddie seem to you?"

"What do you mean?"

"Was he happy? Sad? Agitated? Angry? What kind of mood was he in?"

Geneva frowned slightly and tucked a lock of hair behind one ear. "Eddie was always worked up over something— that's the way he was. His music, his family, his band, his van—didn't really make much difference."

"Was he worked up about anything in particular at the time of his death?"

"I don't think so, but how would I know? I wasn't there."

"Can you think of anyone who might have wanted Eddie

dead? Anyone with a grudge against him or an ongoing battle?"

"No." She met his gaze and her eyes looked hopeful. "Why does it have to be murder? Maybe Eddie gave the insulin to himself."

Fred shook his head. "Not according to those closest to him."

"Oh? Like who? Ricki?" To Fred's surprise, he heard a faint note of bitterness in her voice.

He tried not to act as if he'd noticed. "Yes. And others."

"Sharon?" This time her voice sounded even harsher. And Fred suddenly understood the kind of relationship she'd had with Eddie, and had a new, unwelcome idea about the father of her baby.

The thought of it turned his stomach. He remembered Geneva as a young girl in pigtails, crossing the monkey bars at the school, jumping rope, and playing hopscotch. He didn't like thinking of her as another of Eddie Leishman's conquests. "Is Eddie the father?" he asked softly.

Geneva's face flamed. "What kind of question is that?"

"I don't mean to get personal," he assured her.

"Well, you are." She glanced toward the door as if she thought Donelle might be standing there. "I don't want to answer any more questions. I want you to leave before Donelle comes back."

In that moment, nothing could have made him walk away. He'd found a new trail—or at least a variation on an old one—and he wanted to see how far it ran. "As far as I'm concerned, this can stay between us, unless it ties in to Eddie's death."

Geneva darted a glance at him and tried to look forbidding, but her shoulders sagged a little and she succeeded only in looking young and vulnerable. "Well, it doesn't."

"Just help me understand Eddie so I can help Enos know where to look."

Geneva looked away and pinched her nose between two fingers. "I can't believe this. Will you just leave?"

"I can't."

She stared into his eyes for another few seconds, trying to

decide whether he'd back down or not. Apparently, she decided he wouldn't, because she sighed heavily and looked down at her fingers. "Don't tell my dad. He'd kill me. He hated Eddie."

"Are you sure he doesn't know?"

She smiled sadly. "Positive. You ought to see him around Wayne."

"But your dad knows you're expecting."

She nodded miserably. "He thinks Wayne's the father." She obviously hadn't done anything to change his mind.

"What about Wayne? What does *he* think?"

She still didn't look up. "He knows the truth."

"Wayne knows the baby is Eddie's, but he lets you tell people he's the father?"

"He thinks he's in love with me." As if that excused the deception.

"He *must* love you to agree to lie for you."

She shrugged as if it didn't matter. "I'm not in love with him. He's no Eddie."

That might be true, but Fred couldn't see the negative side to that, no matter how hard he looked. "What about Ricki? Does she know about the baby?"

Geneva pursed her lips and glanced at her stomach. "Of course she doesn't. I never told her, and Eddie wasn't stupid, either."

"Does Sharon know?"

This time a definite head shake. "I don't think so."

Fred considered that for a moment and wondered if Geneva was right. Knowing Eddie had kept yet another woman on the side might have been enough to send either of them over the edge of reason.

He felt Geneva watching him from the corners of her eyes, wary, expecting another question. He might as well find out the rest. "Did you go to Tex's with Wayne the night before Eddie died?"

"What night was that? Thursday? No."

"Did you see Eddie that night?"

"No. I told you, I hadn't seen him for a few days. He hadn't been calling so much."

Fred tried to picture Geneva as a jealous lover but he couldn't imagine her working up enough passion. "Let me get this straight," he said. "You were seeing Eddie at the same time he was married to Ricki but living with Sharon."

A nod.

"Did he know about the baby?"

She tried to look bored. "Yeah. Sure."

"He didn't offer—?"

She interrupted with a laugh. "To marry me? No. It was never an issue." Maybe not to Eddie, but the look deep in her eyes told Fred it might have been an issue to Geneva.

"I see. Where were you on Friday morning?"

"Are you asking for my alibi?"

"I'm really trying to find out if anyone saw him that morning."

She gave an amused shrug. "I didn't. I was home, arguing with my parents."

"So, you have no idea who killed him?"

Some emotion flickered across her face too rapidly for Fred to read it. "No."

"Eddie never told you about any trouble he might have had with other people?"

She flushed. "Well, yes. But—"

"Who might have been angry enough with him to kill him?"

Without missing a beat, she answered. "Sharon."

Fred's heart dropped. "Sharon Bollinger?"

"She's the only one I can think of. Eddie was talking about going back to Ricki, you know, and Sharon didn't like it."

"Who told you that?"

"I overheard him talking to Ricki one night at Tex's."

"When?"

"I don't know. A few days before he died."

"How did *you* feel about that? Did it upset you?"

A casual shrug. "No big deal. Like I told you, *I* never thought he was going to marry me."

Fred forced himself to ask, "And you think Sharon did?"

Geneva laughed through her nose again. "I don't think, I

know." She looked away again, as if the questions were beginning to bore her.

"What can you tell me about the guys in the band?"

She reluctantly dragged her gaze back to his. "Eddie had a hard time working with Bear, I know that. Bear was jealous of Eddie, but I don't think he'd kill him just because Eddie was a better musician." She glanced up at the clock on the wall and frowned back at him. "Will you please leave? Donelle's going to be back any minute and she's already freaking out about the baby. I don't want her to think I'm tied up in something like murder, and I don't want her to hear about Eddie and tell my dad." She stared hard at him, obviously expecting him to turn around and leave.

Half of him wanted to stay and demand more answers. The more logical side warned him not to push. "All right, I'll go. But I may need to come back." He pulled on his gloves and smiled. "Thanks for your time."

She turned away without even returning the smile.

Fred opened the door and stepped outside, sparing one last glance back at the girl behind the counter. He let the door close behind him just as a gust of cold, clean air whipped around his legs.

This time, he welcomed it. He dragged as much of it into his lungs as he could, and stood there for a moment letting his head clear.

The more he learned about Eddie Leishman, the more he understood why Doc felt the way he did. Eddie had gone through life doing as he pleased without looking back at the mess he made. He wanted to blame Eddie's death for leaving Geneva pregnant and alone, but in reality, Geneva would have been in the same straits even if Eddie had lived.

Fred took another deep breath and sighed heavily. He'd picked up some valuable information today. He had several leads to follow, but he felt strangely depressed, frustrated—even helpless.

Standing in front of the video store, he scanned the street and considered his options. He could walk back to his car and drive home, but somehow the idea of being in an empty house didn't appeal to him. He couldn't visit Enos, and stopping by Doc's certainly wouldn't cheer him up.

He needed coffee, and lots of it. And maybe an ice cream sundae with hot fudge sauce. And he didn't want to hear one more word about Eddie Leishman or the women in his life for at least an hour.

Just making the decision helped him feel better. He bent his head into the storm, shoved his hands into his pockets, and headed for the Bluebird Café.

twelve

To Fred's dismay, every stool at the Bluebird's counter already held an occupant, and customers had already claimed most of the tables in the dining room, including Fred's favorite corner booth. With his good humor slipping by the second, he scanned the room for an acceptable substitute.

In the corner by the back window, a group of teenaged boys laughed and tossed straw wrappers at each other. A couple booths up, Pete Scott and his new young wife gazed across the table through soulful eyes. By the front window, Summer Dey sat in a booth and stirred a cup of something hot with a listless hand. She didn't come in often, and Fred was surprised to see her there. The other two window booths held people Fred didn't even recognize.

On the jukebox, Elvis started belting out a version of "Proud Mary," which only served to spiral the boys' antics out of control. Somebody at the counter roared with laughter. With all the noise and confusion, Fred watched his plans for a peaceful cup of coffee evaporate before his eyes.

To make matters worse, George Newman turned around as if he intended to speak to Fred. Anything but that. Fred glanced around again. If he sat by himself, George would join him. But if he sat with Summer, George wouldn't bother him. And Fred would rather sit with Summer than leave himself open to a visit with George.

He started toward Summer's booth when one of the boys tottered to his feet and waved. "Hey, Grandpa."

Benjamin? Even better. Fred reversed direction and came to a stop in front of the boys' booth. He recognized Joshua

Leishman opposite Benjamin, Nathan Grimes and Tyler O'Neal on the ends of each bench.

Since Fred hadn't seen Joshua to offer condolences on his father's death, he thought about saying something. But he didn't want to rake up an unpleasant subject, especially since Joshua looked relaxed and happy.

He worked up a scowl and said what he figured he ought to say. "What in heaven's name are you doing here? Aren't you supposed to be in school?"

Benjamin grinned and caught Joshua's eye as if to say he'd predicted Fred's response. "We had an assembly. Boring stuff. Nathan brought us in his car."

Nathan Grimes waved sheepishly, Tyler O'Neal tried to smile, and Joshua nodded in Fred's direction.

"Wonderful," Fred groused. "A herd of teenaged boys running loose on snow-slick streets. Just what this town needs."

Benjamin's smile faded. "Jeez, Grandpa. Are you in a bad mood, or what?"

"I'm in a perfectly fine mood, but I'd feel a lot better if you were where you're supposed to be."

Benjamin rolled his eyes. "It doesn't matter. Nobody stays for the assemblies."

"As I recall—" Fred began, but broke off when he caught sight of Bear Sandusky in the parking lot. Bear paced into Fred's line of vision, lit a cigarette by the tailgate of his pickup truck, and paced away again. He acted like a man waiting to meet someone.

Without another word, Fred dragged a chair from another table and sat at the end of the boys' booth where he could still see outside without calling attention to himself. He smiled innocently at the boys and pulled an empty coffee cup toward him. "Well, then. Everybody ready for Christmas?"

The other three boys murmured answers, but Benjamin followed his gaze, glanced back once, and looked out the window again. When he turned back at last, he met Fred's gaze with a steady one of his own. "When are we putting up your tree?"

"I thought we could do it Monday evening after the Extravaganza's over. What do you think?"

"That's way too early," Tyler O'Neal said with a shake of his head. "We never put ours up until Christmas Eve."

"We put ours up the day after Thanksgiving," Nathan said. "Every single year."

Bear moved into sight, dragged heavily on the cigarette and flicked ash into the snow. He stood by his truck bed, staring at the street before he moved away again.

Benjamin gave no indication he'd noticed. "Hey, Josh, since my grandpa's here, tell him about your mom's truck. He knows."

Joshua didn't look particularly excited about it, but he shrugged and pushed hair out of his face. "Nothing to tell. It's all right, I guess. Kind of old. It runs."

Based on that recommendation, Fred couldn't imagine why he still resisted the idea.

"It's a great truck, Grandpa," Benjamin said. "Nate's seen it."

Nate nodded and slurped a mouthful of soda. "It's cool, Mr. V. Even my dad said he'd like to get his hands on it."

If Randall Grimes approved of it, Fred felt a little better about Benjamin's scheme. Not much, but a little.

Benjamin bounced back in his seat and said something to Joshua while Lizzie appeared at Fred's elbow and poured from a more than welcome pot of coffee.

"New set of friends?" she asked.

Fred leaned back to give her room to pour, caught a glimpse of the back of Bear Sandusky's coat where he'd stopped pacing near the edge of the window. Fred leaned a little further and tried to see if he'd met anyone yet, but the wall blocked his view.

He cleared his throat to catch Benjamin's attention, but the boy was too deep in conversation with Joshua to notice. He tried leaning a little further, but it didn't get him anywhere. He scooted his chair an inch to the left and leaned again. No use.

Unless he stood and called attention to himself, joined

Pete Scott's wife on her seat, or caught Benjamin's attention, he'd never know if Bear had a companion out there.

He glanced at Lizzie, noticed her quizzical expression, and scooted another inch to the left. She watched him in silence for several seconds, then walked behind his chair and peered out the window. "Your mom's out there, Josh."

Swearing, Joshua bolted to his feet and tried to climb out of the booth over Tyler O'Neal's legs. "I *told* you we shouldn't come here." As he reached the end of the booth, he caught Fred's cup with his hand and toppled it onto the table.

Tyler shouted and leapt up as coffee poured onto his lap. Nathan nearly tumbled from his seat. Benjamin started scooting across the bench.

Fred watched his coffee drain away as Elvis switched to a rendition of "All Shook Up." Reaching for a stack of napkins, he tried to soak up the mess and figure out why Ricki Leishman would meet Bear Sandusky in the parking lot of the Bluebird Café.

Before Benjamin could get out of the booth, the front door jangled open and Ricki Leishman stepped inside. She looked completely different than she had the other day. This time she wore some sort of athletic stretch pants and a ski jacket. She'd pulled her hair into a ponytail and wrapped a muffler around her ears, and Fred realized he'd seen her jogging around town before; he'd just never known it was her.

It took her less than a second to spot Joshua. Her face flamed and she marched across the dining room toward him. She caught him before he'd even put two tables behind him. "What in the hell are you doing here?"

"Nothing. Don't worry about it." Joshua pushed past her and started for the door.

She snagged the arm of his jacket and stopped him in his tracks. "You're supposed to be in school."

"Who the hell cares?" Joshua whipped his arm out of his mother's grasp and started away again.

She lunged after him, grabbed the hem of his jacket, and jerked him back to face her. "Get in the car."

"Get screwed."

"Don't you dare talk to me like that," she warned.

Joshua met her gaze and held it for an uncomfortably long moment. Pivoting away, he crossed to the door and this time his mother did nothing to stop him. But Fred could tell the boy's hostility had affected her deeply. Her coat rose and fell rapidly with each breath she took, her face burned, and the muscles in her jaw jumped.

Tyler sidled toward the front door, Nathan stood in the middle of the floor for a few seconds looking indecisive, and Benjamin bolted after Joshua. When they'd all disappeared, Ricki gave a little gasp and sank into a chair at an empty table.

She buried her face in her hands, and within seconds her shoulders began to shake with the telltale movements of a woman crying. She looked defeated and lonely, and Fred knew he couldn't let her sit there alone.

He pushed to his feet and closed the distance between them. Placing a hand on her shoulder, he took the chair beside hers. "Are you all right?"

She glanced up at him, saw who it was, and sobbed even louder.

Not certain what to do next, Fred looked around for Lizzie. He still needed coffee, and he suspected a soothing cup wouldn't do Ricki any harm, either.

But Lizzie had disappeared into the kitchen, and Fred didn't feel comfortable leaving Ricki alone yet. "Boys that age are difficult," he said.

"He's usually not like this," she said softly. "The past few days have been so strange."

Fred could only imagine. He remembered only too well the days immediately following Phoebe's death and the different ways they'd all expressed their grief. But he didn't know the best thing to say, so he muttered, "Why don't I buy you a cup of coffee?"

"Coffee?" She looked a little confused, but she pulled herself together after only a second. "All right. Coffee."

Fred patted the table as he stood, crossed to the kitchen door, and flagged Lizzie down on her way past with a steaming pan of meatloaf. He placed his order and returned to the table, feeling a little more sure of himself.

"Coffee's on its way."

A few of the worry lines worked their way off of Ricki's face. "Thank you. Maybe it will help."

While Lizzie filled their cups, the jukebox clicked again and Elvis began the opening lines of "For the Good Times."

Ricki wrapped her hands around her cup, sighed, and tipped her head back with her eyes closed.

Fred took a bracing sip. "You look exhausted."

She opened her eyes slowly. "I am."

"Try not to let Joshua upset you. He'll come around."

She smiled bitterly. "I doubt it, but thanks for the encouragement."

"It's been hard on him——" Fred began.

But she lifted one hand to stop him. "I appreciate the coffee, but I don't want to talk about it. All right?"

Fred couldn't think of a polite way to say no. He smiled and drank again, caught Summer watching him from her booth by the window, and watched George pay his bill and leave. He tried to convince himself not to push Ricki. But with Doc and Enos never far from the front of his mind, he couldn't let the subject rest.

"I couldn't help but notice Bear waiting for you in the parking lot earlier. I hope everything's all right."

She seemed surprised by his observation. "Everything's fine."

"I guess he's been very supportive."

Ricki's eyes frosted. "Bear had money for me. He bought Eddie's guitar and amplifier."

Already selling Eddie's musical equipment and his truck? Ricki wasn't letting any moss grow under her feet.

As if she could read his mind, she scowled at him. "Funerals are expensive."

He flushed. "Yes. Of course. I'm sorry." He let her anger dissipate for a few seconds. "I know how hard it is for you to talk about what happened."

She stiffened and glared at him over the rim of her cup. "I don't intend to talk about it."

Fred went on as if she hadn't spoken. "I know how painful the last few months have been for you with Eddie living somewhere else. But I think that's exactly why you need to find out the truth about why he died."

She lowered her cup to the table hard enough to make the dishes rattle. "I know what happened."

"Doc didn't make a mistake."

"Then *that woman* killed him."

"Sharon?"

Her lips pursed into a tight bud. "Yes."

"Eddie had trouble with a number of people before he died."

Ricki didn't move a muscle for several long seconds. When she spoke again, her voice sounded like ice dropping into the room. "I know what happened, Mr. Vickery."

"Tell me about Bear Sandusky."

Nothing in her expression changed, but Fred felt her tense. "What about him?"

"You're friends?"

"He was one of my husband's business associates."

"I understand he and your husband argued often. Can you tell me why?"

Her voice dropped another degree. "I wouldn't know about that."

Fred leaned across the table toward her and lowered his voice. "Listen, Mrs. Leishman, I'm not trying to make this any harder on you. I'm just trying to find the truth, and it seems to me you'd be as anxious as I am to find out what really happened to your husband."

She didn't respond.

"All I'm asking is that you at least consider the possibility that Doc didn't make a mistake when he treated Eddie and that Sharon didn't kill him."

She didn't even blink.

Fred tried not to show his discouragement, but it came out in his next words. "You were separated. Your marriage was in trouble—"

"My marriage was *not* in trouble." The words came out in a hiss so low Fred almost didn't hear her.

"Excuse me?"

"You have no idea what kind of marriage Eddie and I had. It was not in trouble."

"But he'd moved out. He was living . . . in another house."

Her bitter smile flashed again. "Yes. But you'd have to know Eddie to understand."

Fred glanced at the surrounding tables, cursed the lack of privacy, and wondered whether she'd agree to talk with him outside. He discarded that idea immediately, and decided to take his chances where he was. "So, tell me."

"Eddie was a free spirit," she said. "He couldn't stand to be chained down, and commitment trapped him. I understood that. I accepted that. Sharon Bollinger wasn't the first woman he took up with, and she wouldn't have been the last. But she didn't understand Eddie. She thought their . . . arrangement . . . was permanent. But Eddie wanted me. He was always asking me to come to him at her house. To make love to him there. But of course, I wouldn't. I told Eddie he had to make a choice. Well, he did. But when he finally decided to come home to me, Sharon threw an absolute fit."

Fred stared at her, trying to take it all in. She'd known about Eddie's affairs? And she'd accepted them? He didn't know if he'd ever understand that. He tried to imagine Phoebe's reaction if he'd strayed even once, and he knew he'd never have been allowed home again.

He took another mouthful of coffee and rubbed his hand across his chin. "Then you don't know of anyone else who might have wanted him dead?"

"No, I don't." She stood and glared down at him. "Now if you'll excuse me—"

Pulling a couple of bills from his pocket, Fred tossed them onto the table and hurried after her. She made it across the dining room and onto the street before him, and he had to walk quickly to catch her in the parking lot.

"I didn't mean to upset you in there."

She met his gaze squarely and held her silence for several

seconds. "I told you, I don't want to talk about it anymore. It's too difficult."

He lifted his shoulders in a gesture of surrender, though it was the last thing he wanted. He watched her walk away, head high and shoulders squared. She showed strength, and he had the feeling she was going to need every ounce she could muster over the next little while.

When he turned around, he saw Summer Dey watching him from the Bluebird's front window. She didn't avert her gaze, even when he caught her staring.

He managed a fairly pleasant nod before he walked away. He'd had a long, hard day already and he wanted time alone to sort through everything he'd heard. The last thing he needed was Summer spouting some of her mystical mumbo-jumbo at him.

His conversation with Ricki disturbed him more than he wanted to admit. He saw Ricki Leishman, Sharon Bollinger, and Geneva Hart as threads running through Eddie Leishman's life. All intelligent women who'd been swept head over heels by a man Fred could only think of as a loser. In one combination or another, they'd all known about the others, yet they still seemed smitten. Why?

He tried, but failed, to form an image of one of them killing Eddie. He tried to pull a motive out of the few things he'd learned about Eddie's business—such as it was. But every thought led him back to the same place, the women in Eddie's life and the people around them. Wayne Openshaw and Geneva Hart. Bear Sandusky and Ricki. Doc and Sharon. Vance. Or maybe, God forbid, there was another woman out there Fred hadn't even heard about yet. The more questions he asked, the broader the field seemed to grow.

thirteen

Fred walked slowly down the snow-covered trail around the lake and breathed deeply of the cold morning air. His visit to the Bluebird yesterday afternoon still played through his mind, and he needed his morning constitutional to start today off right.

Eddie Leishman left a bad taste in Fred's mouth. Every person he talked to only made it worse. And every story he heard helped him understand why Doc hated Eddie. But that only made him feel more frustrated and helpless. The idea was to find something that would make Doc look *less* guilty—not more.

Fred walked around the southern tip of the lake and headed north where he'd turn around at the far edge of Doc's property just as he'd done every morning for the past twenty years or more. He loved mornings, especially ones like this when he couldn't see another living soul around.

Closing his eyes, he turned his face toward the sky and let the weak winter sun dance there for a minute. Sunlight reflected off the fresh snow, nearly blinding Fred as he walked. It glittered, jewel-like, off the thin crust of ice covering the lake. But it did little to warm the air.

Fred tried to enjoy the scenery, tried finding pleasure in the sun and the snow, the crisp dry air, the deep green of the pines against the stark white snow. He didn't want to think about Eddie today. He wanted to think about the holidays, about taking his granddaughter Alison to dinner at Margaret's tonight, about his son Jeffrey and his family who'd be here for Christmas in less than three weeks. But he couldn't shake the shadow of Eddie Leishman from his thoughts.

When he reached the clearing behind Summer Dey's house, Fred hurried past, ducking his head as if that might make him less visible. He was in no mood for her nonsense today.

He traveled a few feet further, dreading Webb's birthday dinner but looking forward to a rare evening with Alison. But when he rounded a narrow curve in the path and saw Sharon Bollinger standing near the edge of the lake, Fred stopped in his tracks.

She stood with her head bowed and her arms folded across her chest, but she jerked her head up when she heard him approaching, and half a dozen different emotions flitted across her face.

Fred smiled brightly as he stepped off the path and followed her footsteps through the snow. "Morning."

She tried diligently to return the smile. "Good morning, Fred."

"It's been a few years since I've run into you out here so early in the morning. Did you stay over with your mom and dad?"

She nodded. "I let Mom talk me into it."

Fred worked his hands into his pockets and rocked back on his heels. "How are things between you and your dad?"

"Okay, I guess."

"Not any better than that?"

"No. I've managed to make him even madder than he was before." She glanced sideways at him, then sighed heavily and looked away over the lake. "I don't think he likes me much."

"Of course he does."

She shot him a look full of disbelief.

"He just doesn't like what you've done."

This time her glance seemed sharper. "You mean loving Eddie?" She laughed harshly and looked away. "He'll never forgive me for that, will he?"

Fred didn't answer immediately. "He only wants what's best for you," he said at last, but he knew instinctively she wouldn't like him saying that.

And he was right. Her shoulders jerked back and her eyes

glinted with anger. "He doesn't care what's best for me, all he wants is what's best for him."

"I think you're judging him a bit harshly."

"*He's* the one judging *me*. He says he loves me, but he sure doesn't act like it unless I behave the way he wants."

"Well, now—" Fred began, not sure he knew what to say.

But Sharon tuned him out. "He hated Eddie, so he refuses to believe I loved him. And since I couldn't possibly have loved him, I shouldn't feel bad that he's gone. He spent the entire night last night telling me horror stories about Eddie, and he doesn't even care how it makes me feel."

"I'm sure what your dad objected to most was that Eddie was married."

Sharon's face flamed in spite of the cold. "Legally, maybe, but not in his heart. He loved *me*. He wanted to be with me. He was going to divorce Ricki, and we were going to be married after the first of the year."

Fred couldn't hide his surprise. "You and Eddie were going to be married?"

"Yes."

"Does your dad know that?"

She nodded sadly. "I told him weeks ago, but he won't listen. He claims Eddie was lying."

Fred took a step toward her and tried to keep his expression gentle. "Sharon, I don't want to make you feel worse, but I think you should know that I heard yesterday Eddie was planning to get back together with his wife." He said it as kindly as he could, but she looked up at him as if he'd attacked her.

"That's a lie." She spoke sharply, as if she bit each word off with her teeth.

"Are you sure?"

She didn't answer his question, but countered with one of her own. "Who told you that, Ricki?"

Fred didn't want to bring Geneva's name into this, so he didn't say a word.

Sharon's mouth twisted into an ugly sneer. "You don't need to answer, I know it was her. It had to be. Well, did you also hear that she's been trying to get Eddie back for months? Did she tell you that she called him almost every day, trying to win him back?"

"I'm sorry, Sharon. I didn't want to hurt you."

Sharon didn't seem to hear him. She paced a few steps away. "She wouldn't leave us alone. She jogged past our house every morning. She even started going down to the bar, trying to get him back." She paused and studied his face. "You don't believe me, do you?"

"I don't know what to believe," he admitted.

She crossed back to face him. "Ricki's a liar. She always has been. That's what drove Eddie away in the first place."

Fred met her gaze. "I didn't hear it from Ricki." He paused another second, then added, "And I saw Eddie hugging her the night before he died."

She stared at him for a few long seconds, then seemed to lose whatever had held her up these past few days. Her posture sagged and tears welled up in her eyes.

Fred hated breaking it to her that way, but after all the stories he'd heard, he could draw only one conclusion about who'd done the lying. Eddie must have been a master at making women believe what he told them.

Drawing in a deep breath, he looked out at the lake again as if it would tell him what to say next. It lay still, icy and gray, and yielded nothing. "Has Enos figured out how the killer got inside your house?"

"No."

"Is there any possibility Eddie loaned his key to someone? Or maybe he had an extra key made for a friend—"

She began shaking her head immediately. "No. Absolutely not. He knew how I felt about the guys in the band—he wouldn't have given a key to one of them." But her voice didn't sound as definite this time.

Fred tried to think of a tactful way to phrase his next question. He couldn't. "What about other women?"

Sharon's eyes darkened. "*Women*? You mean Ricki?"

"Or someone else."

"You think Eddie cheated on me?"

Fred didn't answer.

Which must have told Sharon what she wanted to know.

She dashed tears away with the back of her hand. "I trusted him."

"Eddie didn't have any other women friends?"

"Yes, he had friends, but they weren't *that* kind of friends."

"What about his wife? Did she have a key?"

"No. Ricki never actually came to my house. I told Eddie I didn't want her anywhere near me."

Fred wasn't convinced that would have stopped Eddie. "Someone overheard him making plans to move back home with Ricki, and I know of at least one other woman who had a relationship with him—while he was living in your house."

"That's a lie," she shouted. "Who told you that? Bear Sandusky? What did he do, overhear it some night at the bar? He's drunk most of the time, Fred. How can you believe him?" She sounded almost desperate to find a way to make it untrue.

"I'm trying to figure out whether there's a jealous boyfriend or husband somewhere."

"And you think I'd know? I thought Eddie loved me."

"I know." He didn't look away from her angry gaze. "Sharon, *somebody* got inside your house last Friday morning. They took the glucagon syringe your dad used and filled it with insulin from your fridge and killed Eddie. Now, either someone else had a key or a way inside, or it was someone in your family."

"That's ridiculous. Who would have done it? Me? I loved him. Vance?"

"Vance hated him," Fred said softly.

She tried to laugh, but her efforts fell flat. "Or my dad, right? That's why you're so worried."

"I don't think any of you did it, but I'm worried one of you will end up paying for it."

She looked at her feet and pressed patterns into the snow with the toe of her boot.

"Sharon, help me." Fred's voice came out a little harsher than he intended. "I've been through this before, remember? Don't make the mistake of thinking Enos won't arrest someone just because they're a friend. He took Douglas into custody without batting an eye."

"What do you want me to do?"

"Tell me about Eddie's friends. Tell me about *anyone* who might have been a girlfriend—even one he wasn't seeing any longer."

"Why are you so sure Eddie was killed because of a woman?"

"What else could it have been?"

"What about the money?"

"What money?"

"The money he and Bear were arguing about."

Fred gripped her shoulders and turned her to meet his gaze. "What money?"

"I don't know details, I just heard them arguing about it a few nights before Eddie died. Maybe even the night before—I don't remember now, it's all so mixed up together. But I heard them arguing, and I heard Bear threaten Eddie—" She broke off, focused on something behind him, and whispered, "Here comes my mother. I don't want to talk about this in front of her."

"Just tell me what you know about the money."

"No." She glared at him and pulled out of his grasp. "Not in front of my mother. She has enough to worry about."

Fred glanced back to where Velma must have been following Sharon's footsteps from the house to the lake. She picked her way across the snow and looked up every few steps to make sure she hadn't lost her bearings.

Once she reached the trail, she stopped and shouted, "Sharon? I need to talk to you."

Sharon smiled and nodded. "I'll be right there, Mom."

Velma shook her head. "No. Now. It's important."

Sharon flicked a glance at Fred, then started away from the lake. "What is it, Mom? Is something wrong?" When Velma didn't immediately answer, Sharon's step faltered. "Mom?"

Velma crossed the trail and slid a few feet downhill toward them. "We have to go to the sheriff's office right away. They've arrested Vance."

Fred's stomach clenched. "Arrested Vance? For Pete's sake, why?" But he already knew the answer to that, and he suspected both women did, too. "Where's Doc?"

"I haven't told him yet. I came straight down here to get Sharon. I'm so angry, I can't even see straight. Ivan told me not to try to see Vance until he's been arraigned and bail is set."

"When will that be?" Sharon demanded.

"Ivan said it might be two or three days, depending on what the judge decides to do."

Sharon started toward the house. "That's ridiculous. Vance didn't kill Eddie. He couldn't have."

Velma followed, muttering under her breath. But Fred knew they were fighting a losing battle. If Margaret hadn't been able to budge Enos when Douglas was in jail, nobody could.

He trudged through the snow after them. "Maybe I should drop by and see what's going on."

Velma turned back to stare at him. "Oh, for heaven's sake, Fred, you sound just like Bernard. What do you think you can do that *we* can't?"

Fred tried to hide his sudden frown. He most definitely did *not* sound like Doc. "I could try talking sense into Enos," he said, but his voice held no conviction. Even he could hear that.

Velma shook her head and took another few steps away. "We'll handle this ourselves, thank you."

Fred trailed after her. "I've been through this before, remember? I know how Enos gets. He won't like it if you show up at his office when he's told you not to. And I don't know if you've noticed, but he's in a pretty foul mood lately. If you go over there now, you'll do Vance more harm than good."

Velma hesitated, reached out a hand and caught Sharon by the back of her coat.

"Enos isn't going to let any of you near Vance," Fred insisted. "Not today. But he doesn't know that I've talked to you. I could drop in for a visit, totally unaware there's any trouble . . ." He let his voice trail off and left Velma and Sharon to think through the possibilities.

Velma eyed him with new respect. "You really think you can help?"

"I'll do my best." It was all he could say. Enos wouldn't have arrested Vance unless he thought he had a reason.

Velma thought for a few seconds, searched Sharon's face for an answer, then nodded. "All right. I won't tell Bernard until I hear from you or he'll race over there like a mad bull. So you call the minute you know anything."

"Fair enough." Fred patted her shoulder, smiled again at Sharon, and turned away. He tried to hold his back straight as long as they could see him, but the weight of responsibility felt heavy on his shoulders. Maybe he'd given them false hope, but he didn't want Doc to make matters worse for himself than they already were, and he didn't want Sharon subtracting points from her own scorecard by saying things to Enos she probably shouldn't.

Imagining how he'd feel with Benjamin under arrest, Fred walked a little faster. This would be harder on Doc than his own arrest would have been. Fred could only hope he'd learned something over the past couple of days that might make Enos think twice about the case he thought he had.

It took nearly twenty minutes to follow the path back around the lake and then make the half-mile trek into town. Fred climbed the boardwalk to the sheriff's office and opened the door, slightly out of breath from walking faster than usual.

Enos glanced up from a pile of paperwork. Ivan Neeley pulled the door shut to the cell area and crossed to stand beside Enos. Fred couldn't see Grady anywhere.

He kept his expression innocent and his tone light as he pulled off his hat and unzipped his coat. "Morning, Enos. Morning, Ivan. It's beautiful out there today, isn't it?"

Enos didn't look exactly pleased to see him. "We're kind of busy here, Fred. Mind if we catch up with you in a minute?"

Fred dropped into a chair with a hearty sigh. "I'll wait. Nothing urgent on my plate." He cocked an ankle over one knee and smiled brightly, as if he hadn't a care in the world.

Enos obviously had several cares, and his expression showed them all. "We're in the middle of something. How about if I meet you down at the Bluebird in half an hour?"

Fred settled himself more comfortably in the chair, and looked up at Ivan. "What's going on? Where's Grady?"

Ivan folded his arms across his chest. "Business, Fred. And Grady's in the back."

Fred lifted an eyebrow. "Oh? You have a prisoner?"

Enos glared at him. "Why would you think that?"

"Well," Fred said slowly. "Because Grady's doing something in the back."

"He might be cleaning up the cells," Enos argued. "Or taking inventory."

"But he's not, is he?"

Ivan scowled as if he'd been caught cheating. Enos didn't move a muscle. "He might be shoveling snow in the alley."

"Or he might be processing a prisoner."

Enos seemed to consider that, then nodded once. "He might be. Like I said, we're pretty busy."

Fred leaned back in his chair and smiled, first at Enos, then at Ivan. If Enos wouldn't admit to having Vance in one of the cells, Fred couldn't very well ask what kind of case Enos thought he had, but he still had a duty to pass on vital information, and he had a moral obligation to Doc and his family to help.

"I had an interesting conversation the other day," he said.

"You're going to have to tell me about it later," Enos said.

But later wouldn't do Vance a bit of good. Fred went on as if Enos hadn't spoken. "I ran into Wayne Openshaw—you remember Wayne, don't you?"

Ivan glanced down at the top of Enos's head. They'd probably already talked to Wayne, but it wouldn't do any harm to pass on what he knew. "Wayne mentioned that he'd had a fight with Eddie Leishman last Thursday night—the night before Eddie died."

Enos stared at him. "Wayne just happened to mention that?"

Fred nodded. "In casual conversation."

Enos's face reddened a little. "I can just imagine. Can't you, Ivan?"

Ivan smirked. "Oh, yeah. People are always doing that."

Enos leaned across the desk. "What else did Wayne mention—in casual conversation?"

Fred held up both hands as if to ward off an attack. "I stopped by to look at a car. A nice little Comet. We got to talking—you know how that happens—and the conversation did happen to turn to Eddie, which I think is understandable under the circumstances."

Ivan rolled his eyes.

Fred didn't care. He'd play the game as long as Enos did. "Anyway, Wayne happened to mention that he didn't like Eddie's way with the ladies, but I suppose you already knew about that."

"Yes, we did," Enos said.

"Wayne's pretty smitten with Geneva Hart—you know her, don't you? Donelle Freckleton's sister? Works over at the video store?"

Enos nodded.

"Wayne told me Geneva didn't know Eddie, and that he and Eddie argued because Wayne had too much to drink. But you'll never guess what Geneva told me when I stopped by to congratulate her on the baby."

Ivan's eyebrows shot up, but Enos didn't even try to guess, he just stared at Fred without blinking.

"She did know Eddie. They were pretty close friends." Fred sat back in his chair and waited for their reactions.

Ivan darted a glance at Enos and took a step forward as if Fred might cower under the weight of Ivan's considerable authority. Fred didn't.

Enos clenched his jaw.

His uncharacteristic silence was beginning to unnerve Fred, but he'd be dipped if he'd show it. "I got to thinking maybe you'd like to know, so I stopped by."

Enos leaned forward and propped his hands on the desk for leverage. "Just exactly what are you trying to do, Fred?"

Fred uncocked his ankle and shifted position again. "I've

run into quite a few people the past few days who hated Eddie. Vance isn't the only one."

But Enos didn't look impressed. "I warned you not to get involved this time."

"I *didn't* get involved. I had a couple of conversations with my neighbors."

"Don't try to pull that on me this time. You and I both know the truth, so let's cut to the chase. You're interfering in an official homicide investigation. Again."

"Somebody needs to do something. You and I both know Vance didn't kill Eddie."

"I'm doing everything that needs to be done."

Fred snorted a laugh. "Have you talked to Wayne? To Geneva? What about Bear Sandusky?"

Enos leveled a finger at him. "You don't need to know what I'm doing."

"Hogwash."

He must have said the wrong thing, because Enos shot to his feet and started around his desk. "Get out of here, Fred."

But Fred didn't move. He wouldn't. Not until Enos came to his senses. "You know as well as I do that boy's innocent."

Enos walked straight past Fred, jerked open the door, and glared back over his shoulder. "Out."

Ivan took a step as if he intended to help Fred comply with the sheriff's orders, but Fred warned him off with a glare, then turned his frown to Enos. "All right, I'll go. On one condition. You tell me what's bothering you lately."

Enos's face looked too red, his eyes too angry. He didn't even look like himself.

"Everybody's been asking me," Fred went on. "And I've been covering up, trying to act as if nothing's wrong. But you're not acting like yourself, not even with me."

Enos didn't seem to care. "Get out of here, Fred, before I arrest *you*."

"For what? Talking to people? What law am I breaking? Or do you think *I* killed Eddie?"

Fred expected Enos to realize how ridiculous he sounded. Instead, the damned fool reached for his handcuffs on the back of his belt, and Fred decided maybe he'd pushed a bit too far.

He stood, clapped his hat on his head, and crossed the room with as much dignity as he could muster. He didn't spare Enos a glance as he passed.

Enos waited just until Fred got both feet on the board-walk, then slammed the door hard enough to rattle the glass in the window.

More worried than angry, Fred walked slowly away. Everyone had problems, he knew that. Enos certainly had his share, and they'd been through a few together. But Fred had never seen Enos's troubles affect him like this before, and he didn't have any idea how to fix things between them. But, to be smart, he'd probably better avoid Enos for a day or two and give him time to calm down.

He walked until he reached the bank, then screwed up his courage and dropped a quarter into the pay phone outside. Drawing a steadying breath, he punched in Doc and Velma's home phone number and prayed he'd know what to say by the time Velma answered. He couldn't offer encouragement, couldn't promise Vance would be home soon, couldn't even say for certain that Enos would eventually see reason. He only knew something was seriously wrong, and he hoped an innocent person wouldn't have to pay the price.

fourteen

Fred held seven-year-old Alison's hand loosely in his own as they walked together toward Margaret's front door. Alison had reached for his hand as they'd left her house, and Fred had taken hers eagerly. After the abuse she'd suffered at the hands of Garrett Locke before his murder, Fred always let her approach him first.

Colored lights along the eaves and on the trees lit the night. The lights on Margaret's Christmas tree blinked on and off in the front window. Alison watched it all with wide eyes as she recited the list of things she'd asked Santa to bring.

When she finished, Fred whistled. "That doesn't leave Grandpa much to pick from. What should *I* buy you this year?"

She smiled up at him and her small face glowed. "A camera."

"A camera? Does that mean you want to be a photographer?"

She nodded and her expression sobered. "I want to take pictures of my daddy when he comes to visit."

Fred smiled softly and squeezed her hand. His youngest son had always been a trial to him, and because Alison craved stability Douglas couldn't seem to provide, Fred made certain to fill in the gaps where and when he could. "Then that's what you'll get," he promised. "I'll add it to my list as soon as I get home."

Alison pulled her hand from his and scampered up the steps as if she hadn't expected any other answer. Her faith in him made Fred feel a little better, but he made a mental note to discuss Alison with Douglas next time he heard from the boy.

Before he could even get one foot on the bottom step, Margaret threw open the door and greeted Fred with a relieved smile. "I was afraid you'd forgotten."

More likely, she'd worried he'd change his mind. Fred looked down at Alison in mock horror. "Me? Forget a birthday party? Never."

With a giggle, Alison gave Margaret a shy hug and passed into the house. Margaret brushed a kiss to the girl's cheek and helped remove her coat, then reached for a hanger from the closet. "Deborah's in her bedroom. Do you want to let her know you're here?"

Without even a backward glance, Alison started toward the hall. But when Webb stepped out of his bedroom door in front of her, she stopped suddenly. And when he reached toward her, probably intending to ruffle her hair, Alison drew back sharply.

Webb stepped aside to let her pass and waited until she'd moved several feet away before he started toward the living room again. But once there, he shook his head and sent Margaret a disgusted look. "That kid's so damned jumpy, she makes me nervous. It'd drive me crazy to have her around all the time."

"That kid's got good reason to be jumpy," Fred reminded him.

Webb didn't seem to care. "Well, she's got to get over it. How many months has she been going to that doctor, anyway? I'll tell you what I think—they're ripping Suzanne off. Charging an arm and a leg for nothing—that's the way they do, you know."

Margaret flicked a warning glance at Fred and answered before he could say a word. "The therapy's helping, Webb, but Alison needs time. She's been through a lot. Anyway, Suzanne's pleased with the results so far, and since she's Alison's mother—"

Webb snorted his response and rolled his eyes. He flopped onto the couch and fumbled through the cushions for the television remote.

Fred settled into his favorite chair and wondered how he'd ever last all evening in Webb's company. He'd promised himself that for Margaret and the kids he'd try, but he hadn't expected Webb to act like an idiot within the first minute.

He worked up his most pleasant smile and turned it on his son-in-law. "It's not the big one today, is it?"

Webb drew his head back as if Fred had tried to hit him. "What? Fifty? No, not yet, thank God. I'm forty-eight today." As if reaching fifty would bring about the end of the world.

Enough small talk. Fred turned his attention to Margaret. "What are you fixing for dinner?"

To his dismay, she started back toward the kitchen as if she intended to leave them alone. "Pot roast. It's Webb's favorite."

And Fred's least favorite meal. Almost. He worked hard at keeping his smile in place.

Margaret paused at the kitchen door. "Do you want something to drink before dinner?"

If Fred had been a drinking man, he'd have jumped at the offer. Instead, he shook his head. "Nothing, thanks." He started to push back to his feet. "Maybe I should give you a hand with dinner."

"No. Stay there. I'll only be a minute." She disappeared around the corner before Fred could blink again. Wonderful. Alone with Webb. What in the Sam Hill would they ever talk about?

He thought of and discarded at least half a dozen topics for conversation, then finally settled on something even Webb ought to be able to discuss. "Think we'll get more snow?"

Webb nodded. "Probably. Heard it's supposed to be a wetter than average winter." He dropped the *TV Guide* into his lap and drummed his fingertips on one knee. He looked nearly as unhappy as Fred at being left alone together.

Fred focused on the Christmas tree and tried to find another suitable topic. "Where are the kids?"

Webb shrugged. "Sarah won't be home for a few more

days, Deborah's here somewhere, and I don't know where Benjamin is. Probably at work, I guess. I don't know—ask Maggie." He leaned forward to grab a handful of peanuts from a bowl on the coffee table. Shelling them into his fist, he tipped his head back and dropped them one at a time into his mouth. "Did Maggie tell me Jeff and Corinne are coming for Christmas?"

For the first time since Margaret left the room, Fred smiled. He loved having his children around, but he didn't see Jeffrey or Joseph and their families often enough. "Yes, on the twenty-fourth. I guess Corinne can't get off work until Friday. Joseph and Gail can't make it this year, though."

Webb fished another handful of nuts from the bowl. "What about Doug?"

Fred lifted a shoulder. "I don't know yet." And knowing Douglas, he wouldn't know until Douglas either showed up on the doorstep, or didn't, depending on his mood.

Webb ate peanuts for another few minutes, then dusted nut particles from his jeans onto the floor, oblivious to the mess he made. "I guess I don't have to ask whether *you* think Doc killed Eddie Leishman."

The question caught Fred off guard and left him speechless for a second or two. "Is that a question you're asking everyone?"

Webb half-smiled. "It's the latest thing. Did he or didn't he? Frankly, I'm pretty sure he did it. It's getting about time for these old geezers to step down. Let younger men have the jobs, know what I mean?"

Fred knew exactly what he meant, and though he wouldn't have expected anything else from Webb, he didn't like hearing it. "Doc is a good doctor."

Webb threw back his head and laughed as if Fred had told a wildly funny joke. "Every time I've seen you for the past two years, all you can do is complain about Doc. Now, all of a sudden, you're on his side." He curled his lip and looked away. "Typical."

Fred didn't hear Margaret return until she spoke up from behind him. "What's typical?"

Webb waved a hand in Fred's general direction. "Oh, your dad. Sticking up for Doc. I don't know why I'm surprised."

Margaret came out from behind Fred's chair and sat on the arm of the couch. "I have a hard time believing he's guilty, too."

Webb snorted. "Look, I'm not like most of the town. I don't think Doc killed Eddie on purpose. I just think the old guy made a mistake. Maybe his eyes are going. Maybe he couldn't see how full he had the syringe."

"He didn't make a mistake. Somebody else killed Eddie," Fred said firmly.

Margaret looked at him out of the corners of her eyes for an uncomfortably long moment. She started shaking her head slowly before she spoke. "Oh, no. No. You're *not* getting involved this time, Dad."

Webb rested his elbow on the back of the couch and grinned. "There's nothing to get involved in. I'm telling you, Doc screwed up."

"Doc *didn't* make a mistake," Fred insisted.

Webb leaned forward a little. "How can you be so sure?"

Margaret didn't pay attention to Webb. She stood, paced toward the Christmas tree and back again. "He's doing it again."

Webb fixed Fred with a steady gaze and asked again. "What makes you so sure Doc didn't do it?"

Margaret raced back across the room. "Don't encourage him, Webb. Don't even talk to him about it."

Webb chuckled. "This is great. I can get the inside scoop here. Maybe sell the story to the *Crier.*"

Margaret scowled at her husband. "Please don't. It's not funny." She turned to face Fred again. "Dad, you're not involving yourself. No matter how Eddie died you simply can't do this again, it's too dangerous. I want you to promise."

She looked so concerned, Fred didn't have the heart to tell her anything else. Besides, it wasn't a lie—not technically. He wasn't involved in the official investigation. He looked her straight in the eye. "I'm not involved."

"You *are*. I can't believe it." She pivoted back to face him. "No, that's not true. I can believe it, that's the problem. You're going to get yourself killed one of these times, Dad. Don't you understand that?"

Frowning, Webb wagged a hand toward her. "Oh, knock it off, Maggie. It's kind of funny when you think about it, your dad snooping around . . ."

Margaret didn't even crack a smile. "It's not a game, Webb."

No, it certainly wasn't. Fred didn't see what Webb found so amusing, and he wasn't at all certain he liked having Webb on his side. But before he could say anything, the front door slammed open and Benjamin stomped inside.

He tossed his coat on the floor of the closet, then crossed the room to kiss his mother's cheek.

"That's not where your coat goes," Webb snarled.

"I know. I'll get it in a minute. I've got to tell you all something." He dropped onto the far end of the couch and smiled at each of them in turn. His smile looked a little too broad, his eyes a little too bright to make Fred comfortable.

Margaret didn't seem to notice. Webb reached into the peanut bowl again. "What are you doing home?" he demanded. "Aren't you supposed to be working?"

Benjamin palmed his hair to put it in place. "Thayne let me off early since it's your birthday."

Webb rolled his eyes and cracked a peanut with his teeth. "Can't earn enough for tuition that way."

Some emotion flashed through Benjamin's eyes, and he flicked a glance at his mother. "Don't you want to hear my news?"

News? For half a beat, Fred worried he might be intending to tell them about the truck. In the next breath, he reassured himself. Benjamin was determined not to discuss the truck with his father until he had his mother firmly on his side. Only Fred's paranoia made him wonder about the truck in the first place.

Margaret smiled at her son. "Of course we do. What is it?"

The boy looked at each of his parents, flashed a grin at Fred, and said, "I bought a truck today."

Margaret's smile disappeared, Webb tossed his unshelled peanuts back into the bowl, and Fred felt a headache start low in the base of his neck.

"What in the hell did you say?" Webb asked.

Benjamin pulled his shoulders back and lifted his chin a little. "I gave Ricki Leishman a down payment on a truck today."

Margaret sighed. "Oh, Benjamin—"

But Webb didn't let her finish. "What money did you use?"

"My savings."

Margaret dropped back to the arm of the couch. "But that's your college money."

Benjamin shook his head. "I don't want to go to college."

Fred tried to make sure he wore an appropriate expression of shock and silently willed the boy to keep his name out of the discussion.

Webb surged to his feet and towered over Benjamin. "What are you, stupid?"

Margaret reached for her husband's arm and spoke in a soothing tone Fred had heard her use many times. "I think we ought to talk about this later. We've got company right now."

But Webb ignored her and continued to glare at Benjamin. "That's not even your money. *I* put it aside for you to go to college."

Benjamin shot to his feet and took a step out of his father's way. "How many times do I have to tell you? I don't *want* to go to college."

Webb glared at Margaret. "The boy's an idiot."

"There's no need to sling names around," Fred pointed out quite reasonably.

Webb ignored him. Ignoring Fred was one of the things Webb did best. "I ought to call the sheriff over here. You didn't have any right spending that money."

Big talk. Webb wouldn't do anything to voluntarily bring Enos into his home.

Benjamin didn't look worried, either. "It's my account, under my name."

"That's your mother's fault." Webb waved his arm toward Margaret. The broader his gestures, the angrier Fred knew he was. "*She* thought we could trust you."

"I don't want to talk about this now," Margaret insisted.

"Neither do I," Webb shouted and windmilled his arms a bit more. "But now that he's stolen the money from me, what am I supposed to do, ignore it?"

"I think that's a bit harsh," Fred said.

"I haven't stolen anything," Benjamin shouted.

Since Webb wouldn't listen, Margaret turned to Benjamin. "We'll talk about this later. This is between you and your father and me. We don't need to involve Grandpa in it."

But Benjamin was obviously too caught up in the argument to use any common sense at all. He wagged a hand in Fred's direction. "It's okay to talk in front of Grandpa. He knows about it already."

Absolute silence fell over the room for about ten seconds, and Fred's stomach clenched at the expression on Margaret's face. "Dad? You knew he was going to do this, and you didn't say anything?"

Webb glared down at him. "It figures. Damned old fool can't keep his nose out of anything."

Benjamin didn't seem to realize what a corner he'd pushed Fred into. He'd come home with his sales pitch ready to deliver, and he wasn't going to let anything stop him. "We're going to use the truck to haul equipment. We're going to line up gigs all over the county. School dances. Parties—"

Margaret looked as if she were having trouble processing everything at once. "You bought a truck for the band?"

Webb shook his head and turned partially away. "Oh, that does it. That really does it." He whirled back and shoved a finger close to the boy's face. "You're going over there and get my money back. And you can forget playing in that band of yours, do you hear me? I don't care what you've got lined up."

But Webb obviously hadn't reckoned on Benjamin's determination. The boy took a deep breath and let it out again slowly. "No, I'm not. I'm not giving up the band, and I'm not getting the money back for the truck."

Fred had faced this moment with each one of his boys. The situations had differed slightly, but they'd all challenged his authority—at least once. Joseph had been satisfied after the first time, Jeffrey had tried it a time or two, Douglas had made a career of it. But tonight's confrontation felt different, more volatile. Webb's temper ran hotter than Fred's ever had, and Benjamin never knew when to back down.

"You either go get that damned money back, or I will," Webb warned.

Benjamin looked down at Fred. "See? I told you he wouldn't listen."

That's all it took to plant Fred squarely in the middle of the argument. Webb turned his hostile gaze toward Fred, which forced Fred to stand and face him. But he'd have given anything at that moment for something to stuff into Benjamin's mouth.

Webb glared at Fred, breathing heavily as if the mere act of controlling himself left him exhausted. "Where in the hell do you get off, interfering with my kids?"

"He's my grandson, and when one of my grandkids comes to me for help, I'm not going to turn him away. Not for you. Not for anybody."

"You have no right."

"I have every right when you're not around for them to talk to."

Margaret groaned aloud. "Don't make things worse, Dad. Please. The bottom line is, Benjamin shouldn't have done something like this without talking to us first."

"What good would *that* have done?" Benjamin shouted. "You'd have said no, just like you're doing now. *He'd* have thrown a fit, just like he's throwing now. It wouldn't have made any *difference* if I'd talked to you first."

"All right," Margaret conceded. "What's done is done,

but I don't want to discuss this anymore tonight. It's your dad's birthday—"

Webb flung his arms wide and nearly hit a table lamp. "He doesn't care about that. He doesn't care about anything or anybody but himself." He turned on Margaret, still swinging his arms like a madman. "You've spoiled him, just like you've spoiled all the kids. The only thing your precious Benjamin ever thinks about is Benjamin. What does Benjamin want today? How is Benjamin going to get his own way? This is *your* doing, Maggie."

Fred stepped between Webb and Margaret. He'd heard enough of Webb's style of argument over the years to last him a lifetime; he didn't intend to listen to one more word.

Margaret tugged on his sleeve. "Don't, Dad. Please."

Webb sent him such a taunting look, Fred figured he must be equally eager to settle things between them. "No, Maggie. Leave him alone. I want to know what he's going to do about it."

Fred started to answer, but Benjamin pushed himself between them and faced down his father. The boy actually stood a few inches taller than Webb, but Webb probably outweighed him by fifty pounds. Benjamin didn't seem to care. "If there's anybody around here who's selfish, it's you. *I'm* not trying to force you to do what *I* want."

"Don't you talk to me in that tone of voice, boy. I'm your father."

Margaret looked as if she might cry. "Stop it, Benjamin. No more."

With Margaret defending him, Webb seemed to grow a few inches. "That's it, boy. From here on out, you'd better give me the respect I deserve or I'll kick you from hell to breakfast."

Benjamin's lip curved and his nose curled, and Fred waited without breathing for his next words. "Respect? You? Why don't you stay out of the bar sometime so I can?"

Webb swung his hand back as if he intended to strike the boy, but Margaret caught his arm. Without waiting to see Webb's reaction, Fred pulled Benjamin away and propelled him to the hallway and out of his father's sight before Webb could make good on his threat.

He pushed Benjamin toward his room while Margaret's voice floated down the hallway after them. He opened Benjamin's bedroom door and nudged him inside. "Stay there for a while. Let your dad cool down before you come out." He started to shut the door, looked back inside, and fixed Benjamin with a stern stare. "I mean it, Benjamin. I don't want anyone getting hurt over this."

Benjamin looked sulky, but he nodded and Fred closed the door between them. He turned back toward the living room just in time to see the door to Deborah's bedroom closing silently. With sinking heart, he realized the girls must have heard every word.

He crossed the hallway and knocked on the door. It creaked open immediately, and two sets of honey brown eyes met his. He bent his old knees and put himself on their level, then worked up his best smile.

"Everybody okay in here?"

Deborah looked resigned, as if she'd witnessed scenes like this many times. Alison pulled the door open the rest of the way and threw herself against Fred's chest. She wrapped her arms around his shoulders and spoke into his neck. "Are they getting a divorce, Grandpa?"

Fred didn't think he should admit how much he wished for that very thing, so he hugged her with one arm and put the other around Deborah's shoulders. "They're just having an argument, sweetheart. That happens sometimes."

He could hear Webb's voice rise and fall petulantly. "This is *your* fault, Maggie, not mine. I've warned you about him, a million times, haven't I? But you never listen to me."

"You're never home so I can listen," Margaret pointed out in a tone Fred thought sounded reasonable enough.

Webb fell silent for half a second, swore violently, and stomped across the room. "That's bullshit, Maggie. But if that's what you want—" The front door slammed and the house seemed to breathe a tentative sigh of relief that he'd gone.

Without missing a beat, Deborah pushed out of Fred's

embrace and ran down the hall to her mother's side. Fred straightened more slowly and followed her into the living room, still carrying Alison.

Margaret stood at the front window beside the Christmas tree and watched her husband storm away. Her shoulders sagged, and she dabbed at her eyes with her fingertips.

Deborah clutched Margaret's waist and leaned her head against her side. After a few seconds, Margaret put her arm around her daughter's shoulders and pulled her close.

Fred held Alison and watched the Christmas lights blink on and off. They highlighted Margaret's hair and the side of her cheek and mocked the ugliness of Fred's emotions, his helplessness, his frustration—his anger.

fifteen

Fred walked slowly down the sidewalk and turned his face from the wind. The rising storm matched his mood; unlike the storm, he couldn't do anything to relieve the tension.

Margaret and Fred had eaten Webb's birthday dinner with Benjamin, Deborah, and Alison in tense silence. The minute they'd cleared the table, Margaret had announced she wanted to go straight to bed, and even though Fred didn't believe her, he and Alison had gathered their things and left.

Now, with Alison safely home, Fred knew he should probably hurry home before this new storm hit. But he also knew he wouldn't sleep until he'd talked to Margaret alone. He wasn't naive enough to believe she'd welcome his interference, but he'd already turned a blind eye on her troubles for too long.

He slowed his step as he approached Margaret's house for the second time that night. The living room looked dark except for the lights on the tree; Margaret might have wanted the world to think she'd gone to bed, but she was too much her mother's daughter to leave the tree lights on overnight. Webb had only been gone a little over two hours; he wouldn't have come back this soon. Still, Fred checked his watch again to be certain.

Margaret didn't answer for several minutes, and when she did, she didn't smile. "Dad? What are you doing here so late? I was in bed." She'd dressed the part by putting on a nightgown and a thick robe, but even that didn't convince him.

"We need to talk."

"It's late. I'll call you in the morning."

"I can't leave, Margaret. I've waited long enough."

She pulled back a little and eyed him cautiously, then reluctantly stood aside to let him enter. She padded on bare feet across the living room floor and curled herself into the corner of the couch.

A blanket lay crumpled on the floor, one dim light burned on an end table, and she'd propped open a paperback novel on the back of the couch. Further proof, if Fred needed any, that she wasn't sleeping when he arrived.

"All right," she said. "Let's have it. I know what's coming, don't I?"

Fred perched on the edge of the seat beside her. "You might," he admitted. "I'm worried about you."

She couldn't meet his gaze. "Don't be."

"Well, I am. And I'm worried about the kids, too. How often do you have arguments like the one you had tonight?"

"I don't think that's something you need to know."

Fred didn't agree, but he knew she'd pull away completely if he pushed for an answer. "Sweetheart, you haven't been happy for years. Why are you still with him?"

She didn't answer immediately, and for a long moment Fred feared she might not. When she did speak, she couldn't meet his eyes and her voice sounded resigned. "He's my husband."

Fred had to admit that was an unfortunate truth. "Where is he now?"

She didn't look up. "You know where he is."

"Where he always is," Fred agreed. "Drinking away his salary at the Copper Penny. You're miserable, Margaret. Why do you stay?"

"We've been married twenty-six years, Dad. We've got three kids—"

"Do you love him?"

This time she didn't answer.

He touched her cheek gently. "Then do you stay because of the kids? Or because staying is easier than starting over?"

Her lips curved into a gentle smile. "That sounds like something Mom would have asked."

Fred smiled back and tried to blink away the sudden tears that filled his eyes. "Then I must be on the right track," he said, but his voice sounded gruff and hoarse. He cleared his throat and waited to speak until he could trust his voice again. "Sweetheart, you aren't doing the kids any favors by staying in a marriage where you're so miserable."

"I won't do them any favors by giving up."

"I'm not talking about giving up. Sometimes you have to advance in a different direction. Do you really want Sarah and Deborah to wind up married to men like their father? Or for Benjamin to act that way when he gets married?"

She turned further away from him. "They won't."

"Why not? No matter what you say, you're telling them this kind of marriage is okay, and they've never seen anything else."

"They saw you and Mom."

"They didn't pay attention to your mother and me. We were old folks."

She tried again to smile, but failed miserably. "You don't know," she said softly. "He's not always like that."

"I know more than you think." He pressed a kiss to her cheek. "I love you, Margaret. I only want what's best for you."

She gazed up at him, blinked rapidly, and looked away. "I know. But keeping Benjamin's plans secret from us didn't help."

"I didn't like doing it," Fred admitted. "But I'd already promised before I knew the whole story."

"But you lied to *me*."

"It was an impossible position, sweetheart. I had to betray Benjamin's trust or betray yours. I didn't like either option."

She shook her head angrily. "Webb's furious. It'll take weeks to put this behind us."

"I'm not saying Benjamin was right. Or that I was, for that matter. But that doesn't make it all right for Webb to talk to you that way, or for him to hit Benjamin."

"He didn't hit Ben."

"He came a little too close for comfort." He waited for her to speak again, but she remained silent for a long time.

He sighed and put his hands on his knees so he could push back to his feet. "Don't be angry with me. I had to say what was on my mind."

"I'm not angry."

"Maybe it's because so many people I care about are having a hard time right now. You. Doc. Enos—"

Her eyes flew back to his face and her forehead creased with concern. "Enos? What's wrong with him?"

"I wish I knew. He's not himself. I don't suppose you've talked to him lately or heard anything?"

She shook her head slowly. "I haven't seen him. Is he sick?"

Fred considered that. "Could be, I guess. But I don't think so. He's just not himself."

"Maybe he's busy. There's a lot going on right now."

Fred shook his head slowly. "That's not it, either. I don't think he's giving the Eddie Leishman case his full attention."

"Oh? And how would you know that, Dad?"

"I've heard a few things."

She pulled back and frowned. "Accidentally, I'm sure."

"Absolutely. In passing."

"What have you heard?"

"For one thing, Enos arrested Vance Bollinger this morning."

"I know. I talked to Sharon this afternoon." She looked deep into his eyes. "I suppose you've decided you need to help Vance now."

"Somebody has to. Enos isn't doing anything, and that muddle-headed Grady—"

"Grady's not muddle-headed. He does a good job. So does Ivan. They don't need your help."

"They need something."

"Oh, Dad." She shook her head in exasperation, but she still hadn't worked up to her usual level of argument. "What am I going to do with you?"

"You don't need to do anything. I can't help it if I pick up bits of information here and there."

She ticked her tongue against the roof of her mouth.

"Don't try that argument with me this time, because I won't believe it."

"It's true."

"I suppose it's nothing more than coincidence that you've been talking to Eddie's friends?"

"Maybe they need someone to talk to."

"And you just happen to be that someone?"

"Your mother always said I was a compassionate man."

Margaret laughed. "She did not. She said you were a stubborn old mule."

"She meant compassionate." This time when she looked at him, her face looked softer and a spark had returned to her eye. It was almost worth getting her angry with him.

Margaret sighed and leaned back on the couch again. "This whole thing is ridiculous, anyway. How could anybody kill Eddie with insulin?"

"The glucagon kit Doc used on Eddie the night before he died is missing. I think someone found that syringe in the trash, filled it with insulin from Eddie's fridge, and killed him with it."

Margaret shook her head slowly. "But who? Eddie wouldn't just lie there while somebody waltzed up to him and gave him a lethal injection. He'd have fought back. Besides, who had a key?"

"Those are two questions I can't answer," Fred admitted. "Sharon claims the house was locked up tight. Nobody else in the world admits to having a key, and there was no other way in."

She shook her head. "Impossible."

"Not if Doc or Sharon or Vance did it."

"No. I can't believe that."

"I don't believe it, either."

"Then somebody had a key."

"It always comes back to that. Trouble is, I don't know who."

"And you're not going to be the one who finds out."

Fred ignored her. "I suppose we'd have heard if Vance knew anything about what happened that morning . . ."

Margaret shook her head. "That's enough, Dad. You've taken this far enough."

"Maybe he heard something. Footsteps. A conversation. Or maybe he saw somebody approaching the house . . ."

"Let Enos do his job."

"I would, if he'd do it. But I *won't* sit back while he keeps Vance in jail and doesn't even bother looking for the real killer. What does Sharon say about the way Eddie died?"

"Sharon?" Margaret shook her head slowly. "She thinks Ricki did it."

That came as no surprise. "Well, that's fair since Ricki thinks Sharon did it."

Margaret sighed. "I hate this."

"I know. Has Sharon ever mentioned anything else about Eddie? Anything that might give Enos something to go on? Something she might have said in the past that seemed unimportant?"

"Like what?"

"Like trouble with somebody. An argument? *Anything*. Did she ever say anything about Eddie going back to Ricki?"

Margaret gaped at him. "Back to Ricki? No." She shook her head slowly and pulled back to stare at him as if he might be making it up. "No. That's not true. Is it?"

"That's the trouble," Fred admitted. "I don't know what's true and what isn't."

"I know Sharon was worried about the band breaking up, but I never heard anything about Ricki."

"The band was breaking up? Are you sure?"

"I don't know details, I just know Sharon told me a few days before Eddie died that he might not be working much longer. She was worried about what her dad would say if he found out."

With good reason. Doc wouldn't have been happy to hear about that. But this and the money Sharon had mentioned made two things Bear had neglected to mention, and Fred couldn't help but wonder why.

Maybe Bear needed money. Maybe Eddie was removing

Bear's only source of it. Maybe Bear Sandusky had a few good reasons for wanting Eddie out of the way.

Fred smiled in satisfaction, cast an anxious glance at Margaret to make sure she hadn't noticed, and pulled his face back into line. "Well, it's all upsetting, that's for sure. But I guess you're right, there's nothing I can do about it." He tried to sound resigned.

Margaret sent him a sideways glance and spoke hesitantly, as if she didn't know whether to trust him or not. "No, there isn't."

"All I can say is, it's a good thing you're here for Sharon. She needs a friend."

"I know."

He checked his watch and pretended surprise. "It's late. I guess I'd better let you get to bed." He kissed her cheek again and stood.

Acting much more like herself, she followed him to the door. "What are you trying to pull?"

He turned back to face her. "I don't know what you mean."

"Just like that, you're willing to give up and let Enos do his job? I don't believe it. You're planning something."

How had he managed to raise his daughter to be so suspicious? Or had she learned it being married to Webb? Purposely keeping his face innocent, Fred nodded toward the Christmas tree. "Don't forget to unplug that. Fire hazard."

"The only good thing is that I think it's too late tonight for you to go anywhere," she muttered. "I'm coming by to check on you first thing in the morning, and you'd better be there."

"I might go Christmas shopping."

"Where?" She looked suspicious and angry. Her eyes gleamed with that peculiar golden light that had always signaled a temper in her mother.

Fred didn't mind seeing a little of her sass back, he just wished she'd use it where she needed it most—on Webb. He waved a hand over his head as he started down the steps. "Oh, I don't know. Here and there. I've got lots to do."

"I don't believe you," she called after him. "If you go chasing around town sticking your nose in where it doesn't belong, I'll hear about it."

That was certainly true, but he couldn't change that, so he'd have to stay a step or two ahead of the gossip. He waved again when he reached the sidewalk and turned toward home. With a shake of her head, she stepped back inside and closed the door. A second later, he saw the Christmas tree lights flicker out and he knew now she'd be able to sleep.

But for Fred, sleep would be a long time coming. He had a lot to think about. He didn't want to chase over to Enos's office and accuse Bear of murdering Eddie unless he was positive he'd found the right person.

Neither Geneva nor Ricki seemed hostile or angry enough with Eddie to kill him—though each of them probably had good reason to be. Bear and Wayne each admitted arguing with Eddie. Each had lied about why. Bear and Eddie had argued about money. Wayne was obviously in love with Geneva who was pregnant with Eddie's baby. Other men had been killed for less.

With sinking heart, Fred realized he didn't have enough to take to Enos. Not yet. He needed to know more about Bear and Eddie. About the money. He needed to talk to someone who'd seen Bear and Eddie together, someone who didn't have reasons to lie.

He crossed Lake Front Drive and started down his driveway when the solution came to him. Tex's Tavern.

He smiled, dug his key from his pocket, and climbed the front porch. Checking his watch again, he considered driving out there tonight when he knew the place would be open. But he didn't want to run into anyone involved in the case—certainly not Bear Sandusky. So he'd wait until daylight, when Bear was almost certain to be home sleeping.

With a satisfied smile, he let himself in the front door and locked it behind him. And he promised himself that by tomorrow afternoon, he'd have what he needed to get Vance out of jail.

sixteen

Fred didn't even try to visit Tex's Tavern until nearly noon. He doubted whether it would be open any earlier than that, and he didn't want to call too much attention to himself by showing up at an odd hour. He found the bar in a low building made of dark, weathered wood on the highway outside Snowville. It occupied one end of a wide dirt parking lot, and the number of tire marks in the frozen mud told Fred it was a popular hangout.

Today, the parking lot stood empty except for one pickup truck near the building. But neon beer signs glowed in the windows, leading Fred to believe the place was open. Couldn't hurt to try, he supposed. He'd slip inside, order lunch, and engage the bartender in casual conversation that he hoped he could turn to Eddie. And Bear.

He parked near the door and hurried inside, pausing to let his eyes adjust to the sudden dim lighting and his nose adjust to the layers of old cigarette smoke. When he could see again, he gave the room a quick once-over. The bar stood at one end of the long, narrow room. A tiny stage holding a drum set, three or four amplifiers and two microphone stands occupied the other. A dance floor cut through the middle of the room with tables lining either side and filling a small carpeted area in front of the bar.

Delightful.

A muscular young man of about forty watched Fred expectantly from behind the bar. Thick brown hair curled over his ears and touched his collar, a heavy mustache hid his mouth, and the kind of lines a person earned from living hard etched his face.

Fred turned toward him with a friendly smile and hitched himself onto a bar stool. "Afternoon."

The bartender inclined his head and swiped at the counter in front of Fred with a damp cloth. "What can I get you?"

"Do you serve lunch here?"

The bartender shook his head. "Sorry. No kitchen. But we've got jerky, chips, and eggs." He used his chin to point to a bottle filled with eggs floating in a foul-looking liquid.

Fred decided against lunch. He'd stop at the Tastee-Freeze on the way home. "What kind of chips?"

The bartender nodded at a variety of bags clipped to a piece of cardboard. Fred settled on one, and pulled money from his pocket.

The bartender tossed the chips onto the bar and reached for Fred's money, then stopped. "You want something to drink?"

"Water?" Fred asked hopefully.

To his relief, the bartender nodded as if he could fill the request, pulled Fred's money off the bar, and turned around to make change.

"Is the owner around?"

The bartender looked back over his shoulder. "You're looking at him."

"Tex?"

"You got it. What's on your mind?"

Fred shook his head to indicate he had nothing special to ask, then glanced around again. "You have a band in here?" Fred asked.

"Four nights a week." Tex slapped change on the bar in front of Fred and filled a glass with ice and water.

"Are they any good?"

"Why?" Tex asked with a smirk. "You going to come dancing?"

Impudent young whelp. Fred fixed him with a glare. "Any reason why I shouldn't?"

Tex stopped smiling at his own joke and attacked an imaginary spot on the counter with his cloth. "No, I guess not." He swabbed again, shrugged, and looked at the stage. "They're pretty good, I guess."

Fred munched a stale chip and gave the room another look. And he couldn't help wondering why Benjamin thought making a living in places like this sounded glamorous. The chairs were old and faded. A dozen or more broken ones lay in a heap on one side of the stage. The tables had definitely seen better days, and the few patches of carpet were stained and filthy.

"Is the band a local group?"

Tex nodded without volunteering anything.

"My grandson's a musician."

"Oh, yeah? What are you, his manager?" A hint of the smirk returned in a flash across the man's craggy face.

"No. But I wonder if he'd know any of the folks in your band."

"He might, I guess. Let's see, there's Bear Sandusky, Mike Anderson, and Franco something-or-other."

Fred nodded thoughtfully. "The first name sounds familiar. Doesn't he play with a guy named Eddie?"

This time Tex's expression changed just a little. "Leishman? Yeah. He used to be in the band, but he died last week."

"Oh?" Fred tried to look surprised and shocked, appropriate expressions, he imagined, under the circumstances. "What happened?"

"I don't think anybody knows yet. I heard rumors that the doctor was too damned old to know what he was doing." He glanced quickly at Fred as if he'd suddenly realized how tactless his remark was, and shrugged. "But I've heard other rumors, too."

"Oh? Like what?"

"Like I heard the doc killed him because Eddie was living with the old man's daughter . . ." He broke off, lifted his eyebrows suggestively, and left Fred to fill in the blanks.

Fred had to force himself not to set the record straight and to keep his expression one of polite interest. He ate another chip. "That must be hard on the rest of the band."

Tex worked a stopper into place in the bottom of a deep sink and turned on the water to fill it. "I don't know. I guess. To tell the truth, I'm not sure they're exactly brokenhearted.

Eddie wasn't what you'd call a real nice guy." He filled the sink with glasses and swished a couple through the suds.

Chewing thoughtfully, Fred nodded as if he understood the man's comments completely. "That's my worry with Benjamin," he said honestly. "Too many of these fellows seem to get caught up in the wrong sorts of things."

"How old is this kid?"

"Sixteen."

Tex whistled and whisked another couple of glasses through the water. "I got a kid about that age myself. I don't want to see him get into this life. There's women, liquor, drugs . . ." He let his voice trail off and met Fred's eyes. "The kind of things that can lead to real heartache if you get involved, you know?"

Fred knew. "So, was that what happened to this guy?" He gestured vaguely in the direction of the stage.

"Eddie?" Tex reached for two more dirty glasses. "Yeah, I guess. Eddie was burning himself out. He always did too much of everything, and he got on people's nerves. Even the women—" He broke off with an embarrassed laugh, then obviously decided Fred could survive hearing about it. "I've never seen anything like that guy. Women loved him, man, but I never got it. He wasn't that good-looking. He wasn't even that smart."

"But the women liked him."

Tex laughed. "Yeah. At first. But they all got tired of him. Tell your grandson that. It never lasts with guys like these. It's all surface, you know what I mean?"

Fred did, but he didn't want to derail the man's train of thought, so he just nodded.

"I mean, the guy had a decent enough wife, but he was always cheating on her, you know? And then he'd cheat on *those* women with others. It was something." He upended the clean glasses in a rack and reached for two more. "But sooner or later, they all got tired of him. Except his wife. What kept her coming around, I'll never know."

"She came to see him often?"

"Yeah. Every other weekend or so. Even when they were having problems. Sometimes Eddie would seem real glad to see her, but at other times . . ." He let this one dangle, too. Another fill-in-the-blank answer.

Had Fred been on the wrong track? Should he be looking at Ricki's motives a little closer? He leaned forward a little. "She came to see him right up until the time he died?"

Tex pondered that for a few seconds. "Yeah. I think so, anyway."

"What about last weekend? Did you see her last weekend?"

Tex stopped washing dishes to stare at him, and Fred knew he'd gone beyond typical grandfatherly concern. "Why do you want to know?"

Fred popped another chip into his mouth and smiled around it. "Just curious."

But the suspicion didn't budge from Tex's eyes. "I don't think so, bud. Just what do you want?"

"I'm a friend."

"Of *Eddie's?* No way."

"Of Doctor Huggins. And of his daughter."

It took a second for the connection to register, but Tex pulled back a little when it did. "You know Sharon?"

"Do *you?*"

Tex nodded. "Sure. She used to come in here all the time."

Fred glanced around again and tried to picture Sharon here. He couldn't. "Is this where she met Eddie?"

"It's where they *all* met Eddie."

"Then you know Geneva Hart, too?"

"Little Gennie?" Tex looked surprised. "Yeah, I know her."

"What about Sharon and Geneva? Did either of them come in last weekend?"

He didn't even have to think about that question. "Nope."

"You're sure?"

"Sure, I'm sure. Some of us were talking about it, you know? I mean, since Sharon stopped coming in, it was pretty obvious Eddie was cooling it with her, then Geneva stopped coming in." He chuckled as if he found the memory amusing. "In fact, right at the end, Eddie had a couple of

guys come in to see him, but no women. We laughed about
it, if you know what I mean."

Fred figured he did. "Who were the guys?"

Tex unstopped the sink and dried his hands on his apron.
"I don't know, but they were both pretty upset with him.
There was one guy who started shoving Eddie around,
Eddie and Bear got into a big one between sets Thursday
night. And then there was that kid—"

Fred didn't ask, he already knew. "Wayne Openshaw."

To his surprise, Tex shook his head and leaned one hip
against the counter. "It wasn't Wayne. It was some other kid.
Dark-haired. Too young to be in here, probably, and hotter
than a pistol at Eddie."

"Could it have been Eddie's son?"

"No, I know Josh. He used to come in once in a while to
pick up Eddie's guitar or to help his old man set up the
equipment. No, this was somebody else I'd never seen
before."

Fred could think of one more possibility, but he didn't
like it. Vance. And if Enos knew Vance had been here
arguing with Eddie, was that why he'd been arrested?

Tex nodded toward the stage. "You could ask Bear about
the kid. He knew who he was."

Fred would do exactly that. He tried to push away the
new concern and concentrate on what he'd come in to find
out. "You said that Eddie and Bear argued. Do you know
why?"

Tex barked a laugh. "It'd be easier to tell you what they
didn't argue about. Women. Music. Booze. Money. They
argued about everything."

"What about money?"

The man shrugged. "I don't know exactly. I gave Bear
their pay the other night and before I knew it, I heard the
two of them going at it. I couldn't tell you details, though.
I was too busy to pay much attention."

The door opened and sunlight split the gloom. Tex looked
away, nodded toward his new customer and reached into a
cooler for a bottle of Coors. "Hey, Leroy. Didn't expect to
see you up and at 'em so early."

Fred didn't want to lose his attention. Not yet. He leaned across the bar. "You didn't hear anything of their argument?"

"Enough to know it was about money. Nothing else. Sorry, man. I wish I could help you." He twisted off the bottle cap and started toward Leroy.

Fred watched him go, watched him push the beer toward Leroy and lean across the bar. Within seconds, they were deep in conversation and Fred knew he'd been dismissed.

Fred climbed the stairs to the second level of Bear Sandusky's apartment building, followed the walkway to the end, and pressed the doorbell. No answer. He rang again and waited, but with every passing second, he grew more frustrated. He rang again, then again until Bear answered, sleepy-eyed, spiky-haired, and clad only in his briefs.

"What in the hell do *you* want?"

"I need to talk to you."

"Come back later." Bear tried to shut the door, but Fred blocked it and the door bounced back open. "What the hell? I'm *sleeping*, man."

"Five minutes of your time. If I have to come back later, I'll bring the sheriff with me."

Bear hesitated long enough to make Fred worry he'd call the bluff, then groaned and stepped aside to let Fred enter. "What do you want?"

"I want to know what you argued with Eddie about Thursday night—and be honest with me this time. I don't want to hear about professional differences or who's the better musician. I want to know about the money. And I want to know why Eddie was worried the band might break up."

That certainly got Bear's attention. He scowled and tried to look innocently confused. "What money?"

"I know you and Eddie had trouble over money. Everybody knows you and Eddie had trouble over money. I want to know what, and I want to know why."

"Why should I tell *you*?"

"Because I'm just about convinced it's a motive for

murder, and I'm about ready to take what I know to the sheriff."

Bear's eyes widened. He dropped to the couch and lolled his head from side to side as if it might help him form a coherent thought. "Okay," he said at last. "But you've gotta know right off that I didn't kill him."

Fred perched on the edge of a chair and waited, but his expression didn't concede a thing.

Bear scowled, huffed about for a second or two more, then finally started talking. "I found out Eddie was skimming money off the top of the band's pay. I told him. We argued. There. Now you know. Satisfied?"

"No." But neither was he surprised. Eddie's loose moral fiber had weaved its way through every part of his life.

"Well, I *didn't* kill him."

"That's what everyone says. When did you find out what Eddie was doing?"

Bear managed to look utterly miserable. "The night before he died."

"Thursday?"

Bear nodded. "It was in between the third and fourth sets, and I was at the bar getting a beer. Eddie always collected our pay at the end of the night, and none of us had a problem with it—he'd just bring it back to the table and divvy up the cash, you know?"

Fred didn't know, but he nodded anyway.

"Well, that night, Tex had to leave early, so he catches me and asks if I'll take the band's pay. I figure no big deal, right? So I go with him, and he hands me the cash, and I count it. But there's fifty bucks more than we usually get." Bear raised an eyebrow and pulled a bitter smile from somewhere. "So I tell him he overpaid us, and he counts it back and says no, he didn't. Well, I know right then and there what Eddie's been up to. He's pocketing the extra fifty and splitting the rest of the money four ways, right?"

Fred nodded again.

"So this time, *I* pocket the fifty and I give Eddie his share of the four-way split. Well, he looks at me, and he knows that I know, and he catches me by the jukebox a few minutes later and tries to explain how he's worth the extra cash because he's the lead singer, and how we all agreed to work for so much a night, and how I don't have any right to be upset because he's making more than the rest of us."

"Nice guy," Fred said.

Bear laughed bitterly. "Yeah. So, anyway, we get into it right there in the club, and I tell him we're through and I'm going to the other guys, and he offers to split the fifty with me every night as long as I don't break up the band."

"Did you agree?"

Bear flushed a little and darted a glance away. "I told him I'd think about it." He turned back wearing an earnest expression. "By the next day, I knew I wasn't going to go for it, and I was going to tell the other guys at practice and let *them* take Eddie apart, but I never got the chance. He was dead before I ever saw him again."

Fred pondered the story and looked at the ceiling thoughtfully. "You didn't pay him a visit Friday morning?"

"No," Bear almost shouted his answer. "Why would I?"

"Seems to me, I'd want to know what Eddie was going to do about all the other nights he skimmed money off the top of my pay."

Bear flushed a deep red. "Yeah. Well."

"Maybe after I thought about it a while, I'd decide to confront Eddie about that," Fred suggested.

This time, Bear didn't say a word.

"So, did you?"

Bear still didn't speak.

"Maybe you did," Fred suggested. "And maybe Eddie refused to do anything about it. Or maybe he laughed at you, and you got angry enough—"

"To what? Shoot him full of insulin?" Bear interrupted. "That doesn't work, does it? Can you picture it? I got so mad, I stormed into the kitchen, filled a syringe with insulin and shot Eddie full of it. Man, if I was going to off Eddie, I'd have used his own gun to shoot him, or I'd have hit him with something, or *maybe* I'd have stabbed him."

Fred hung onto the first of Bear's options. "Eddie had a gun?"

Bear nodded. "Carried it in his boot."

"All the time?"

"Never left home without it." Bear smiled a little at his joke. "You're way off base here, man. Way off base."

Fred's mind raced. Where was the gun? Did Sharon have it? Had the killer taken it? The possibility of a murderer on the loose with a gun put a little different spin on the picture. But in that case, why hadn't the killer used the gun on Eddie? Why use insulin as a weapon instead?

"If you didn't kill Eddie, who did?"

Bear shrugged lazily. "What does it matter?"

Fred's face froze into the expression he'd used on his sons when they were misbehaving. "Humor me."

Evidently, Bear didn't feel like humoring anyone. He met Fred's gaze and held it without blinking.

Tightening his hold on his temper, Fred tried another tack. "I spoke with Tex today. He mentioned a young kid, dark hair, who came in the night before Eddie died. He said the kid argued with Eddie and that you knew who he was."

Bear's eyes cleared and he almost smiled. "I'd forgotten about that."

"Who was it?"

"The kid? Sharon's son. Vance."

Fred's spirits plummeted. "You're sure?"

"Sure, I'm sure. I know Vance. Saw him every time we had practice. I've even had a beer or two with him."

"He came into Tex's and argued with Eddie the night before Eddie died? What about?"

"Take your pick. Vance hated Eddie living with his mother, hated the way he kept Ricki coming around all the time, hated him screwing around with other women." Bear laughed aloud, then sobered. "Vance hated Eddie. Period. He told Eddie to pack up and move out, or he'd kill him."

Fred tried to keep his voice steady when he spoke again, but despair tweaked at him as if Vance were his own grandson. "He used those exact words?"

Bear nodded and met Fred's gaze, a little surprised by the memory. "Yeah."

Fred willed it to be untrue. A misunderstanding.

Bear stood, looking as dignified as a man can in nothing but his underwear. "I don't know what you're so worked up about. They've already got the killer, haven't they?"

"Vance didn't do it," Fred insisted.

Bear smiled slowly. "I'm not talking about Vance. Haven't you heard? The old man confessed this morning."

"What old man?"

"Doc. Walked right in to the sheriff's office and spilled his guts."

seventeen

Fred's breath caught in his throat and he stood to face Bear. "Doc *confessed?*"

"Yeah. Ricki called earlier to let me know. She's pretty happy that it's finally all over."

"It's not true," Fred insisted. "He didn't kill Eddie."

"Doesn't matter what you say, Doc says he did." Bear looked pleased with himself, almost as if he enjoyed Fred's discomfort. "Look, if you want to know what happened to Eddie, ask the old man. But get out of here. I'm beat. I didn't get to bed until after four, and you're the second person to wake me up."

More than a little numb, Fred turned toward the door. He had nothing more to ask, anyway. He struggled to keep his face expressionless and his walk steady all the way back to his car. But there, he leaned his forehead against the steering wheel and battled the heartache that suddenly threatened to overwhelm him.

He sat that way for several minutes, until the shock wore off and a little common sense returned. Nothing would make him believe Doc killed Eddie—not even a confession. The old fool had obviously confessed to keep Vance out of trouble. Fred could hear him now, moaning that his own life was nearly over and Vance had his whole life in front of him. Ridiculous.

At least, Fred had the consolation of knowing that Enos would see right through Doc's confession. He'd laugh Doc right out of his office. And he managed to hang onto that hope halfway back to Cutler. Then, a niggling doubt pushed its way to the surface of his mind. If Enos hadn't believed

Doc, if Doc wasn't in jail, how had Ricki found out about Doc's confession?

Maybe she'd been there when Doc came storming in. Or one of Enos's big-mouthed deputies had carried the story to the Bluebird and given it wings. Doc might even have gone for a cup of coffee and laughingly told the story on himself.

Fred refused to even consider the possibility that Enos had taken Doc seriously. Refused to picture Doc in jail. But Enos hadn't been himself lately, and Fred knew that anything—even the unthinkable—was possible. In the end, he decided it might be smart to stop by Enos's office so he could see for himself that Doc wasn't in jail and set his mind at ease.

He drove as quickly as he dared back into Cutler, parked beside Enos's truck, and hurried into the sheriff's office. He expected to see Enos behind his desk and Doc in one of the old chairs across from him. Instead, he found an empty room.

A pot of stale coffee heated on the burner of the coffeemaker, several stacks of files teetered on the edge of Enos's desk, and somebody's blue parka hung on the coat rack. Doc's old overcoat lay across one of Enos's chairs and the door into the cell area stood partway open, but Fred couldn't see Enos, Grady, Ivan, or Doc anywhere.

Not a good sign. Fred started across the room, fully intending to deal with Doc and Enos at the same time.

Before he even reached the open doorway, Ivan Neeley pulled the door open the rest of the way and planted his stocky body squarely in Fred's way. "What can I help you with, Fred?"

Fred didn't have the time or the patience for games. "I just heard that Doc confessed to killing Eddie Leishman."

Ivan nodded once. "That's true."

"Well, for Pete's sake. You don't believe it, do you?"

"I can't talk about the case—especially not with you."

To tell the truth, Fred didn't want to talk with Ivan, either. He wanted Enos. Scowling, he nodded toward the cell area. "Have you got Doc back there?"

"We might."

"Then let me see him."

"Sorry. Restricted area." Ivan firmed up his stance as if he suspected Fred might try to bulldoze past him.

Fred thought about it, but decided not to push his luck. "You're not allowing Doc any visitors?"

"Not unless the sheriff clears it first."

"Let me talk to him, then. Where is he?"

"He's in the back, but he's busy. He sent me to deal with you."

Fred pushed down a rising seed of resentment. He didn't need to be *dealt with*. "Now listen, Ivan—"

But Ivan held up both hands in defense. "I'm just following orders, that's all. If you don't like it, take it up with Enos next time you see him."

The muscles in Fred's neck tensed and he had to struggle to keep his voice level. "Do you have any idea when that might be?"

"I don't have a clue."

That didn't surprise Fred a bit. "I'll wait. Let him know I'm here." He started toward the chairs in front of Enos's desk.

Ivan hustled around him and planted himself in Fred's path again. "I don't think that's a good idea. I'll let Enos know you were here, and he can call you—"

"Apparently, he already knows I'm here. What's he doing back there, questioning Doc?"

Ivan worked so hard not to react, Fred knew it had to mean yes.

"He *believes* Doc's ridiculous confession?" Fred demanded. "For crying out loud, Ivan, you know as well as I do why Doc confessed. And if Enos was in his right mind, he'd know it, too. What in the hell is he thinking?"

Ivan leaned a little closer and lowered his voice. "We've got evidence, Fred. We've questioned everybody who lives anywhere near Sharon's house, and nobody saw anybody go near that house. And Doc knows enough details to make the case pretty tight."

"He's a doctor for hell's sake. He could make up the details. For that matter, *I* was at the scene of the crime—I could probably make up a pretty convincing story myself."

Ivan glanced over his shoulder as if he thought Enos might loom in the doorway any second. "Maybe, and maybe not. Look, we all know how you feel about Doc. Enos has been expecting you to show up all afternoon. But he's not in a good mood, and he's given us orders to lock you up if you try to interfere."

"You can't be serious."

Unfortunately, Ivan looked completely serious. His mouth formed a thin line, his eyes narrowed, and his shoulders rose to meet his ears. "Do yourself a favor, Fred. Leave. Enos isn't going to take any crap from you this time."

"*Crap?*"

Ivan's expression soured. "I mean it, Fred. Leave it alone."

"If I leave this to you idiots, Doc will wind up in prison."

"If you don't, *you* might. Now, will you get out of here?"

Fred wanted to argue, but considering Enos's mood lately, maybe it would be a good idea to leave while he could. Doc needed help, and Fred wouldn't do him a bit of good from inside a jail cell. "Just tell me whether Enos has let Velma see him."

Ivan nodded and lowered his voice another notch. "She was here for a minute, but Doc didn't want to see her."

"Damned fool. When are you expecting Judge White to set bail?"

"I don't know. Look, you've got to leave. If I don't get back in there, Enos'll come out here in a minute—"

Fred patted the boy's arm. "I'm leaving, don't worry. I won't get you into trouble." He took a step or two toward the door, then thought of one more thing he needed to know. "I guess you've released Vance?"

Ivan nodded. "We processed him out a couple of hours ago."

"Did he go home?"

"I don't know, Fred. He didn't say where he was going, but if you're smart, you'll stay away from him."

Fred didn't bother to respond to that, he just yanked open

the door and stepped outside again. He didn't have time to quibble.

Fred rang the bell on Sharon's front door and slipped his hands into his pockets. Through the cloudy glass on the side of the door, he saw a shadowy figure start down the stairs and a second later Vance opened the door.

The boy wore an oversized flannel shirt with a crisp white T-shirt underneath and jeans that had definitely seen better days. "My mom isn't here," he said without preamble, and started to shut the door.

"I didn't come to see your mom." Fred caught the door with his hand and pushed it back open none too gently, but he kept his face as pleasant as he could. "Do you mind if I come in?"

Vance shrugged elaborately and turned away to lead Fred up the stairs into the living room. There, he dropped into a chair and kicked his feet onto the coffee table. With a flick of the remote control, he muted the sound on the television, but the black and white figures of Jimmy Stewart and Donna Reed still danced on the edge of Fred's vision.

"So, what do you want?" Vance demanded.

Fred lowered himself onto the couch and tried not to wince at the twinge in his knees. "I need to ask you a few questions about Eddie."

"I've already answered enough questions."

Fred's patience, already stretched taut, snapped. "You know your grandpa's in jail right now, don't you?"

To give the boy credit, he did look uncomfortable when he nodded.

"Why do you suppose he's there?" Fred asked.

Vance shrugged.

"He confessed to help you. You know that, don't you?"

Vance nodded slowly. "I didn't ask him to do it—"

"I know that. But he did it anyway, the damned fool, and for some silly reason, I thought you might want to help him now."

"Yeah? Well, what can I do? Go back to jail? No way. I didn't kill Eddie."

"Neither did your grandpa."

The boy looked away. "I know that."

"Good. So, let's get to work."

A flicker of uncertainty crossed the boy's face. "Doing what?"

"Let's talk about the day Eddie died. You were downstairs, right?"

A hesitant nod.

"Where's your room?"

"Right underneath the living room."

"Good. I'm assuming you can hear people moving around upstairs—maybe even voices—from there?"

Another nod.

"So, did you hear anything that morning?"

"No."

That didn't leave much room for discussion. "How about keys to the house? Who has one?"

"Me, my mom, and Eddie."

"Nobody else?"

"No."

"You're sure?"

Vance slouched a little lower in the chair and slanted a glance over at him. "Yeah, I'm sure."

"You didn't hear *anything?*" Fred demanded. "You didn't see *anybody?*"

"No."

"Dammit, boy, think harder."

"Nothing." Vance sounded convincing, but a fleeting shadow behind his eyes made Fred wonder if he was hiding something.

"What time did your mother leave that morning?"

Vance shrugged and the shadow flitted past again. "Same time as always. Seven-thirty."

"And she came home when?"

"A little after ten."

"And in between seven-thirty and ten you didn't hear anything?"

"I was sleeping," Vance said.

"Then how do you know she left at seven-thirty?"

Vance's gaze flickered a little and he licked his lips. "I was awake when she left. I went back to sleep."

"Right away?"

"Right away."

"And the next thing you heard was your mother coming home from work and finding Eddie dead?"

"Yes."

"Nobody else came by?" Fred asked.

"No."

"When was the last time you saw Eddie alive?"

"I don't remember." Vance didn't even blink, but the irises of his eyes flicked, and Fred knew he was lying. The same way he'd lied about the broken window in the elementary school when he was eight, the tear gas in the girls' bathroom in junior high, and setting off the fire alarm in high school.

"Tell me about the argument you had with him the night before he died."

To his surprise, Vance looked faintly amused by the question. "Which one?"

"The one at Tex's Tavern."

"I don't know what you're talking about." Vance's jaw tightened and his eyes continued to jump around.

"There were witnesses who saw you there and who heard you arguing with Eddie. They say you threatened to kill him."

"That's a lie."

"I don't think so."

Fear darted across the boy's expression, and Fred knew he'd either crumple or lash out soon.

"I didn't kill him," Vance said at last.

"You threatened to."

"Yeah, but I didn't." He shot to his feet and slapped the television control with the palm of his hand to turn it off. "If you only knew what he was like."

"I've been getting a pretty good idea," Fred said.

"You can't even begin to imagine. The guy was a dirtbag. Totally. And when I came home that day and found him—" He broke off, refusing to say more.

"Found him doing what?" Fred pressed.

Vance spun around and pointed at Fred's spot on the couch with a trembling finger. "Right there. He was *right there*."

"Doing what?"

"Getting it on with some girl. In my mother's house. On her own damned couch." Vance pushed the hair out of his face and old anger tightened his face.

Fred looked at the couch and wished he'd chosen someplace else to sit. "Who was the girl?"

Vance's gaze shifted. "Geneva Hart. She got up and ran out when she saw me, and Eddie ran after her. I waited for him. I wanted to kill him right then and there, but he didn't come back inside, so I went to the bar that night and told him to get out of here."

"What did he say?"

"He laughed. Thought it was so funny. I told him I was going to tell Mom what he'd been up to, but he didn't care. He said Mom was so desperate, he could talk her into anything. And you know what? He was right."

"Is that when you threatened him?"

Vance nodded.

"Did you tell your mother about Geneva?"

"No! I don't want her to know. Ever."

"You don't think she knows already?"

Vance laughed scornfully. "No. She trusted Eddie."

"Did your grandpa know?"

Vance's smile faded and he looked miserable. "Grandpa came by that afternoon. He could tell I was upset, and he pried it out of me. But that's why Enos believes Grandpa, isn't it? Because I told Grandpa about that afternoon."

Fred crossed the room and touched Vance's shoulder. "I don't know what Enos is thinking. Let's concentrate on finding something that might help. Now, who do you think killed Eddie?"

Vance shook his head. "I don't know. It could have been anybody."

"Even your mom?"

Vance whipped around to face him. "No. I'm telling you, she didn't know about Eddie and Geneva."

"Maybe there were other things going on between her and Eddie you don't know about."

Vance's expression grew a tad more guarded. "She *didn't* do it."

Fred stared at the boy for a long second. "What is it you're not telling me?"

"Nothing."

"You think your mother's guilty, don't you?"

"No." The word cracked with tension.

"What happened, Vance? Did you see her come back that morning earlier than she claimed?"

"No."

"Then, what?"

Vance looked away for a second, and clenched his jaw several times before he spoke again. "I heard footsteps upstairs."

"When? That morning?"

Vance nodded.

"Your mother's?"

"I don't know. I mean, the more I think about it the less sure I am. I didn't hear anybody talking, I just heard somebody moving around up there. It could even have been Eddie for all I know."

"So, you've been trying to protect your mom?"

"She didn't kill him."

"Then who did?"

"I don't know," Vance shouted. "How about Geneva Hart? Or her boyfriend?"

"Wayne?"

"Or Bear? Or Eddie's wife? Or what about Carl Fadel?"

The last name caught Fred by surprise. "Carl Fadel?"

"Yeah. He'd been hanging around the last few weeks. What about him?"

Fred struggled to remember what the schoolteacher had said about Eddie. He'd denied knowing him, and Fred had been suspicious of his reasons for that at the time, but he'd never imagined Carl as a suspect in Eddie's murder. "Carl and Eddie were friends?"

Vance smirked. "Eddie didn't have any friends, not once people got to know him, anyway. But Mr. Fadel called a few times, and I saw him here the day before Eddie died."

"When?"

"I don't know. That afternoon. It was still light."

Before Eddie paid his visit to the school. "Do you have any idea what they were doing together?"

"I don't know anything about Eddie's business. I didn't talk to him any more than I had to."

"Do you think your mother knows?"

"Probably not." Vance's voice sounded bitter. "Eddie didn't exactly value her for her mind, you know?"

"Can you think of anyone else who might have wanted him dead?"

Vance laughed aloud. "Everybody who knew him, does that narrow it down?"

Fred had heard that before. He waited to see if Vance would list anyone else by name. When he didn't, Fred breathed a sigh of relief that at least the list hadn't grown again. He stood to leave and got as far as the stairs. "One more thing," he said. "Were you aware that Eddie had a gun?"

Vance's mouth thinned. "Yeah. Eddie made sure I was aware."

"Do you know where it is now?"

The boy shook his head and pushed the hair out of his eyes again. "No," he said tentatively, then more positively. "No. I haven't seen it."

"It wasn't in your mother's bedroom when Eddie died?"

This time, Vance looked definite. "No. I know it wasn't there. I helped her clean things up."

"You don't think she put it away somewhere?" Fred suggested hopefully.

"No. She hated that thing. Eddie'd come home drunk and wave it around, especially if he was mad about something." He shook his head again. "No. If it was here, she'd have given it to Ricki when she came after Eddie's things. But

Mom didn't give it to her, because I heard Ricki say something about it not being in with Eddie's stuff."

Then what had happened to it? Maybe Sharon had quietly given Eddie's gun to Enos. But surely Enos would have said something—or Grady would have let it slip. He patted Vance's shoulder again. "You keep thinking. If you remember anything—no matter what it is—you call me. We'll get your grandpa out of this."

For a second, Vance looked wide-eyed and full of hope again, like the young boy he'd been only a few years ago. "Thanks, Mr. V."

Fred started toward the door, not at all surprised that Vance didn't follow him. He hurried back to his car and cranked the engine to life one more time, anxious now to get to the school before Carl Fadel left for the day.

eighteen

Fred pulled the gearshift into drive and inched away from the curb, remembering the night Eddie had interrupted Benjamin's rehearsal, the look on Carl's face, and Carl leaving the boys to have a private conversation with Eddie. The next morning, Eddie had turned up dead.

Was there a connection? Possibly. Should he tell Enos about this? Probably. And under other circumstances, he would have. But Fred couldn't go back there until he had something more than gut instinct to offer. Not unless he wanted to spend time in jail with Doc.

At the high school, he parked close to the front doors and hurried up the walk just as the snow started falling again. He passed the school's office and waved to Becky Grimes at her desk by the photocopy machine, then turned down the hall toward the music department.

He found Carl digging through a box of sheet music on the desk of the second classroom he checked. "Carl? Do you have a minute?"

The younger man jerked upright, spun around, and smiled in confusion when he saw Fred standing there. "Sure. What can I do for you?"

"I need to ask you a couple of questions about Eddie Leishman."

The confusion evaporated and distrust immediately took its place. "Why? I don't know anything about Eddie Leishman. I told you, I only met him once."

Fred took a couple of steps into the room, and hoped furiously Carl wasn't hiding a gun in the waistband of his

Dockers. "Someone mentioned that you called Eddie on the phone several times before he died."

"Who did? Sharon? Well, I guess I may have. For parent-teacher conferences or something."

"And is that why you went to visit him?"

Carl frowned. "Eddie? No. I never visited him. I didn't even know him."

Fred tried a bluff. "Someone saw you at Sharon's house the day Eddie died."

Carl's frown deepened and he took another step away. "That's not true. Whoever told you that is lying. I wasn't there that day. I was here, teaching."

"Then, when *did* you go to Sharon's?"

Carl didn't speak, he just folded his arms across his chest and stopped retreating. "What makes you think I did?"

"Someone saw you there."

"Impossible."

"I've spoken with a witness," Fred said. "Why don't you think about it again?"

Carl didn't want to think. He stuck his chin out like a stubborn little boy. "I don't have to tell you anything."

But Fred's patience was wearing thin and his time was running out. "You're right," he snapped. "You don't. I'll just tell the sheriff what I know and let him ask you about it. It'll probably be easier that way, anyway."

Carl didn't react by so much as a blink.

"I don't think Andy Martinez will mind Enos coming to take you out of class, do you?"

At the mention of the principal's name, Carl's cheek twitched. Andrés Martinez was a hardline administrator with an unsympathetic view of troublemakers, both within the student body and on staff. He wouldn't be pleased by one of his teachers having even a marginal connection to a murder investigation.

Carl continued glaring, but his shoulders sagged a little. "What do you want to know?"

"How did you know Eddie Leishman?"

"His son is in one of my classes. I've been worried about

Josh's performance since his parents separated, and I
wanted to talk with Eddie about helping him."

"So you called him?"

A nod.

"And you went to visit him at Sharon Bollinger's home."

Carl nodded eagerly. "Yes."

"When?"

"The day before Eddie died. Thursday."

"How long did you stay?"

Carl hitched one hip onto the corner of the desk and
shook his head. "I didn't. When I got to the door, I heard
Eddie and Sharon arguing. They were really going at it, so
I decided not to disturb them."

"Could you hear what they said?"

Carl shrugged and looked a little nervous. "Not the whole
thing."

"What *did* you hear?"

"Eddie. I heard him telling her some real ugly stuff. How
he didn't love her, never had. How he'd just been using her."

"Maybe it wasn't Sharon," Fred suggested hopefully.

Carl shook his head. "No, it was her. I could hear her
crying. Begging him not to leave her. But Eddie didn't care.
He was like that."

Fred stared at him for a moment. "He was? I thought you
didn't know him."

This time, Carl flushed. "Well, I mean . . . I didn't.
Like I said, I only met him once, but—"

Fred took a couple of steps closer. "Sounds like you knew
him better than you've been admitting."

"No, I didn't. I didn't know him at all."

Fred planted his fists on the desktop and leaned closer.
"Look, Carl, I might be an old man, but I can still recognize
a lie when I hear one. Now, why don't you tell me the
truth?"

"I don't have to tell you anything," Carl insisted.

They were right back where they'd started. Fred straightened and glared at him. "All right, since you don't want to
discuss this with me, I'll let the sheriff figure it out."

He started for the door, hoping that Carl would get

nervous enough to call him back, fearing that he'd let him walk away. At the door, he forced himself not to look back. He kept his shoulders straight and his head high as he walked out the door. He left the school slowly, to give Carl plenty of time to come after him, but he made it all the way down the corridor and out to his car and Carl still hadn't changed his mind. Fred unlocked the Buick, glared at the snowflakes that had already managed to cover his windshield, and slid behind the wheel.

He sat there for another few minutes, dreading the drive home on the slick snow-covered highway and wishing he'd played that interview with Carl some other way. Thick, heavy flakes of snow fell onto the car while Fred sat.

Cursing, Fred started the Buick's engine and left it to warm up while he climbed back outside and started brushing the windows. He didn't hear Carl approaching until he was only a step or two away; even then, the movement caught his eye a second before the sound reached him.

Carl had slipped on a light jacket, but he looked far too cold to be outside in this weather. His breath formed clouds as he walked.

Fred stopped brushing and waited for him to speak.

The younger man stood in the snow and shivered for several seconds. "All right," he said at last, as if Fred had been badgering him to speak. "I'll tell you the truth, but you have to promise that what I tell you is strictly between us."

"That depends on whether it has any connection to Eddie's murder."

"It doesn't," Carl said quickly. He paced a few steps away, then doubled back. "Okay, you're right, I knew Eddie. I've known him for years. And I hated him. But I didn't kill him."

"How did you know him?"

"I used to play the bars down in Colorado Springs. Eddie's band played the same circuit, so we knew each other. Rivals, I guess you could say. I was a different man, then. I drank too much, chased around with women—the same sort of things Eddie did. But I've changed since then.

I've really cleaned up my act, and I'll lose this job in a heartbeat if that part of my life ever gets out."

"I see."

"A few years ago, I cleaned myself up, got married, stopped drinking, and I came to Cutler to start over. And I've been doing great. My wife and I are happy. I'm good at what I do. And I think I understand these kids better than somebody who never got into any trouble at all."

Fred thought that might be true, but he didn't comment.

"And then Eddie showed up." Carl strode away again, quick, jerky steps that betrayed his agitation. "He recognized me, of course. Saw me at Lacey's or someplace. And he came by the school to renew old acquaintances. But I didn't want anything to do with him. I'd *changed*." His tone pleaded with Fred to believe him.

Fred didn't say a word.

Carl paced for another few seconds. "I told him I didn't want my past to get out. I told him I'd lose my place here, lose everything I'd worked so hard for. I thought—no, I *hoped*—he'd understand."

Obviously, he hadn't.

"He thought it was funny. He kept threatening to spill the beans, kept threatening to *accidentally* let things about my past slip. Then, for some reason, he needed money and guess who he decided to ask for it."

"Why did he need money?"

"I don't know. He didn't tell me and I didn't ask. With Eddie, it was best not to know."

"He didn't say anything to give you an idea?"

"No. Not Eddie. He seemed pretty anxious to get it, though. And I guess I always thought it had something to do with a woman."

"He must have said something that made you think that."

"Not necessarily." Carl stuffed his hands in his pockets and hunched his shoulders. "Eddie was always having trouble with women. Besides, Eddie talked a lot, but he didn't really say anything you could put your finger on. I knew he'd left his wife—*everybody* knew that. But I got the feeling things weren't going real well with his new lady."

"What made you think that?"

"I know her old man hated Eddie and wanted him to leave. Eddie said he was pretty desperate to split them up. And, of course, Eddie thought that was funny. He probably goaded the old man, you know?"

Fred didn't even want to think about Doc's reaction to Eddie goading him about Sharon. "Did you give him the money?"

"I didn't have any to give him. I'm a schoolteacher, for hell's sake." Carl managed a thin laugh, saw that Fred wasn't laughing with him, and sobered again. "He didn't believe me. He kept coming around, trying to push me into finding the money somewhere. Kept threatening to tell Andy who and what I was. I'll be honest with you, I thought about finding the money somewhere. I've worked hard to set myself up here. I didn't want to lose everything. But in the end, I didn't get the money, and I didn't kill him." He glanced over his shoulder at the school as if he thought somebody might be watching him. "Promise me you won't say anything to anyone about this."

Fred gave his windshield a final swipe, pulled open the car's door, and slipped behind the wheel. "I'll do what I can." He shut the door without giving Carl a chance to respond, and tugged the gearshift into reverse.

Carl took a step backward, but his expression didn't relax. Fred refused to worry about that. Probably a good portion of the story he'd just heard was actually true. But Carl had lied before to protect himself. Fred had no reason to believe he wasn't doing the same thing now.

Fred clutched a glass of holiday punch and worked his way through the high school's crowded corridors. Stalls full of homemade gifts lined the hallways, holiday music blared from the loudspeakers, and the whole place smelled like Fred's kitchen used to after Phoebe'd done her holiday baking.

He waved and smiled at people he hadn't seen since last year's Extravaganza and tried to pretend he was thinking about something besides Eddie Leishman's death. Fred missed the excitement that had filled his house in the days before the event. He missed seeing Phoebe's flushed face in the crowds. Missed pulling her under a sprig of mistletoe and kissing her soundly in front of anyone who wanted to watch.

Phoebe had loved the holidays, and the Extravaganza had been one of her favorite events of the whole year. She'd worked for months making things to sell; embroidered pillowcases and tablecloths, crocheted dolls. One year she'd even found enough time to make half a dozen afghans.

The party didn't feel the same these days, but he came anyway. He couldn't, in good conscience, do anything else. But he had trouble concentrating on the festivities. Benjamin's band was scheduled to play in less than twenty minutes, and he wanted to make sure Margaret got a chance to hear her son play. He couldn't count on Webb behaving with any decency.

Someone jostled his elbow and sloshed punch over his fingers, then pounded his back in laughing apology and moved on. Someone else stopped too quickly in front of him and leaned to pick up a wailing child. Fred lost a little more punch, gave up trying to drink the blasted thing, and looked around in vain for a garbage can.

"Fred?" Someone grabbed his arm and spilled the rest of his punch onto his fingers.

He turned around to glare at the offender and came face to face with Janice Lacey. Of all people.

She wore a bright red sweater with huge white snowflakes knit into the design, fire-engine red stretch pants, and boots that tried to come all the way up to her knees. She'd done something to her hair, but Fred couldn't figure out what, and he didn't want to take the time to work on it.

"I wondered if you'd be here." She leaned in close to be heard over the crowd. She smelled like gingerbread. "It's a wonderful party this year, isn't it?"

"Wonderful," Fred agreed.

"I was worried about it, you know, what with everything that's been happening. I wondered if anyone would dare leave their homes to come out. But even the Leishman murder hasn't had much of an effect, has it?"

"Not much," Fred said, and tried to take a step away only to discover that she hadn't released his coat sleeve. "Listen, Janice," he said with as much patience as he could muster. "You don't have anything to worry about. Eddie Leishman's killer isn't going to come after you."

She pursed her lips at him and planted a hand on her hip. "And how do you know that?"

"Eddie wasn't murdered by some roving psychotic who's out looking for his next victim."

Anger glinted in her eyes. "I never said it was a roving psychotic, Fred Vickery. But you know I live right across the street from Sharon Bollinger, and after the things I saw and heard that day, no one could blame me for being nervous. For all I know, I saw the murderer."

In spite of himself, Fred's pulse flickered. "You were home the day Eddie was killed?"

"No, but I was there the day before, and there were all sorts of goings-on."

Fred's pulse steadied. Everybody admitted to visiting Eddie the day *before* he died. And he'd already talked to Janice once—he didn't think he'd learn anything new from her that had any basis in fact.

But Janice went on as if he were paying attention. "Car doors slamming, people shouting, women crying. I told Bill, a man like Eddie Leishman living in the neighborhood could make property values drop overnight."

A man like Eddie Leishman dying in the neighborhood wouldn't do it any good, either. Fred glanced over the crowd again, stretched as high as he could, but he still couldn't see Margaret. He checked his watch again and scowled. They'd all miss Benjamin's performance at this rate. With a vague smile in Janice's direction, he tried to walk away.

She bounced after him. "Naturally, I heard the car doors first. I mean, I couldn't miss them, could I? He'd parked right outside of my house, if you can imagine that—"

"Who had? Eddie?"

"No. Wayne Openshaw."

Fred stopped so suddenly, she bumped into him. "Wayne Openshaw?" he demanded. "He was at Sharon's house that day?"

"He was. I think he followed Geneva there. Anyway, he lurked around outside for a while—right in front of *my* house, of all places—"

"Where was Eddie?"

"Inside with Geneva," Janice said in a tone that suggested she thought Fred had missed something.

Fred scowled at her. "Why didn't you tell me about this the other day?"

She drew herself up and glared at him. "Because you said you weren't helping Doc." She sniffed and looked away, then slanted a glance up at him. "Besides, Carl Fadel was standing right there, lying about knowing Eddie. I knew he was lying because I saw him there that day, too."

"For hell's sake, Janice. You could have told me anyway." She picked a fine time to withhold gossip. "So, what happened?"

Janice looked pleased with herself. "Geneva came running out of the house crying, and Eddie came after her."

"What did Wayne do?"

"He stood there in front of my house and watched them argue for a second or two. Then he ran across the street and hit Eddie before Eddie even realized he was there. It was horrible," she said, and shuddered at the memory.

"Then what?" Fred demanded, but when she pulled back and glared at him, he softened his tone and asked again. "Then what?"

"Then Eddie hit Wayne back and they got into a horrible argument right there on the street." She stopped as if she thought that might be all he needed to hear.

"And then—?"

"Then Eddie went back into the house and Wayne tried to get Geneva to go in his car with him, but she wouldn't. She got in her own car and drove off, and Wayne followed her."

"What about Carl?"

"He came later."

Fred tried to pull fragments of other conversations from

his memory and piece them together with this new information. Almost everyone else connected with Eddie had admitted being at Sharon's house on the first—the day before Eddie died. Except Wayne.

"Have you told Enos about this?" he asked.

Janice glanced across the corridor, and for the first time all evening, Fred noticed Enos standing against the wall with his wife. Jessica didn't look any happier than Enos had for the past few weeks.

Janice turned her nose into the air and shook her head. "Heaven knows I've tried, but he doesn't seem to think I know anything important. Honestly, I don't know what's wrong with that man lately."

Fred didn't want to get Janice started speculating on Enos's troubles—whatever they were. "I'll make sure he knows what you've told me."

"That's not even the important part. Wayne and Geneva set up a ruckus, but that Bear Sandusky's the one who really frightened me, shouting at the top of his lungs—"

Bear Sandusky? "What was he shouting about?"

"About how much money Eddie owed him and how Eddie'd better pay up or he'd be sorry."

"You're sure about that?"

"Of course I'm sure," Janice said with a sniff.

"And you told Enos this?"

"I *told* you, Enos wouldn't even listen to me."

Fred glanced at his friend again. Janice's claims disturbed him more than he wanted to admit. Enos never discounted the word of a witness—especially one with an eye for detail like Janice. "And you're sure Bear said something about money?"

"Now you sound like Enos. I'll tell you the same thing I told him. I was home from work with that horrible cold—you remember how sick I was?"

Fred didn't, but he pretended as if he did.

"Well, I was watching television, and I happened to have the front windows open for a few minutes, and it just worked out that all this business with Eddie happened during that time, so I heard everything quite clearly."

Fred could only marvel at the coincidence.

Janice tried to tug the hem of her sweater over her backside, and scanned the crowd. "I don't suppose you've seen Bill anywhere around?"

"Not yet," Fred admitted.

"Well, that figures. He saw Ricki Leishman over by the table with the wreaths and raced off to offer his condolences. I haven't seen him since. You could have knocked me over with a feather, I was so surprised to see her here. And just a week after her husband was murdered."

Fred didn't want to get caught up in Janice's speculations about Ricki's behavior. "Her son is playing in the band with Benjamin," he said and checked his watch again. "In fact, they're scheduled to play in just a few minutes, and I still need to find Margaret."

"Well, of course," Janice agreed somberly. "And I admire Ricki for supporting her son in spite of everything that's happened, I really do. But heaven only knows whether I'd be able to come to a party if Bill had died just a week before." She tugged the hem of her sweater again and tried to look sweetly understanding. She failed miserably. "If you're looking for Margaret, I saw her and Webb going into the auditorium a few minutes ago."

Great. That made one less thing to worry about. "Are you going in?"

She shook her head. "Gracious, no. Rock and roll's not my style of music at all. Why the committee ever allowed those boys a part on the program is beyond me." All at once, someone across the corridor caught her eye and she lost interest in Fred. She waved eagerly and dashed away, still tugging at the hem of her sweater.

Fred breathed a sigh of relief and started toward the auditorium. It had been a rare, profitable conversation with Janice, but that didn't make him any less relieved to be finished with it.

He thought back over what she'd told him and smiled to himself. He'd known all along that either Bear or Wayne had to be Eddie's killer, but which? Both had lied to him.

Both were obviously still lying. Of the two, Fred could most easily imagine Bear killing Eddie in cold blood, but he wouldn't rule Wayne out—especially now. Much as he hated to admit it, Janice may have handed him a trump card.

nineteen

Fred pressed through the throng into the auditorium, grateful that someone had adjusted the temperature to a more moderate level than the last time he'd been here. He sidestepped down the aisle, searching for an empty seat at the end of a row. He always claimed that he needed an aisle seat because he hated climbing across laps, but the truth was, he didn't like sitting in the middle of a row even when he was the first to arrive. He liked knowing he could stand up and walk away at any time.

He found a likely looking seat about halfway to the front and claimed it immediately. Peeling off his coat, he wedged it into the seat with him and leaned back, trying to get comfortable. He didn't recognize Summer Dey as the woman in the next seat until she'd already seen him sitting there.

She propped one booted foot on her knee and smiled at him—a vague sort of smile, as if her spirit guides had come to the Extravaganza and left her home.

Maybe if he ignored her, she'd leave him alone.

No such luck. She studied his face and frowned. "You're still searching, aren't you?"

Fred ignored the question and pretended to scan the auditorium for Margaret and Webb.

"I could teach you how to connect your higher consciousness with all the higher consciousnesses in the universe."

Fred increased his efforts. In spite of Webb's obvious faults, an hour in his company might actually be preferable to one in Summer's.

"You could draw upon their energy."

"Whose?"

"The higher consciousnesses. You're searching for a way to unlock the questions surrounding the death of a dark soul. The universe would help you if you'd listen. The universe will always help you."

Fred wondered if the universe would convince Summer to leave him alone if he asked. He turned his attention toward the program photocopied slightly off-center on a sheet of green paper so dark he couldn't read the type in the dim overhead lighting.

Summer leaned toward him and a lock of her baby-fine hair fell into his line of vision. "I'd love to help you. I could teach you to communicate with others through energy alone."

Fred hoped Summer's energy could read the unmistakable message his was sending.

She smiled softly.

Obviously, it couldn't. Well, he'd just have to help it along. "Look, Summer," he said in the kindest voice he could manage under the circumstances. "I'm not interested in energy or consciousness or readings or anything else. I'm here to listen to my grandson's band."

Her smile faded, but she seemed to understand his verbal message without trouble. She settled back into her seat and watched the stage for several seconds without speaking.

Fred relaxed slightly and made himself comfortable in his chair while he waited for the program to begin. As the house lights dimmed a notch further, Enos stood up from a seat near the front of the auditorium and climbed across a dozen people to the aisle. He waited there while Jessica worked her way out behind him, then started up the incline slightly ahead of her.

They marched, silent and apparently angry, toward the back of the room. Fred watched them approach, grim-faced, and pass without acknowledging anyone they knew—behavior so unlike Enos, Fred knew something had to be wrong.

He shifted in his seat and followed their progress into the brightly lit hallway where they turned toward the school's front doors. But Jessica loved the Extravaganza as much as Phoebe had, and Fred couldn't imagine her leaving before the end.

As he turned back to the front of the auditorium, he caught a glimpse of Ricki Leishman watching Enos and Jessica from a couple of rows behind him. She sat stiff, shoulders back, as if she expected her friends and neighbors to judge her—and Fred figured they probably would.

Sudden applause jerked him back to the moment, and he struggled to focus on the stage where Carl Fadel strode toward a microphone. He wore a dark suit, a white shirt, and a holiday-red tie. He looked entirely at home on the stage, every inch a teacher, and Fred had trouble imagining him an Eddie Leishman act-alike. He also understood with sudden clarity how desperately Carl wanted to cling to the new life he'd made.

"You're searching in the wrong place, you know." Summer shouted into his ear, but he could barely hear her over the applause.

He pulled away sharply and scowled at her. "Not now, Summer. I don't want to hear it."

"But you need to know," she insisted. "You can find the solution if you put your desires out to the universe. She will answer you."

"Who will answer?" he demanded a little too loudly.

Carl Fadel had finished speaking, the first group on the program was taking a quiet moment to set up its equipment, and Fred's voice bounced back at him from the auditorium walls. Two little girls in the row ahead started giggling, several anonymous people shushed him, and Carl tried to see through the stage lights into the audience.

Summer lifted a finger to her lips and leaned closer. "The universe. Where everyone's energy mingles."

Fred didn't want his energy to mingle. It liked being alone.

"You must watch closely," Summer whispered. "There is evil around you."

"Where?"

Another round of shushers and more giggling from the little girls.

Summer shook her head and looked disturbed. "I don't know, but I can feel it."

"You can feel its energy, I suppose," he muttered under his breath.

But apparently she heard him because she beamed and tossed a lock of limp blonde hair over her shoulder. "Exactly. I *knew* you'd make an excellent student."

"Not interested."

"But you have the gift."

"Don't want it."

"You're a natural."

Fred pushed to his feet and glared down at her, but under the curious stares of people around him, he managed to keep his mouth shut. He pulled his coat from the seat and strode up the aisle in dignified silence, searching for another empty aisle seat. But he was out of luck. Every aisle seat had someone in it, which left him no choice but to stand at the back of the room. Well, at least he'd have peace and quiet and he could concentrate on Benjamin without interruption.

He leaned against the wall and made himself as comfortable as he could under the circumstances. He crossed one leg over the other, uncrossed it, hitched a shoulder against the wall, straightened up again, and scowled down at Summer.

A row or two from the back, a man's blond head caught his eye. Bear Sandusky leaned forward to speak to a companion, then sat back with a silent laugh. At first, Fred thought he was watching the stage, but after a few minutes he realized what held Bear's attention—Ricki Leishman.

Fred leaned against the wall again. Maybe standing back here wouldn't work out so badly, after all. He could watch Benjamin's performance, keep an eye on Bear, and he'd notice Summer if she tried to approach him again.

He knew Bear hadn't seen him standing here, and Fred wanted to keep it that way. Because the minute the performance ended, he planned to have one more chat with

Bear, and he intended to get to the bottom of this puzzle once and for all.

Even before the applause stopped at the end of the program, Fred started moving toward the auditorium door. He planted himself to one side where he could easily approach Bear as he came through, and he waited. He smiled at passersby, commented favorably on the performance, and planned what to say to Bear once he had him alone again.

When Bear appeared in the doorway a few minutes later in the company of his friends, he looked as if he were having a grand time, grander than Fred might have expected a man like Bear to have at the Extravaganza. But when he got a little closer and Fred caught a whiff of the alcohol fumes on Bear's breath, the unsteadiness of his gait and the brightness of his eyes, he understood why. Bear had obviously started celebrating early.

Fred stepped into his path. "Evening, Bear."

It took Bear a moment to get Fred into focus, but Fred knew the instant he did because his smile slipped. "Oh, my hell. Not *you* again. What do you want now?"

"I didn't expect to see you here tonight," Fred said.

"Why not? This is the high point of the year, isn't it?" Bear sneered over his shoulder at his companions; they grinned back as if he'd made a fine joke.

When Bear started away, Fred fell into step beside him. "I don't suppose you have a minute . . ."

Bear's smile faded altogether. "No, I don't. Leave me alone."

"It's just that I've thought of another question or two you can answer for me."

Bear shook his head and increased his pace. "Leave me alone."

Slinging his coat over his shoulder, Fred matched the other man's gait and tried to look unconcerned. "All right. I just thought you might like a chance to tell me why you lied about the money before I talked with the sheriff."

Bear scowled over at him. "I didn't lie."

"You didn't?" Fred looked puzzled. "My misunderstanding, I guess. Someone mentioned that they overheard you arguing with Eddie about the money early Thursday afternoon. I thought you told me you found out about it for the first time later that night."

Bear looked over his shoulder to see if anyone could hear them before leading Fred a few steps away from his friends. "Who told you that?"

"I'd rather not say."

"They're lying."

"I don't think so."

Bear's eyes narrowed. "You think *I'm* lying? Is that it?"

Fred shrugged. "Somebody is."

A group of high school aged boys jostled past Bear and earned a dark look in response. None of them seemed to notice, but Bear looked angry enough to kill, and Fred wondered whether he'd been wise to confront him.

"Look," Bear said at last, leaning close enough for his foul breath to drift up Fred's nostrils again. "All right. I knew about it. I found out about the money a few days before."

"So you went to Eddie's house on Thursday to confront him about it."

Bear nodded and waited while a group of flirting teenagers passed. When he spoke again, he lowered his voice so Fred had to strain to hear what he said. "Yeah. That's exactly what happened."

"Why did you wait until Thursday to talk to him? Why didn't you confront him as soon as you found out?"

Bear pondered that for a few seconds, then tried to smile as if Fred's questions didn't bother him. "I waited because you had to catch Eddie in the right mood with that sort of thing, and I knew he was distracted. He'd been complaining about trouble at home, about—what would you call him? The old man wasn't really a father-in-law."

"Complaining about Doc?"

"Yeah. I guess the old man was getting real bothersome, you know? He didn't like Eddie, and he didn't try to hide it. But Eddie and the old man had it out—at least that's what

Eddie told me Wednesday night—and he acted as if he'd won the argument, so I figured that was a good time."

Doc argued with Eddie on Wednesday? The damned fool. Fred wondered whether Enos knew about it, then decided *he'd* be a fool to ask. "So, you went to see Eddie on Thursday—" he prompted.

"Yeah. But I didn't see him because he and Sharon were arguing, so I left."

"How did you know it was Sharon?"

"Well, there weren't any cars around, and when she came home for lunch, it was always about that time."

"You didn't actually see her?"

A shake of the head.

"What time was this?"

"A little after noon."

"What time did you go back?"

Bear shook his head again and tried to look confused.

But Fred's patience was wearing thin. He had no time for games. "Someone overheard you and Eddie shouting at each other," he reminded Bear.

Bear's confusion evaporated. "I guess it was about an hour later."

"What happened then?"

"I figured Sharon would be back at work and Eddie would be alone. I drove over there and confronted him about the money. The rest happened just like I told you—he offered me half and I told him I'd think about it."

"Was Eddie alone when you came back?"

"Yeah—at least, I thought he was. But if somebody heard us, maybe he wasn't."

Fred had no intention of setting him straight. Janice Lacey would never forgive him if he brought her into this.

Bear checked over his shoulder again and leaned a little closer. "Look, man, you've gotta understand. I'd worked with Eddie for two years, and he'd been skimming that whole time. I've been busting my butt to make ends meet while he's been stealing my pay and living off women. He tried to tell me he'd pay me back. That we had a good sound together and I was a fool to let something *little* like this come between us. He told me not to tell the other guys yet, and that he'd make it worth my while."

"Two years' worth?"

Bear nodded and sent Fred a wry smile. "That's what he said."

"So you decided to give him another chance?" Fred asked.

"Yeah, sure. I decided to see if he could really come up with the cash. But even if he had, I was still going to walk. I couldn't trust him anymore."

Trust wasn't a word Fred would ever have associated with Eddie Leishman, either. "Then, why did you argue at Tex's that night?"

"He couldn't come up with the money," Bear said simply.

That seemed to back up Carl Fadel's story. "So you told him you were through?"

Bear nodded. "Just like I said."

"He didn't like that," Fred guessed.

"I didn't care."

Fred pondered a moment, then asked, "Tell me, do you know where Eddie kept his insulin?"

Bear's eyes narrowed and his face grew red. "In the fridge except what he carried with him."

"You saw him give himself a few injections over the years, I'd imagine."

"No. Eddie was kind of embarrassed about it for some reason. He never did his thing in front of us."

"Never?"

"Never." Bear looked quite definite, then his expression shifted abruptly as he focused on something or someone over Fred's shoulder.

Before Fred could even look around, a hand gripped his arm. "Dad? We've been looking everywhere for you."

Fred tried not to look disappointed when he smiled at Margaret. "I've been around, sweetheart."

"What are you doing?"

"Passing the time of day. Did you hear Benjamin's band?"

Margaret nodded, but she narrowed her eyes. "Did you?"

"Of course. Wouldn't have missed it."

"So, what are you doing now?"

"Just getting ready to check out the booths, saying hello to Bear, here—"

Bear muttered something that might have been a greeting, hitched up his pants a little, and took advantage of the interruption to slip away.

Margaret took Fred's arm and nodded toward the auditorium doors where Deborah stood with Webb. "Come and join us."

Fred hesitated a split second longer, but he could see Bear rejoin his friends and slip out of the building. Fred wasn't likely to get close enough to ask questions again.

twenty

Fred tried to look pleased and happy when he waved to Deborah, but he and Webb ignored each other by unspoken mutual agreement. He could think of a hundred things he'd rather do than spend an evening in Webb's company, but it didn't look like he'd get the chance.

Now Fred would have to wander from booth to booth and listen to Webb argue with Margaret about wasting money on trinkets. Later, Webb would race off to the Copper Penny where he'd drink everything he wouldn't let Margaret spend.

Well, Fred would give Webb half an hour, but only for Deborah and Margaret. After that, he'd find an excuse to wander off—if Webb hadn't invented a reason to leave before that.

He pasted on a smile and allowed Margaret to lead him across the corridor. He hugged Deborah warmly and planted a kiss on the top of her head.

For some reason, Margaret seemed to want Fred to like Webb—or at least to tolerate him. Fred figured the best he could offer would be ignoring him.

Margaret slipped an arm around Deborah's shoulders and looked around as if she needed to take stock. "What do you want to see first?"

"The gingerbread houses," Deborah voted.

Fred shrugged. "Sounds good to me."

Webb scowled. "We're not buying one, so don't even ask. All this crap they sell here. It's a rip-off. Nothing but a waste of money."

Fred didn't usually buy trinkets, either, but he knew

Margaret liked them. And with everything Webb put her through, he didn't think spending a few dollars on a gingerbread house or carved Santa once a year was out of line.

Even so, it wouldn't do him a bit of good to voice his opinion. He clamped his mouth shut and took Deborah's hand as they started off through the crowd. "Emma Brumbaugh makes a mighty fancy gingerbread house," he told her. "Of course, they're not anything like what your grandma used to make."

Deborah grinned up at him. She loved hearing about her grandmother, and Fred never tired of sharing stories that would help her remember. "Did you help her?"

Fred smiled. "No. She wouldn't let me. These big old hands of mine are too clumsy, I guess."

"If I'd been big enough, *I* would have helped her." Deborah bobbed her head and stuck out her chin, and her expression reminded him so much of Phoebe, his eyes grew misty. But before he could say anything in response, something at the next table caught her eye and she skipped ahead to get a closer look.

Margaret paused at a table filled with carved Santas. She touched one gently, almost reverently, and looked over at Webb with a hopeful expression. "Isn't he wonderful?"

"It's a piece of crap," Webb snapped. He jerked the Santa up from the table and shoved it under her nose. "It's a damned hunk of *tree*, Maggie. You can pick one up on the ground any day of the week."

The hope in her eyes flickered, but didn't die completely. "But look at how intricately it's carved."

Her expression didn't even touch Webb. He glared at Margaret and put the Santa back on the table. "I'm not wasting money on something like that."

Watching Margaret's face fall, Fred gave up trying to tolerate Webb. He moved a little closer and muttered, "Not when you can spend it on something valuable, like beer."

Webb pivoted to face him. "I don't need any comments from you."

"Who *do* you need them from?" Fred asked.

Margaret's expression sobered instantly, and she glared at Fred. "Dad, don't start. Please."

"I'm not starting anything," he pointed out. "I made an observation."

"You're starting trouble," Margaret insisted.

Webb's frown deepened into the self-pitying expression he always used to get his own way with Margaret. "You know, I've had just about enough—"

Fred nodded his understanding. "Yes, we know. Just about enough. Can't take any more. And now you're going to have to run over to the Copper Penny to soothe your hurt feelings. Well, go on. You've already been here longer than any of us expected."

Margaret made a noise and tugged at Fred's arm, but Webb firmed up his stance and raised his voice. "Don't push me."

Voices in the crowd around them hushed, and Fred sensed increased interest in their conversation. For Margaret's sake, and for the kids', he forced a smile and hoped it looked more genuine than it felt. "Push you? I wouldn't dream of it."

But Webb wasn't buying it. "You don't like me, Fred, I know that. You never have. But that's okay, I can live with it because I don't care for you, either."

"No great loss in my books," Fred told him.

"Stop it, both of you," Margaret demanded in a harsh whisper. "People are listening."

As if he'd been waiting for an audience, Webb turned a mocking face to the crowd. "There must be something in the water around here. First, Doc Huggins kills Eddie for messing around with his daughter. Now Fred's picking a fight with me. So, what is it, Fred? Am I next?"

At that moment, Fred thought removing Webb from the census sounded like a particularly good idea, but he didn't say a word.

Obviously embarrassed, Margaret pulled on Webb's sleeve. "Stop it, Webb. Right now."

"It's not my fault," he protested. "Your dad started in on *me*." He shook his head and whipped his arms around.

"Well, I don't have to stay here and take it." He tugged his sleeve away from Margaret's grasp, turned on his heel, and pushed through the pack of people.

Fred watched him go with mixed emotions. The jerk had gotten his own way, after all. And their exchange had embarrassed Margaret. Worst of all, it wouldn't end here. There'd be talk for a day or two.

Deborah pushed her way back through the tiny throng of onlookers and took Margaret's hand. "Did Daddy leave?"

Margaret nodded, and shot an angry glance in Fred's direction as if he were somehow to blame. "Yes, sweetheart, he did."

Fred glared at those in the crowd closest to them, and waited to speak until they'd started milling around again. "He engineered that argument, Margaret, and you know it."

"You started it, Dad."

"Maybe," Fred conceded graciously. "But he was looking for an excuse to leave, and if I hadn't given him one, he would have found some other reason."

Margaret didn't look as if she appreciated that observation. Holding Deborah's hand tightly, she followed Webb's lead and turned away.

Fred pointed to the Santa Margaret wanted and shouted to the clerk, "Hold that for me. I'll be right back." As quickly as his knees would carry him, he followed Margaret and Deborah through the crowd. "Margaret, wait," he said when he got close enough. "You're going to need a ride home."

"Not from you." She increased her pace and pulled an unwilling Deborah after her.

Fred tried to keep up, but determination moved her through the crowd more rapidly than he could manage. She easily put several feet between them, and within seconds Fred lost sight of her completely.

He slowed, then stopped in the center of the foyer, confused and saddened by the whole episode. Had he been wrong to point out the obvious? No. The longer Margaret's marriage went on, the worse it seemed to Fred. Under most circumstances, Fred didn't believe in divorce, but neither did he believe in staying with a bad marriage.

The only mistake he'd made was in pushing Webb in public and so close to the holidays. Margaret and the kids would suffer for Fred's self-indulgence. Webb would spend more time at the Copper Penny—if there *was* any more time he could spend. Thank goodness Albán traditionally closed the bar on Christmas Eve and Christmas Day or Margaret would have probably spent at least half that time alone.

With his nerves rubbed raw by the constant chatter and piped-in music, Fred stood in the foyer a moment longer, then headed back to the stall to pay for the Santa. He didn't care what Webb thought, Margaret would have it for Christmas.

Besides, he supposed he owed her an apology—not for what he'd said, but for saying it here and now. If he hadn't been so worried about Doc, if Enos hadn't been constantly in the back of his mind—if Eddie Leishman's death wasn't such a puzzle, maybe he'd have done better at keeping his mouth shut.

Fred meandered through the hallways for nearly half an hour, watching for some sign of Margaret and Deborah. He saw Grady Hatch once in the distance and waved to Olivia Simms while she smoked a cigarette outside the gymnasium, but after his third circuit around the building, he finally had to admit Margaret and Deborah must have found another way home.

He started back toward the front of the school, determined to leave himself, when he saw Geneva Hart ladling hot cider at the refreshment table. As if she felt Fred watching her, she met his gaze, and then jerked her own away.

Well, well, well. Maybe he ought to stick around for a few more minutes, after all—in case Margaret and Deborah wandered by. He lowered his wrapped Santa to the table and placed an order for cider and a cookie.

Geneva avoided looking at him as she handed him the cup of cider, took his money, and counted back his change. She turned her back as if she expected him to leave; when he didn't, she flicked an uneasy glance at him.

He smiled and used his cup to gesture toward the crock pots of cider. "How are things going this year? Are sales up?"

"I don't know. I've never worked this booth before." She rubbed the back of her neck with one hand and placed the other on her back as if she had a kink there.

Fred sipped the too-hot cider and pulled the cup away quickly when it burned his lip. "You look tired. Is somebody scheduled to relieve you soon?"

She glanced at her watch. "I thought so. Half an hour ago. I just don't know where she is."

"Who is it? Maybe I've seen her."

"Linda Applegate."

As long as Fred had known Linda, she'd never been on time for anything. Even her children had been delivered late. He shook his head slowly. "I haven't seen her yet. You want me to help? I can serve the cider. You sit on that stool and take care of the money."

Geneva managed a thin smile. "No thanks, Mr. V. There's not much to do, anyway." She gathered the hair off her neck with one hand and let it drop again, then crinkled her nose at the crock pot of cider as if she didn't like the smell.

Fred let a few seconds pass and tried another sip. "This is good," he said, lifting the cup toward her again. "Is it a new recipe?"

She shrugged indifferently.

"They've got some great carved Santas over by the biology lab. Have you seen them?"

She didn't look even mildly interested.

He gave up trying to make small talk and checked over his shoulder to be sure nobody else was within hearing distance. "Do you mind if I ask you a question?"

"Not more questions. I told you, I don't want to talk about it."

"Didn't you tell me you saw Eddie for the last time a couple of days before he died?"

"I'm not talking to you."

"Wouldn't you rather talk to me than to the sheriff?"

Geneva glared at him. "I've already talked to the sheriff. Now, leave me alone."

"This is important."

"No."

Fred sipped cider and smacked his lips a couple of times. "You know, this is pretty good. Maybe I'll stay here and have another cup or two."

Geneva sighed, looked away for a couple of seconds, then looked back. "All right. Yes. I saw Eddie a couple of days before he died. Now, go away."

"That's odd. Someone's saying you were over at Eddie's on Thursday—the day before he died."

Her face clouded. "Who said that? Wayne?"

Fred couldn't help feeling a little sorry for Wayne if he was always the first person she suspected of leaking her secrets. "Were you?"

She didn't answer immediately, but she worked hard to keep looking bored. "What makes you think I was?"

"I told you. Someone saw you there."

This time, she scowled darkly and looked away.

Without taking his eyes from her, Fred sipped again and waited. When she still didn't respond, he lowered his cup to the table and glanced behind him. "All right. You don't have to answer. I don't mind asking Wayne about it. Have you seen him tonight? Is he here?"

"Ask him about what? That day at Eddie's?"

Fred nodded.

She scowled up at him. "Oh, like Wayne's going to tell you the truth." She put a heavy dose of sarcasm into the words.

"You don't think he will?"

"After what he did? I doubt it."

"What did he do?"

"He *followed* me there and sat outside like some crazy, obsessed weirdo all the time I was inside with Eddie, and when I came out, he came charging over and started threatening Eddie. He even hit him."

"Threatening him? How?"

Geneva rolled her eyes with impatience. "Threatening.

He told Eddie he'd better leave me alone or Wayne would make sure he did. Stuff like that. Big talk. Like he could have hurt Eddie if he tried."

Fred didn't bother pointing out that the great Eddie Leishman hadn't been as indestructible as Geneva obviously wanted to believe.

"I don't know what Wayne was thinking. I guess he thought I needed him to protect me or something."

"What did Eddie do?"

"He was upset," she said, but she shook her head as she spoke as if she could dilute the words that way. "He was mad at me for leaving, mad at Wayne for being there, mad at Vance for coming home when he did . . ." She let her voice trail away and her head slowed down.

"Do you think Wayne killed Eddie?"

She tucked a lock of hair behind an ear and shrugged. "I don't know. Maybe. He seemed fine when he found out about Eddie and the baby, but then he kind of went crazy."

"Jealous?"

"Insanely."

"How did he find out? Did you tell him?"

She nodded, and for the first time, she looked a little embarrassed. "I've known Wayne all my life, but we didn't start going out until last year. It only lasted for a month or two. Then I met Eddie . . ."

The rest, Fred supposed, was history. In Eddie's shadow, poor Wayne had lost his appeal. "How long ago did you and Eddie start seeing each other?"

"Six months, I guess."

Before Eddie left Ricki? Before Sharon? That threw all Fred's mental calculations off track. He'd been imagining Geneva as third in the chain all this time, and her affair with Eddie as very recent. "Why would Wayne suddenly fight Eddie over something that happened six months before?"

Geneva seemed to wrestle with herself for several long seconds before she spoke again. "Eddie didn't know I was pregnant until Thursday. That's why I went to Sharon's—to tell him about the baby. I *told* Wayne to stay away. It was supposed to be between me and Eddie. I knew Wayne would just make everything worse. But he followed me."

"Did you know it at the time?"

"No. Not until I came out." She looked down at her fingernails and sighed. "You know, I didn't think Eddie would marry me when he found out about the baby. I mean, he'd already started up with Sharon, and Ricki was always there in the background. But I didn't expect him to accuse me of trying to pass off somebody else's kid as his."

"That was his reaction?"

Geneva nodded and blinked a tear away. "When he said that, I went cold. Like I didn't love him anymore, you know?"

Fred could only imagine.

"So, I figured to hell with him, you know? I told him to forget it, I never wanted to see him again. I told him I wished it *was* somebody else's baby, and I got up to leave. All of a sudden, Eddie changed. It was like seeing me angry turned him on or something. He was all over me. He wanted to *do it* right there on the couch, but I couldn't. I didn't want to anymore."

Fred thanked his lucky stars—he didn't want details. "Was that when Vance walked in on you?"

She nodded quickly. "He blew up. I know he thought it was all my fault, but it wasn't. Honest. By that time, all I wanted was to get out of there—fast."

"So you ran outside and Wayne was there?"

"Yes. And then *he* went crazy." She shuddered at the memory. "I guess he could tell I'd been crying, or maybe he was just upset, but he went after Eddie like a lunatic. They were shouting and pushing each other around. I was really scared."

"What happened then?"

"Then Eddie went back inside and Wayne tried to get me to go home with him. But I didn't want to. I needed to be alone. The next day, I heard Eddie was dead."

"Is Wayne here tonight?" he asked again.

She fiddled with a tie on her apron. "I haven't seen him, thank God. I don't *want* to see him."

Fred could have kicked himself for concentrating so hard on Bear he'd all but pushed Wayne out of the picture. "Do you think Wayne killed Eddie?"

Geneva lifted one shoulder. "He said he would, and he was crazy jealous, but no. I don't think he killed Eddie."

"Do you know if Wayne's home?"

"I don't know where he is. I don't *care*. All I want is for him to leave me alone." She leaned down to pick up a worn backpack from the floor, pulled the apron over her head, and dropped it onto the table. "And I want *you* to leave me alone." She started through the crowd.

Fred stared after her for a second, then closed the lid on the cash box and placed it under the table. He scrawled "closed" on a napkin and anchored it to the table beneath a couple of filled cups, then picked up the Santa and walked slowly away.

If Wayne loved Geneva, and Geneva loved Eddie, and Eddie rejected Geneva—why would *that* lead Wayne to murder Eddie? It seemed to Fred, Wayne would find hope in Eddie's rejection. Geneva was more likely to be the killer than Wayne.

Pushing the crash bar on the door, Fred stepped outside. The snow had finally stopped, but every car in the lot stood shrouded in snow, every silhouette in the distance looked about the same to him. None of them seemed to be in the company of a ten-year-old girl.

He stood on the sidewalk, clutching the carved Santa package in one hand and shielding his eyes with the other. He felt old and tired and frustrated. Maybe he was too tired. He had too many other things on his mind to concentrate. All the stories seemed to bounce off each other, and nothing made any sense. And for all the time spent and questions asked, Fred didn't feel any closer to a solution to Eddie Leishman's murder.

As far as motives went, the killer could be anyone— Geneva, Wayne, Bear, Carl Fadel. For that matter, it might have been Ricki or Sharon, Joshua, Vance or even Doc. Eddie had given everyone who knew him plenty of provocation to want him out of the way.

Fred didn't even like to think about opportunity because that narrowed the list to Sharon, Vance, and Doc. And means? Well, the insulin had been sitting right in Sharon's refrigerator and Doc had left the syringe in the garbage. Doc and Sharon had made it easy for the killer—whoever it was—to fill the empty syringe with insulin and use it on Eddie. But who would have known insulin could be lethal?

Fred sighed heavily. He'd like to believe only a few people could have recognized such an opportunity and taken advantage of it. Ricki, maybe. Doc, certainly. In reality, anyone could have picked up that information from any-where—the newspapers or television, or even a book.

And Eddie's gun remained a mystery. If he'd kept it with him all the time, where was it now?

Walking slowly toward the Buick, Fred had to admit this puzzle had gotten the best of him. He'd grown obsessed, to use Margaret's word for his unusual ability to focus, and he'd let everything else slide. Since he couldn't seem to figure out the answers, maybe he should listen to the advice of others and let it go.

The more he tried to get things under control, the more out of control he felt. He might as well pull himself together and concentrate on family and the holidays. He'd let Enos handle the investigation into Eddie Leishman's death. Fred wasn't doing anyone any good this time. Not Doc. Not Enos. And especially not Margaret.

twenty-one

Fred turned off the snowblower and admired his handi-work in the bright morning sunlight. Though he'd resisted when the kids suggested he use the silly machine, he'd actually started growing quite fond of it—especially after a wet, heavy snowfall several inches thick. This morning, he'd cleared the driveway and the sidewalk to the front door in record time. Tomorrow, he'd have to do it all over again. Already, clouds were forming on the western horizon.

He wound the cord around his arm, then pushed the snowblower back into the garage and headed into the house. He slipped off his boots and hung his coat on a hook, then padded to the coffeemaker and poured a mugful. He inhaled the aroma and let the steam from the cup warm his face.

As he turned toward the table, he glanced out the window and caught a glimpse of Doc and Velma's house between the trees across the lake and wondered how Velma was holding up with Doc in jail.

Pushing aside the sudden urge to walk around the lake and pay her a visit, Fred snagged his glasses and the Sunday edition of the *Denver Post* from the kitchen table and headed into the living room. He reminded himself he was cold and tired, he hadn't read the newspaper in days, and he needed to come up with a plan for doing his shopping in the time left before Christmas. No, he wasn't getting involved. Not in any way.

He settled into his rocker by the front window, unfolded the paper, and scanned the headlines. But he didn't find anything worth reading. Another budget crisis in Washington, D.C., a debate over foreign policy, and the latest Congressional scandal—nothing new there.

Maybe the local section would have something more interesting. He skipped yet another article on the new Denver International Airport, skimmed one about an eight-car pileup on Interstate 70 near the Eisenhower Tunnel, and glanced at a couple of sports headlines, but to tell the truth, he didn't want to sit in his rocking chair and read the paper.

He lowered the newspaper to his lap, stared out the window, and cursed under his breath. He might as well admit it, he wanted to be out there doing something. He could sit here all day pretending to read the paper, but he couldn't accomplish a thing that way. He couldn't find out about Doc, couldn't learn anything helpful about Eddie Leishman's murder, couldn't make up with Margaret or even start his Christmas shopping with his backside in a chair.

He dropped the newspaper into a pile on the floor and trudged back to the kitchen. He knew he'd feel better if he told Enos everything he knew, and he might even pick up a piece or two of information. After that, he'd head over to Margaret's and make amends.

Within minutes, he'd bundled up and headed out again. He plodded through the fresh powder along the side of the road and tried to think of an acceptable excuse to offer Enos for barging in again. But try as he might, he still hadn't thought of anything clever by the time he reached Main Street.

He hesitated for a few seconds on the corner, then drew himself up and marched across the intersection, up the steps to the boardwalk, and into Enos's office without giving himself time to back down.

The aroma of coffee left too long on the burner filled the air, a bite of doughnut sat on a paper towel near Enos's elbow, and a tinny-sounding country version of a Christmas song spilled from a radio on the filing cabinet.

Enos looked up, slapped a file folder closed on his desk, and creaked back in his chair. "Well, what brings you here this morning?"

Fred didn't waste any time on small talk. He jerked his

head toward the door leading to the cells as he pulled off his gloves and unzipped his coat. "Have you still got Doc back there?"

Enos closed his eyes and wagged his head back and forth. "Don't start with me, Fred. It's Sunday morning, for crying out loud. Can't you let me have *one* day of rest?"

"Not as long as Doc's in jail."

Enos refocused on him as if it took some effort. "This is none of your business."

"You couldn't be more wrong. What in the world are you thinking, putting Doc in jail like this?"

"He confessed."

"Horsefeathers."

Enos sat a little straighter. "I have a signed confession."

"And you're going to tell me you believe it?" Fred planted his fists on Enos's desk and leaned closer. "What in the hell is wrong with you lately?"

He could see Enos's face shutting down. His eyes dulled, his jaw clenched, and his lips thinned. "You're pushing it, Fred."

"Not as hard as I intend to. Now, are you going to talk to me or not?"

Enos shot to his feet and leaned so close Fred could smell doughnuts and coffee on his breath. "I don't have to talk to you about a damned thing, Fred. Get out of here."

"No."

Enos started to speak, clamped his mouth shut again and jerked back. "You want me to throw you in jail? Is that it?"

"I want you to tell me how you can believe Doc's confession. Even *I* know he confessed to save Vance."

Enos wiped his face with the palm of one hand and shook his head. "You're some piece of work, do you know that? Does Maggie know you're here?"

Fred didn't bother thanking him for the compliment or answering his ridiculous question. He just waited for an explanation.

Enos paced a few steps away, flicked off the coffeemaker, and glared back over his shoulder. "Do you think you could trust me if I asked you to?"

That took a little of the wind out of Fred's sails, but he tried hard not to show it. "You know I trust you."

Enos barked a laugh. "Yeah. That's obvious. All right, I'll tell you this much. Doc is in jail, but not because I believe he's guilty. Okay?"

"You mean it's a trick?"

Enos nodded. "We're trying to get the killer to relax a little. Make a mistake. Give him or herself away."

Fred lowered himself into one of the battered chairs in front of Enos's desk. "Why didn't you tell me?"

"Because it looked more genuine to have you racing around town asking questions and trying to save Doc's hide."

Fred digested that slowly. "You mean, you used me."

Enos had the grace to flush. "I wouldn't put it that way—"

"I would. You purposely got me riled up and sent me out there to ask questions to throw Eddie Leishman's killer off track. Tell me one thing, does Margaret know?"

Enos studied the fingernails on one hand. "No." He looked so uncomfortable at the idea, Fred felt slightly better.

"Well, you'd better hope she doesn't find out. Do you know who killed him yet?"

"No."

"Do you have any ideas?"

Enos flicked a glance at him. "Of course I do."

"Such as—?"

"I have several suspects."

"Wayne Openshaw?" Fred demanded.

Enos turned to face him. "Yes, I'm considering Wayne Openshaw as a suspect."

"Geneva Hart?"

Another nod, this time he looked a little angry. "Yes. Listen, Fred—"

"What about Bear Sandusky?"

"He's my top suspect. In fact, I'm almost convinced he's the one who did it. Now, we're just waiting for him to get careless."

Fred snorted in response. "Are you going to keep Doc in jail until then? How long do you intend to wait?"

Enos shoved his fingers through his thinning hair. "I won't wait too long, I promise you that."

That didn't make Fred feel much better. "Maybe we should do more than sit around here waiting. Maybe we should force the issue a little."

Enos shook his head. "No. When I catch him, I want it to be a good arrest. I don't want to do anything that'll get the case tossed out of court. That means you don't go anywhere near him—right?"

Fred nodded reluctantly. "Fine."

Enos didn't look as if he believed him. "I'm going to be gone tomorrow, so Grady'll be in charge. I don't want you giving him or Ivan any trouble."

"You're taking another day off?"

"Believe me, I'd rather not." Enos's shoulders sagged a little and he glanced away again. "I'm driving Jessica down to Denver again."

Fred knew he shouldn't pry, but he couldn't leave it alone. "Are things okay between you?"

"Yeah. They're fine."

"You don't sound fine." Fred pushed out of his chair and closed the distance between them. He put a hand on Enos's shoulder. "Look, I know it's none of my business, but what's going on between you two? Are things getting worse?"

Enos didn't answer immediately. He kept his eyes trained on the drawer handle of the filing cabinet until, after what felt like forever, he looked up and met Fred's gaze. His eyes were too bright, his mouth too thin, and Fred thought his chin quivered slightly. "It's not what you think."

"What is it, then?"

Enos looked away again and when he spoke, Fred could hear emotion clogging his voice. "I'm taking her to the doctor, Fred. She's found a lump in her breast."

Fred's mouth dried and his heart raced as he relived memories he'd tried for three years to forget. "It's not serious, is it?"

Enos lifted one shoulder. "She's got an appointment for a

biopsy tomorrow. If it's malignant, they'll do surgery while she's already on the operating table. We've had to make some pretty tough decisions the past few days. But, then, you know how that is."

Fred tried desperately to focus in spite of the tears that suddenly filled his eyes. "I'm sorry."

Enos attempted to look as if he had some strength left. "We're hopeful it will be benign, or that if she needs surgery they'll get it all."

Hopeful. What a weak, useless word. Fred and Phoebe had been hopeful, too. "I guess Doc knows about this?"

Enos nodded. "He's taking it hard. He's blaming himself for not finding it sooner. Jessica thinks he's blaming himself for Phoebe and for her."

Fred glanced at the door to the cell area. "The damned fool. That's just exactly the kind of backward thinking he'd indulge in."

Enos tried to smile. "Yeah."

"And you've been trying to solve a murder while you've had this on your mind?"

"Yeah, well, you've been a big help."

This time, Fred almost laughed. "Glad to hear it."

With visible effort, Enos managed to pull himself together again. When he straightened his shoulders, Fred patted his arm one last time and pulled his hand away.

"So, now you know," Enos said. "All I ask is that you let things run their course. Let Bear tip his own hand. Let Grady and Ivan pull him in when the time comes."

Fred nodded. "Of course."

Enos's lips twitched, but they couldn't quite form a smile. "Of course." He glanced at the phone, then back at Fred. "Listen, I hate to ask you to leave, but I promised Jessica I'd call . . ."

Fred lifted a hand to show he understood. "No problem. I've got to stop by and see Margaret, anyway." He nodded toward the telephone. "Give Jessica my best. Tell her my prayers are with her."

Enos nodded. "I will. Thanks."

Fred stepped outside and pulled the door closed behind

him, but his heart ached for his friend. He made the return trip down Lake Front Drive, then hurried through the frigid air down Arapaho Street to Margaret's house.

She opened the door when he knocked and peered out at him through wary eyes that looked even darker than usual. "Dad? What are you doing?"

"Got a minute?"

"Deborah's not feeling well. Maybe you shouldn't come in and risk exposing yourself to whatever she's got."

Fred knew Deborah regularly got an upset stomach after one of her father's episodes—it didn't surprise him a bit. "This can't wait."

Margaret hesitated long enough to let Fred know she didn't really want to talk to him, then nodded briefly and stepped away from the door to let him pass.

"Is Webb here?" Fred asked on his way through the door.

Her face clouded. She pulled a hanger from the coat closet and held out her hand for his coat. "No. He's picking Sarah up in Granby. She's riding that far with a roommate."

"Good. It'll be wonderful to see her." He put a hand on her shoulder and held her gaze. "I want to talk with you alone, anyway."

Margaret worked his coat into the closet, then followed him to the couch. "I'm not going to argue with you," she warned.

"I didn't come to argue, sweetheart. I stopped by to bring you some news. I've just come from Enos's office."

As he'd known it would, Margaret's expression softened. "How is he?"

Fred leaned closer and took her hands in his. "Jessica has a lump in her breast, sweetheart. They're doing surgery immediately, so it sounds as if it's pretty large, but they're trying to be hopeful about the prognosis."

Fred felt as if he were watching Margaret's reaction in slow motion. Every emotion he'd been expecting flitted across her face—shock, disbelief, horror, dismay. She had trouble making herself speak again. "I had no idea."

"Enos hasn't said much—he's playing it close to his chest. Doc knows, and now you and I know. I don't think it's common knowledge or we'd have heard before today."

"When is the surgery?"

"Tomorrow. After that—well, it depends on what they find."

Margaret blinked tears away, studied her fingers for several long seconds, and tried to meet his gaze again.

"Apparently, Doc's blaming himself for not finding the problem sooner."

"That's ridiculous."

"You know that, and so do I. But Doc has a tendency to expect too much of himself."

Another lengthy pause stretched between them while Margaret worked through the news. "Enos doesn't blame Doc, does he?"

"I don't think so. But I do think it explains why he's having such a hard time concentrating."

"You mean, on Eddie Leishman's murder?"

Fred nodded.

"Oh, I see. So, you're using all this as an excuse to keep yourself involved in the investigation?"

He pulled back a little, surprised at the leap in logic. "No. I'm out of it. I've reached a dead end, anyway. I've talked to everyone who knew Eddie, I've heard a dozen different stories, and I still can't piece it together. It's Enos and Doc I'm worried about now."

Margaret eyed him as if she suspected a lie. "You don't have *any* suspects?"

"I have too many suspects," Fred admitted.

She studied him for too long, then nodded slowly and started to say something else, when the front door flew open and Benjamin stomped inside.

He smiled when he saw them sitting there. "Hey, Grandpa. Mom."

Margaret stiffened noticeably and refused to smile back. "Where have you been, and why didn't you stay and talk to your dad this morning?"

Benjamin shrugged out of his coat. "What was I supposed to say?"

"He wants you to go get that money back from Ricki," Margaret insisted. "Today."

"Oh, come on, Mom—"

She lifted her hands as if warding off an attack. "I'm in the middle of this argument, Benjamin. I understand where you're coming from, but you went behind my back to get there. There's nothing I can do. You'd better get that money back before your dad gets home because I don't want to hear any more about it."

Benjamin glared at her, but he didn't argue. Instead, he stormed through the living room and started down the corridor to his bedroom.

"Don't make me tell you again," Margaret shouted.

Benjamin lifted one hand over his head as he walked away in silent signal that he'd heard her.

Margaret sighed and turned back to Fred. "He's not going to go. I'm going to have to take him over there myself."

"He'll go," Fred assured her.

But she shook her head vehemently. "Six months ago, I'd have agreed with you. Now, I don't think so." She stared down the hallway again. "Can you do me a favor, Dad?"

"Anything, sweetheart."

"Can you wait here with Deborah while I take Benjamin over to Ricki's house?"

Fred patted her knee and pushed to his feet. "How about I do you one better? You stay here with Deborah—she needs you more than she needs me. I'll go with Benjamin."

"You won't let him come back without the money, will you? I don't want to spend all evening arguing about that damned truck again."

"I'll convince him."

She stood to face him and tried to look severe. "Good luck. He's almost as stubborn as you are."

Fred pressed a kiss to her cheek. "I can be mighty persuasive."

She pulled away and tried not to smile. "Just persuade yourself to get that money back."

Waving one hand over his head, Fred followed Benjamin to the end of the hallway. After knocking softly, he pushed the door open a crack and peered inside. "Mind if I come in?"

Benjamin sat on his bed, a picture of dejection. He shook his head and shrugged at the same time. "I guess not."

Fred slipped inside and closed the door behind him. "Your mother wants us to get the money back for the truck."

"It's not what *she* wants, it's my dad."

"That's true, but I guess that's why your mother wants it. Seems this truck business is causing quite a rift in the family."

Benjamin shrugged again. "Oh, well. It's not like there isn't a rift there, anyway."

Fred knew that, but it hurt to know the children were so aware of the problems. He lowered himself to sit beside Benjamin. "Listen, son, I'm not going to lecture you about going behind your parents' back on the truck. Part of the blame is mine, anyway. And I'm not going to tell you what you should do in the future. I'm not even going to tell you to forget the truck or to go to college like your mom and dad want. What I am going to suggest is that we get the money back for this particular truck and you talk it over with your parents before you make a deal like this again."

Benjamin scowled at him from under furrowed brows. "Why? They won't let me do what I want."

"Maybe not, but knowing your mother as well as I do, I'd guess she'll be more likely to compromise with you if you don't push her into a corner."

Benjamin grunted.

"She's a lot like your grandmother in that way."

Benjamin smirked. "*You* don't compromise with her."

"In my own way, I do. Besides, I'm her father. *She's* supposed to compromise with *me*."

That earned a genuine smile. "That's not what she says." The smile faded again and he glanced out the window. "I guess I don't have much choice, do I?"

"The way I see it," Fred said, pushing back to his feet, "you've got two choices. Dig your heels in and wait for your dad to go with you to see Ricki. Or go with me."

"I could go by myself."

"Okay, three choices."

Sighing, Benjamin stood to face him. "You want to go now?"

"I've got nothing better to do," Fred said honestly.

The boy snagged his coat from the floor and put it on with just enough hostility in his movements to let Fred know he'd have liked another choice. "Oh, all right. Let's go."

Fred followed Benjamin down the hallway to the front door, and though he looked for Margaret on his way through, he couldn't see her anywhere. He hated dropping a bombshell like the one he'd just delivered about Enos and Jessica, but neither would he have felt right leaving Margaret in the dark.

Besides, he had no intention of doing anything else that might put another barrier between himself and Margaret. He had a sinking feeling he'd be digging himself out of the mess he'd made with Benjamin and the truck for a long time.

twenty-two

Fred and Benjamin walked in silence most of the way to Ricki Leishman's house. Somewhere nearby, a snow shovel scraping against a sidewalk or driveway broke the stillness. Further distant, a snowmobile hummed to life and buzzed off across a field. Children shouted as they played in the snow. But Benjamin didn't speak, though he did scowl at Fred once or twice along the way.

Fred didn't push him to conversation. He knew the boy needed a few minutes to work through his anger. Fred shoved his hands into his pockets and whistled a tune his father had whistled when Fred was a boy. His knees twinged a little in the cold, and he checked the sky for signs of another storm moving into the valley.

He tried to ignore the cold and find pleasure in the walk, but even this late in the morning, the temperature hovered so low the ice and snow hadn't even begun to melt. When they finally reached Ricki's house, Fred's knees ached, his fingers throbbed and his face had grown almost numb.

The house looked warm and inviting, but instead of heading for the door, Benjamin paused at the end of the driveway. "I don't know, Grandpa. She's not going to like this."

"You're worrying too much," Fred assured him. "She'll understand."

Benjamin glanced around as if someone might be listening. "I'm not so sure. Josh says she really needs the money."

Fred scowled over at the boy. He hadn't walked all this way just to turn around and head back. And they didn't need

Webb to rush over here, offend Ricki, and make everything worse.

Without another word, he plodded through the unshoveled snow toward the porch. Benjamin followed more slowly and stepped into place by the door only after Fred had already pressed the doorbell.

Ricki smiled when she opened the door and saw Benjamin standing there, then sobered almost immediately. "Ben? I hope you didn't come out in this weather to see Josh. He went skiing with Nate and Ty early this morning."

Benjamin shook his head and glanced once at Fred, then smiled an apology at Ricki. "No. I . . . I came to see you. I need to talk to you about the truck."

She looked faintly surprised, but she stepped aside and pushed open the storm door with one hand. "You'd better come in. You must be frozen."

Fred followed Ricki up a short flight of stairs into a small but pleasant living room. Not surprisingly, she had allowed few concessions to the holidays. No tree, no gifts, no lights, but she did have Christmas music playing on a stereo somewhere. A soft-looking couch sat on one side of a narrow fireplace with its matching love seat facing it. A television took up most of one wall, and a china cupboard, too large for such a small room, stood against another.

She worked up a thin smile as she steered Fred toward the couch. Benjamin had already plopped himself down on the opposite end. Fred sat, sank into the cushions, and wondered how he'd ever get back up on his own.

Ricki arranged herself into a corner of the love seat so she could face them both. Beside her, a small table held a notepad and a cordless telephone. "So, what about the truck? Did you get the rest of the money together already?"

Benjamin looked up, then back down at his hands. "No. I . . . uh . . . I've got a problem. My dad says I've got to get the down payment back."

She laughed as if she thought he was joking, but when neither Benjamin nor Fred laughed with her, her smile faded and her eyes darkened. "You what?"

"I've got to get the down payment back," Benjamin said

again. "I'm sorry. I know this is bad, but my dad's being a real butthead about it." He flashed a guilty glance at Fred.

"But that's impossible. I've already used the money."

Benjamin sent Fred a look clearly designed to prove his point, and leaned back against the couch as if Ricki's answer settled things.

But Fred wasn't the one Benjamin needed to convince, and he didn't think Webb would care whether or not Ricki had the money. Webb had never been known for thinking logically. Fred leaned forward a bit and took up the argument. "I know this puts you in an uncomfortable position, Mrs. Leishman, but Benjamin isn't a legal adult, and his father doesn't want him to buy the truck."

"Well, I'm sorry about that. But Ben never gave me any idea the sale was in question." She uncurled herself slowly and straightened her shoulders. "If he had, I would have made other arrangements."

Fred conceded that point. "Still, I'm sure we can work something out."

"There's nothing to work out, Mr. Vickery. I can't afford to refund Ben's money and I don't think I should. He told me he'd talked it over with his parents. It's not my fault he lied." She fixed Benjamin with a stony stare. "You don't go back on your word, Benjamin. Not ever."

Fred frowned over at Benjamin. "Did you tell her you'd talked to your parents?"

Benjamin nodded without looking up.

Well, for Pete's sake. "Why?"

"I wanted the truck. I didn't want her to sell it to anybody else."

Fred sighed. "Did you sign an agreement?"

Benjamin shook his head.

"That doesn't matter," Ricki insisted. "He gave me his word."

Fred supposed he should be thankful they didn't have to worry about breaking a legal contract. "Did you get a receipt for the money you paid her?"

This time, Benjamin couldn't even move his head to respond.

Fred held back a groan. Ricki gave every indication of putting up a fight, but Benjamin had left them without any tools to fight back. "Look, Mrs. Leishman. The bottom line is, Benjamin gave you a down payment for the truck, but he can't pay you the rest. I don't think you'll have any trouble finding another buyer—I'd even be willing to ask around for you. I know it must be difficult to think about selling the truck at a time like this—"

Ricki interrupted with a bitter laugh. "Difficult? Yes. But I don't have the luxury of waiting for things to get easier. Eddie may have died in Sharon's bed, but he left *me* with his bills."

Fred blinked in response. Then, because Benjamin was in the room, tried to steer the discussion away from Eddie's extracurricular activities. "I'm sure it's difficult. Unfortunately, we're in a tight spot."

"*I'm* in a tight spot." Her eyes hardened and her nostrils flared slightly. She obviously didn't intend to give an inch.

Fred cast about for another tack to take; Ricki watched him, almost as if she could anticipate his next move. Benjamin slumped down in the corner of the couch and held up his chin with his fist.

When the cordless telephone rang at Ricki's elbow, Fred breathed a sigh of relief. At least he'd have a few seconds to think. But to his surprise, she made no move to answer and after the third ring, an answering machine clicked on in a nearby room. Eddie's recorded voice blended with the Christmas music, demanding that the caller leave a name and number. It sounded eerie to Fred, and he could tell by the way Benjamin suddenly sat up a little straighter that the boy reacted much the same way. Ricki didn't even bat an eye.

"Ricki?" A man's voice blared much louder than Eddie's. "Ricki, are you there? If you're there, pick up the phone."

After only a few words, Fred recognized the caller's voice as Bear's, and he didn't sound happy. Surely Ricki would react now, if only to keep such a dangerous man from growing more agitated. But when she still didn't make a move, Fred realized she had no idea how dangerous Bear could be or what part he'd played in Eddie's death.

"Come on, Rick," Bear commanded. "I know you're there. Pick up the damn phone."

"Maybe you should," Fred suggested softly.

She hesitated a second longer, then snatched up the telephone and used her thumb to turn it on. "I've got company," she snapped into the receiver. "I'll have to call you back." She paused to listen, then flicked a glance at Fred and Benjamin. "Ben Templeton and his grandfather." She nodded eagerly, as if Bear could see her. "Yes, that's the one. What's your problem, anyway?"

Her face creased into a frown as she listened. She rolled her eyes with impatience, then stood quickly and took a couple of steps toward the television. When she spoke again, her voice came so much softer, Fred had to strain to hear. "What do you mean, the amplifier doesn't work? Of course it works. It always worked for Eddie. It was his best one, you know that."

Bear must have argued, because her face grew stony. "You're lying. What did you do to it?"

Fred watched her expressions while she talked and decided he might have been wrong, after all. She swore, strode to the china cabinet, and yanked open one glass door. Lifting a serving bowl, she retrieved a small key and unlocked the top drawer of the cabinet. Looking over her shoulder once more at Fred and Benjamin, she turned her back firmly and tugged the drawer open so quickly the wood groaned in protest.

She kept her movements small, her hands hidden from view, her shoulders hunched to keep Fred and Benjamin from seeing what she was doing. But with every passing second, she seemed to grow more agitated and her movements more broad.

Twice, she peeked over her shoulder to where Fred and Benjamin waited on the couch then turned back to her task. With every secretive glance, Fred's curiosity rose a notch.

She muttered into the receiver, swearing softly at first, then complaining more loudly. "You want the warranty?

Fine." Fred didn't think she sounded fine at all. "No," she snarled. "I've got it here somewhere."

At long last, she found what she'd been looking for. Pulling out a small book, she pushed the drawer shut. The wood creaked again, probably swollen from the moisture in the air. Instead of returning the key to its original hiding place, she slipped it into the pocket of her jeans. "All right," she snapped. "I found it. Come and get the stupid thing."

Fred could still hear Bear's voice, rising and falling with agitation through the telephone line.

"You're *not* changing your mind," Ricki warned, and her voice tightened with irritation. "I don't give a damn whether it works or not. That wasn't our deal." She took a couple of steps toward the hallway, glanced back once more at her guests, then slipped out of the room. "Look, dammit, I don't need this from you. You're acting just like Eddie now."

Benjamin watched her go, then turned to Fred with a serious expression. "Don't you think it's kind of creepy?" he whispered.

Fred didn't know if *creepy* was the word he'd choose to describe his apprehension. "What's creepy?"

Benjamin leaned a little closer. "That she still has Eddie's voice on the answering machine. I mean, he hasn't lived here in months, don't you think she'd change the recording?"

"It's hard to say," Fred admitted. "I still have things of your grandmother's around, and she's been gone three years."

"That's different. You weren't in the middle of a divorce. She didn't hate you."

"Eddie and Ricki weren't in the middle of a divorce, either," Fred reminded him. "And from what I hear, they didn't hate each other."

"*She* didn't hate *him*, but you should have heard the way he talked to her. He wasn't very nice to her—especially after she said no to the divorce."

Fred stared at Benjamin. "Eddie *wanted* a divorce?"

"Yeah. At least, that's what Josh says, and he ought to know, right?"

Fred rubbed his forehead and tried to readjust his thinking. Eddie wanted a divorce, but Ricki didn't? So did that mean Sharon was right? Had Eddie actually loved her? Had he been planning to marry her, after all? If so, it sure put a different spin on things.

But if Ricki had lied about Eddie, what else had she lied about? And what did she have in the china cabinet she didn't want anyone else to see?

Maybe Enos and the boys were on the wrong track, after all. Maybe Ricki and Bear *did* have more of a relationship than either wanted to admit. Maybe they'd engineered Eddie's death together.

Without giving himself time to think, Fred pushed to his feet and pulled out his pocketknife. In two steps, he'd closed the distance to the china cabinet.

Benjamin followed him across the room. "Grandpa? What are you doing?"

Fred carefully worked the blade of his knife between the drawer and the cabinet's frame. "Nothing. I want you to slip outside and find a neighbor who'll let you use the phone. Call the sheriff's office and tell Grady to get over here."

Instead of obeying, Benjamin leaned his chin on Fred's shoulder so he could see better. "Why?"

"I'll explain everything later. Now, get out of here."

"If she catches you, she's going to be really pissed, Grandpa. She doesn't even let Joshua get into this drawer."

If Ricki caught him and Fred's suspicions had any basis in fact, she'd be more than upset. With his heart dancing in his throat, his ears straining for sounds of Ricki's return, and his fingers trembling, Fred somehow managed to trip the lock. He cast a glance toward the hallway and eased the drawer open partway.

Mindful of the swollen wood he worked slowly, and after what felt like an eternity he managed to get the drawer open about halfway. A wooden box, probably containing her silver, took half the drawer's width. Two stacks of papers took up the rest of the space. Carefully, Fred thumbed through the first few documents, but nothing looked out of the ordinary.

Had he been wrong? If Ricki *was* hiding something, would Fred even know it when he saw it?

Benjamin jostled his shoulder. "Grandpa, close the drawer."

But Fred couldn't. Not until he knew for sure. He worked the drawer open another inch or two, then still further until he saw something hidden behind the silver chest. He peered into the drawer, unwilling to touch what might prove to be a crucial piece of evidence.

Benjamin gasped almost silently, but the sound seemed to echo from the walls. "That's Eddie's gun."

Fred flicked a glance at him. "Are you sure?"

Benjamin nodded. "Yeah. He used to carry it all the time." Eddie's missing gun. Fred's stomach knotted as he thought through the stories he'd heard. Nobody had seen the gun since before Eddie died. Everybody swore Eddie never parted with it. Ricki must have taken it from Eddie when he died, or Bear had given it to her later. Either way, she'd been involved in Eddie's death.

He started working the drawer back into place. "Get out of here, Benjamin. Right now. Before she gets off the phone."

This time, Benjamin didn't argue. Fear told Fred to shove the drawer closed quickly or to leave it hanging open and run. But if he did either, Ricki would know she'd been caught and she might escape before he could get word to Grady and Ivan.

Benjamin tensed behind him, then shook his arm. "Grandpa? She's coming. Shut the drawer. Please."

Without hesitating, Fred shoved the drawer closed and hurried back to the couch a step behind Benjamin. They dropped into place just as Ricki entered the room, and Fred willed himself to take deep, even breaths. He cast one last glance toward the china cabinet and realized too late the drawer hadn't closed completely on one side.

It took every bit of concentration he could muster to drag his eyes away from the drawer and to keep his expression bland. He had to fold his hands together to keep them from trembling in his lap.

Ricki crossed so close to the cabinet, Fred had to force

himself to draw breath. But she didn't notice the drawer. She dropped the cordless phone back to the table and turned to them with a smile. This time, Fred could see the ice in her eyes.

"Sorry for the interruption," she said. "Getting rid of Eddie's things has been such a pain. Which is exactly why I'm not inclined to let Benjamin back out of our deal. I don't have the energy to go through this over and over."

Fred forced himself to speak. "I understand. Actually, Benjamin and I were talking while you were out of the room. We've decided maybe we *should* talk to Benjamin's dad again."

She looked surprised and pleased, and her smile widened and some of the ice melted. "Good. I'm glad. Tell him *I'm* not responsible for his son's lies. *I* don't go back on my word."

Fred nodded as if he had every intention of passing on the message. He worked himself back out of the couch and stood. He tried to keep his knees steady. He willed himself not to glance at the china cabinet and draw Ricki's attention to it.

Benjamin popped to his feet behind Fred. "Yeah, I'm gonna . . . um . . . talk to my dad."

Fred started toward the stairway, forcing himself to take steady steps, to walk slowly, and behave normally.

Ricki didn't follow. Instead, she took a step closer to the china cabinet but she kept her eyes on Fred. "Tell Webb next time he has a problem, he can talk to me himself. I'm sick to death of irresponsible men. I don't need to be lied to anymore."

If Fred could get himself and Benjamin away before she realized what he'd done, he'd be willing to tell Webb anything she wanted.

She turned then, still holding the warranty in one hand. She reached into her pocket for the key, then tensed with her eyes on the open drawer. She whipped back around to look at Fred. Her face had grown hard, cold, bitter. Her eyes had turned to steel. In that moment, Fred knew she was a woman more than capable of killing her husband.

Without thinking, Fred shoved Benjamin toward the stairs. But he'd either underestimated Ricki or overestimated his own abilities because he heard the click of the hammer a split second before she spoke again. This time, her voice sounded deadly. "I wondered why the sudden change of heart, Mr. Vickery. I'd heard what a nosy old man you are, but I never expected *this*."

He turned slowly to face her and felt Benjamin stiffen at his side. She leveled the gun, first at Fred, then slowly adjusted her aim to Benjamin.

Fred's heart raced and his pulse nearly deafened him, but he couldn't move. "Let the boy leave."

She brayed a laugh. "You must really think I'm stupid. You really think I'll let Benjamin leave so he can bring back the sheriff?" Her smile died. "Not on your life."

"I don't want him hurt."

"You should have thought about that before you started snooping around. You've defiled me. You've violated my trust." She closed the distance between them and nestled the gun against Benjamin's temple. "I'm sorry about this, Ben. I really am." She gestured toward the china cupboard. "You didn't do this, did you?"

Benjamin shook his head slowly.

"I didn't think so. It was your grandpa. He's no better than the rest of them. He had no business breaking into my things. But I'm not going to prison. Not for some man who betrays my trust."

Fred could taste bile in his throat. "That's exactly where you'll go if you hurt my grandson and live long enough afterward to stand trial."

Her eyes narrowed even further. Fred waited for her to look nervous or for her gaze to shift. But she showed no sign of weakness. "I am *not* going to prison," she repeated. "My son needs me. I'm the only parent he has left."

Did she really expect sympathy? Fred couldn't feel a thing for her, though he worried a great deal about Josh. "You and Bear won't get away with this. Enos is right on your trail."

Ricki stared at him for half a beat, then laughed again. "He thinks Bear did it? I'd never have imagined that."

"No," Fred said quickly. "He knows it's you. He's right behind me on his way here. He knows you and Eddie argued the day before he died and again that night. He knows you took Eddie's keys and had one made for yourself. He knows Eddie wanted a divorce but you didn't."

"Shut up!"

He'd touched a nerve. He kept pushing, hoping to make her angry enough that she'd grow careless. "He knows Eddie planned to marry Sharon after the first of the year—"

"Sharon? Eddie didn't love Sharon. In fact, I know now that Eddie didn't love anyone but himself. It was almost funny at first, watching other women believe he loved them but knowing he'd come home to me. He *always* came back to me. Until this time." She broke off and shook her head. "It took me weeks to figure out what she used to hold him."

"Sharon loved him."

"Sharon?" Ricki laughed wildly, met Benjamin's frightened gaze and laughed again. "Sharon couldn't hold him, either. And he'd have dumped that little slut, too—if he hadn't found out she was pregnant. *Pregnant*, when he made me have my tubes tied after Josh was born so he wouldn't have to be tied down to a bunch of kids. *Pregnant*, and suddenly he wanted her and the little bastard more than he wanted me. More than he wanted Josh. I didn't know how much I could hate until he told me that."

Fred could only gape at her. She was talking about Geneva, not Sharon. Geneva and her unborn baby. He held her gaze, hoping she'd waver, show some sign of uncertainty or weakness.

She stared back for a full minute, then tightened her grip on the gun and rechecked her aim. And Fred knew with a dreadful certainty she wouldn't hesitate to kill them both.

twenty-three

Fred glanced around for a weapon to use against Ricki. But even if there'd been something close at hand, she'd have killed them both before he could reach it.

She seemed to realize what he had in mind. Nudging Benjamin with the gun's barrel again, she jerked her head toward a corner of the room. "That's enough. You, Mr. Vickery. Stand over there. By the wall. Don't move."

Fred inched toward the corner. She knew he wouldn't make a move while she had the gun on Benjamin, but she had to be crazy if she thought he'd stand here with his nose against the wall and let her take his grandson.

"You're making a mistake," he said. "You'll never get away. Too many people know we came over here."

She stopped moving and waited for several long seconds before she spoke. "Turn around."

Fred turned and made eye contact with Benjamin. They hadn't moved far, but the boy looked frantic.

Ricki gestured toward the door. "We're all going outside. You first, Mr. Vickery."

Fred reluctantly led the way to the front door, aware that any second she might panic and squeeze the trigger. Any move he made might be the end of Benjamin. By using Benjamin, she stayed Fred's hand more surely than if she'd put the gun to his own head.

Pulling open the door, Fred stepped outside. He half slid across the icy porch and prayed he'd keep his footing, that Benjamin wouldn't lose his, or Ricki wouldn't slip and accidentally pull the trigger.

He searched in vain for something he could say that

might touch her, but everything he thought of would probably only make her angrier or more frightened. And Fred didn't want an angry, frightened person on the other end of that gun.

If he'd only had himself to worry about, he might have ducked suddenly and tried to catch her off balance. But he wasn't willing to increase the risk to Benjamin.

Fred looked back at her, silently asking directions. She nodded toward the driveway. Slowly, Fred made his way through the frozen footprints in the snow and across the patches of solid ice. He could hear Benjamin and Ricki moving behind him.

When he reached the edge of the driveway, Ricki finally spoke. "Stop there."

He turned to face her again, anxiously searching Benjamin's face for signs of panic. She'd tucked the gun under her jacket, and prodded Benjamin in the side with it every few inches.

She dug a set of keys from her pocket and held them out. "I think we ought to take the truck for a test-drive." She nudged Benjamin again. "Everybody knows how close you and your grandpa are. Everybody knows you'll want his opinion before you take the truck home. Right?"

Benjamin somehow managed to nod.

Fred met the boy's gaze and tried to send him some reassurance.

"No signals," Ricki shouted and held the keys out for Fred.

He held out his hand for them, then slowly worked his way across the uneven ground to the front of the truck. Using the truck's seat and the steering wheel for leverage, he hoisted himself onto the driver's seat and slid the key into the ignition.

While Benjamin climbed into the truck, Fred cranked the key. When Ricki propped one foot on the running board, Fred jammed the truck into gear, and when she grabbed the back of the seat and started to pull herself into the cab, he released the clutch so the truck would jump forward and knock her off balance.

"Get the gun," he shouted.

As Ricki stumbled backward, Benjamin lunged across the seat and tried to wrestle the gun from her. Fred worked the truck out of gear and leaned across to help. But the steering wheel held him in place for several seconds too long. Before he could reach them, Ricki pulled the gun from Benjamin's grasping fingers and turned the barrel toward Fred. "You stupid old man. I *warned* you." She climbed into the cab and slammed the door. "Now, put the truck in reverse—*gently*."

Cursing himself silently for increasing the risk to Benjamin, Fred manipulated the gearshift into position and backed out of the driveway. The truck whined onto the street, bucked a little when he shifted into second, and fishtailed when he accelerated toward the intersection.

"Keep it slow," Ricki ordered. "Don't call attention to us."

Again, Fred tried to think of some way to save them. In desperation, he considered and discarded a dozen different courses of action—all too dangerous for Benjamin. If he'd been alone, Fred might have tried jumping from the truck at an intersection, but if the steering wheel had kept him from moving a minute ago, he knew Benjamin wouldn't be able to leap to safety with both it and the gearshift in his way.

He slid to a stop by Alan Lombard's insurance office and glanced eagerly inside, as if Alan might have decided to stop by the office on a Sunday morning. He accelerated slowly past the Bluebird and waited for someone to look up and see them pass. But for the first time in weeks, nobody sat by the front windows, and their passing went unnoticed.

Ricki sat on the opposite side of the truck, edgy and nervous. She held the gun on Benjamin but she darted frequent, anxious glances out the window. Her increasing nervousness was the only thing in their favor, but Fred didn't know how to make it work to their advantage.

When his fingers started to grow numb, he forced himself to loosen his grip on the steering wheel. The silence between them stretched like taut wire, broken only by the ragged sound of someone's breathing.

"What about Joshua?" Benjamin asked suddenly. His voice sounded unnaturally loud in the small space.

"What about him?" Ricki demanded.

"You're leaving town without him?" Benjamin asked.

Fred drove through a patch of ice, struggled to keep the truck from sliding onto the shoulder, and decided not to try to watch her face. It would be all he could do to keep them alive until she was ready to kill them.

When she didn't answer, Benjamin looked over at Fred. "She's not leaving, Grandpa. She's going to kill us." His voice sounded softer. More frightened.

"I don't want to kill you, Ben," Ricki said. "I've always kind of liked you."

Small consolation to the boy with a gun in his ribs.

Fred didn't speak, but he flicked a reassuring glance at the boy, trying to say everything in that one look he couldn't say aloud. "Killing us isn't going to keep you out of prison," he said to Ricki. He struggled to keep his voice soft, soothing, almost monotone.

Ricki jerked the gun up and aimed it at Fred again. "Shut up. I don't want another word out of you. I don't want any more smart moves. I'm warning you now, if Benjamin gets hurt, it will be *your* fault."

Just as Eddie had brought about his own death, no doubt. But Fred didn't respond. In her heightened state of agitation, he'd be a fool to push when he couldn't fight. He had to get her outside the truck and make her angry enough that Benjamin had a chance to get away.

When they passed Jefferson's One-Stop and drove out into the forest, Fred tried to keep his hopes up. Now, even if they somehow managed to get away from Ricki, their chances for survival seemed remote. Trees so dark they looked almost black under the cover of new snow loomed on either side of the highway. Winter wind gusted and moaned all around them and flung bits of snow across the pavement.

Steering around the first steep curve on the switchbacks, Fred tried to keep close to the mountain wall to avoid flirting with the drop-off on the far side of the road. With the wind picking up and snow blowing across the highway and reducing visibility, they might soon be in as much danger from the elements as they were from Ricki.

He searched his memory for a place on the highway where he could force the truck off the road, close enough to the trees to provide cover without heading into the mountain on one side or over the cliff on the other.

When they hit a dense patch of fog, Ricki leaned forward to watch the highway. "Turn on the lights."

Without appearing to look at her, Fred obeyed and drove cautiously for the next several minutes until the sun broke through the fog again. Twice, he let the truck skim an icy patch and let the wheel slip slightly from his fingers so Ricki wouldn't immediately suspect anything when he made his move. Several times, he had to force himself to relax his grip on the steering wheel to keep the circulation moving through his fingers.

Benjamin sat beside him, alert, watching, ready for anything. They both knew Ricki intended to kill them. But Fred didn't know where. Or when. He only knew they wouldn't reach the bottom of the mountain alive.

Following curve after endless curve, Fred watched for his chance. Snow whipped across his line of vision and nearly obscured the road in some spots. Fog hung low over the highway, forcing him to slow down to maintain control of the truck.

Ricki leaned forward again and stared out the windshield, shoved the hair out of her eyes in a jerky, agitated movement, and Fred realized her own tension was mounting at the same rate as his. He'd have to make a move soon.

He remembered a wide spot in the road near the inside of an S curve less than half a mile ahead. It wouldn't be his first choice—the trees were too far away to provide immediate cover, and they'd be a good five miles outside of town—but he couldn't wait until Ricki did something, he had to catch her off guard.

Not much further now, Fred watched the highway until his vision threatened to blur. Finally, at long last, they hit the switchback he'd been waiting for. He cranked the wheel hard to send the truck into a spin, jammed his foot onto the brake, and steered into the skid, using muscles he'd forgotten he had to keep the truck sliding in the direction he intended.

The truck shot off the highway, bounced nose-down into a ditch, and flew back up into a snowbank. Fred held onto the steering wheel and braced himself against the impact, but his elbows buckled and the steering wheel drove into his chest as a shot rang out and the horn began to blare. Somewhere inside the cab, glass shattered.

Benjamin lurched forward into the dashboard. Ricki's head whipped up, then back again and she braced herself with both hands against the dash.

Fred tried to see Benjamin, hoping against hope the boy was still alive. He hurled himself out the door and pulled Benjamin after him. Thank God, he couldn't see blood anywhere. "Get out," he shouted. "Get moving."

They jumped into the snow and landed in powder so deep it covered their knees. Fred turned toward the truck, fully intending to dive under the body for shelter, but it had landed in snow up to its running board and the wheels were completely buried.

Inside the cab, Ricki started moving toward Fred's open door. He could see the gun in her hand and he knew they had just seconds to save themselves.

"I'm going to get the gun away." Fred had to shout to be heard over the horn. "You get into the trees and hide."

Benjamin shook his head. "I'm not leaving you here alone."

"Dammit, boy, get out of here."

Ricki dropped one foot onto the running board. Fred tried to push Benjamin behind him, but the boy lunged at Ricki instead. He leaped too soon. He caught her arm and jostled her, but she remained firmly rooted inside the truck.

Benjamin stumbled in the snow again, lost his footing, and fell into the powder several feet away.

Fred watched, as if in slow motion, while Ricki slid to the edge of her seat and took aim at Benjamin. The gun loomed in front of his face. Thrusting at her with every ounce of strength he could muster, Fred landed solidly against her shoulder. The pain in his chest exploded and knocked the wind out of him. The gun fired, but the shot flew high and wide and left Benjamin unharmed.

Scarcely able to breathe, Fred drove at her again. This time Ricki tumbled from the truck into the snow, but she kept a firm grip on the gun. She flailed at Fred and struck him with her fists. She kicked and pummeled and bit as he fought to subdue her. He could hear her swearing, even over the blare of the horn.

Powder stung his cheeks, filled the space between his coat and his neck, and flew down his irritated chest. He clutched her gun hand with both of his and forced it up and back as they rolled into the snow together. He fought to hold her down, to keep her in place until he could get the gun away.

"Get out of here," he shouted to Benjamin again.

From the corner of his eye, he could see Benjamin moving. But instead of moving into the trees, Benjamin crawled through the snow toward Fred and Ricki.

Ricki lunged up and fastened her teeth on Fred's wrist. Only the band on his coat kept her from doing anything worse than applying uncomfortable pressure. Fred used the wrist to push her back into the snow. Dragging shallow breaths into his burning lungs, he pressed down on her neck with all the strength he had left and worked an aching knee onto her chest to pin her in place.

She released his arm and bucked against him. She tried to roll away, but Fred managed to keep her planted in the snowbank. He released her neck and gripped both of her wrists, then pressed her back into the snowbank.

His heart thundered in his chest, his mouth and throat burned, his ears roared from the exertion and the blaring horn, and his mind played tricks on him. Through the fog he thought he could see Phoebe coming for him from the edge of the highway.

He focused on drawing each breath and tried to force his heart to beat in rhythm in spite of the pain. He watched Benjamin, crawling closer, and prayed the boy would reach him in time to get the gun from Ricki's hand before Fred's heart gave out.

He tried not to look at Phoebe again. He had to make sure Benjamin was safe before he could go with her. Ricki's energy seemed to flag for a moment, then she gathered strength and fought to push him off her.

Using instinct more than reason, Fred gripped both her wrists with one hand and tightened his hold. With his other hand he pressed his thumb and one forefinger against her larynx, hoping to cut off her air supply and weaken her.

She gasped for breath and increased her efforts to shake him. Fred doubled the pressure and prayed Benjamin could get the gun away soon.

"Grandpa? Are you all right?" At last! Benjamin had crawled close enough for Fred to hear him over the horn.

Fred tried to speak, but he couldn't make himself heard. "The gun," he croaked. "Get the gun."

In horrid fascination, he looked toward Phoebe again. She seemed to be moving toward him. Mist swirled around her feet and she lifted her arms to beckon him toward her. He could almost see her hair whipping in the wind, could almost see her coat flapping, could almost hear her voice calling him.

He pulled in a jagged breath that burned all the way into his lungs. His chest ached, his arms trembled, and he gripped Ricki's arms tighter.

"Grandpa?"

"The gun," he croaked again. But even if they got the gun, what would Benjamin do then? Fred didn't have much strength left. He didn't know how much longer he could hold out. He couldn't die and leave Benjamin alone with Ricki.

Even if he managed to survive for a while, what would they do? Benjamin couldn't endure this bitter cold weather for long. He'd never get the truck out of this snowbank, and they were too far from town for the boy to walk back.

By some miracle, Benjamin seemed to finally understand what Fred wanted him to do. He lunged at Ricki, battled with her grip on the gun, and finally managed to pry her fingers from it. He turned the barrel toward Ricki and held it there, but his hands shook and his aim was far from steady.

The pain in Fred's chest seemed to grow worse by the minute. He could hear Phoebe more clearly now. He stole a glance at her, closer than ever. She lifted her hands to cup her mouth and called out again.

"Benjamin?"

This time, Benjamin must have heard her too. He stopped moving and looked back toward the highway. Dropping to his knees, he clutched the gun in both hands and struggled to catch his breath.

Fred looked once more at Phoebe. This time, she'd moved close enough for him to realize something looked different. Her hair, maybe. Or her coat.

All at once, Benjamin's lips curved into a smile and his fear seemed to evaporate. He collapsed in the snow, inches from Fred's left leg and croaked, "Mom."

twenty-four

Fred made himself as comfortable as he could in his rocking chair while Benjamin stretched out on the couch and adjusted a blanket over his legs. With the telephone receiver in one hand, Margaret stood behind her son and touched Benjamin's shoulders every few seconds while she talked to her brother, as if she feared Benjamin would evaporate. Deborah sat on the ottoman by Fred's feet and smoothed an afghan across his legs.

Fred leaned his head against his chair and savored their company. Only Sarah was missing from the picture, but with luck she'd be here soon. Webb's presence, Fred could do without.

Margaret laughed into the telephone. "I couldn't believe it. Picture it, Jeff. *Dad* rolling in the snow, fighting this crazy woman with a gun. You should have seen him."

Fred didn't think *he'd* want to see it. It would probably give him a heart attack.

Jeffrey said something that made Margaret nod with enthusiasm. "He saved Benjamin's life, he really did. Once I realized what was happening, I couldn't even move. I just stood there and watched the whole thing—terrified."

Fred saw no need to point out how frightened he'd been. He reached for his coffee cup, winced when his bruised chest protested even the tiniest movement. Deborah slid the cup closer on a TV tray and handed him a fresh chocolate chip cookie. Now, if he'd only had a little almond toffee crunch ice cream . . .

"No, actually Benjamin was fighting, too," Margaret said. "They were *both* wonderful. It was unbelievable. It was

Benjamin's idea to tie her with the cords from his jacket and Dad figured out how to get her back to town. You should have *seen* the look on Grady's face when we got to the sheriff's office and Dad opened the trunk."

Fred grinned at Benjamin, sipped his coffee, and wrapped his aching fingers around the cup in the hope the heat would soothe away some of his aches. Benjamin had been something, all right. Without him, Fred wouldn't have survived.

"Wait until you see him," Margaret said with a nod and a concerned look in Fred's direction. "He's stiff and a little sore, but otherwise he's fine."

More than a *little* sore. But Fred had no intention of showing it.

"Doc?" Margaret sounded surprised. "No, he's out of jail. Velma called a few minutes ago to say he's on his way over to check on both of them."

Fred tried his best to look hearty and robust. "Tell Jeffrey I can't wait for them to get here. I'm anxious to see them."

"Dad says hello. He's getting excited for Christmas." Margaret paused again to listen. "Well, Dad thinks Ricki went over there, intending to kill Eddie with his own gun. But when she found the empty glucagon syringe in Eddie's garbage, she decided to use the insulin instead. He had it all figured out."

Fred decided not to set Margaret straight on that point, either.

Margaret nodded for several seconds. "I'm sure once Jessica's out of surgery and Enos gets a chance to question Ricki himself, we'll find out a lot more." She blushed a little when she spoke of Enos and turned away when she caught Fred watching her. "We *all* felt sorry for her." She covered the mouthpiece with her hand and whispered, "He wants to know how you figured it out."

"Process of elimination," Fred said, and managed to keep a straight face in spite of Benjamin's sudden grin.

Margaret waited for him to elaborate. He didn't see any need to. Reluctantly, she turned her attention back to Jeffrey.

Fred sipped his coffee again as the front door opened.

Sarah, home for the holidays and looking more like her grandmother every day, slipped inside. Which meant Webb must be somewhere nearby. With any luck, he'd head straight for the Copper Penny and not waste time coming inside to ruin the rest of Fred's day.

Sarah unwrapped a scarf from her neck and let her dark brown hair tumble to the middle of her back. Running across the room, she ducked under the phone cord, and pressed a kiss to Fred's cheek. "Dad and I found Mom's note at home. What's the matter, Grandpa? Are you sick?"

Fred shook his head. "Benjamin and I had a little set-to with one of the neighbors."

"Nuh uh," Deborah protested. "Benjamin helped Grandpa catch a murderer. She had a gun and everything. Mom and I were even there."

Sarah wedged herself between Benjamin's feet and the end of the couch. "You *what?* Are you kidding?"

Benjamin's chest swelled to twice its normal size, but he leaned back and tried to look nonchalant. "No, she's not kidding. Why?"

"She had a gun?"

"Yep." Benjamin crossed one foot over the other and tried to look as if he wrestled guns from murderers every day. "What do you think, Sis? Benjamin Templeton, private investigator. Sounds good, eh?"

Sarah rolled her eyes at her younger brother and turned back to Fred. "I've been telling my roommates about you, Grandpa. They already think you're awesome. Wait until they hear about this."

The only awesome thing about Fred at this moment was the way his muscles ached. But he smiled modestly.

Margaret lowered the mouthpiece of the telephone again. "Jeff and Corinne want to know what you'd like for Christmas."

Fred started to give his usual response, "Whatever they'd like to send me." Then paused, gave the request a little more thought, and added, "Or you could all go in on a videocassette recorder."

Margaret stared at him for a second, then repeated his

request into the telephone with a laugh. "He wants a VCR. No. Really. That's what he said."

Sarah leaned across Fred's TV tray and helped herself to a cookie. "What were you guys doing there?"

"Well, you know I was going to buy that truck——?"

Sarah didn't even look surprised. Benjamin must have enlisted her as an ally.

"And Dad wouldn't let me buy it——?"

Another nod.

"Well, Grandpa and I went over to get the down payment back and Mom decided to follow us," Benjamin explained. "She said the more she thought about it, the less she trusted me and Grandpa to get my money back, so she brought Deborah with her to make sure we did what we were supposed to. They turned the corner to Ricki's house just as we were driving off the other way."

"She thought we were actually taking a test-drive," Fred said with a chuckle, "and came after us."

"And you saw the whole thing?" Sarah asked Deborah.

Deborah moved from the ottoman to the edge of Fred's chair——the closest she came these days to actually sitting on his lap. "Almost. When they drove out of town past the One-Stop, Mom was so mad . . . you should have seen her. Then we thought we lost 'em in the fog until we heard the horn honking and Mom said, what the h-word is your grandpa doing now?"

As if she could tell they were talking about her, Margaret replaced the receiver and perched on one arm of the couch. "Jeff said he'd call Joseph. He thinks he'll be able to explain what happened and keep him from flying out here."

"You know," Fred said thoughtfully. He almost stretched out his legs, then quickly decided against it when the pain hit. "I'm not convinced we need to tell Joseph about this."

For some reason, Webb chose that moment to join his family. He stomped snow from his shoes and stepped inside. Even from across the room, the smell of fresh alcohol hit Fred and left no doubt how Webb had filled his minutes alone.

Margaret glanced toward him and frowned, then continued speaking as if she hadn't been interrupted. "Can you imagine what Joe'd do if we didn't tell him and he found out later?"

"There's nothing that says he has to find out," Fred reasoned. "All you kids do things *I* never find out about."

Webb brushed snow from his hair and scowled over at Fred. "Now's a fine time to worry about Joe. You shoulda thought of that before you decided to play hero again."

Fred opened his mouth to answer, but Margaret cut him off with a wave of her hand. She frowned at her husband. "Don't start on Dad. He's been through enough already."

"That's nobody's fault but his own."

"I mean it, Webb. I don't want to hear it."

Webb stared her down for another few seconds, as if he had to decide whether or not to argue. He must have decided not to, because he brushed past her and clomped into the kitchen. Fred could hear bottles in the refrigerator door rattle when Webb pulled it open. A second later, he slammed it closed again. He must have forgotten Fred didn't keep beer in there.

Webb reappeared in the doorway and caught Margaret's eye. "How much longer do you want to stay here, anyway?"

Fred expected Margaret to follow her usual pattern. To placate Webb and urge Fred to keep the peace. To bundle up the kids and hustle the whole family away just to make Webb happy. He'd seen it happen hundreds of times over the years.

But to his surprise, her frown deepened and she crossed her arms on her chest. "Knock it off, Webb. Have you forgotten that without Dad, Benjamin wouldn't be here?"

"Without *Dad*," Webb argued, "Benjamin wouldn't have been in trouble in the first place."

Margaret didn't back down. Her eyes glinted with that peculiar golden light, her lips thinned, and her shoulders squared. "I don't even want to think about what might have happened if Benjamin had gone over there alone."

"I could have gone with him," Webb insisted.

"If *you'd* gone," Margaret said, "you'd both be dead."

For the first time in recent memory, Webb's mood didn't

appear to phase Margaret, but her mood definitely affected him. He strode across the room and yanked open the front door like a spoiled child. "I've had enough of this, let's get out of here." He stood there, waiting, fully expecting Margaret and the kids to leap up and follow him outside.

Showing magnificent restraint, Fred managed to keep his mouth shut, but he held his breath and waited.

Margaret's gaze faltered for only a second. "You can leave if you want," she said at last. "We're going to stay with Dad for a while."

Fred tried, and failed, to keep his expression indifferent. He knew he shouldn't find joy in the expression of defeat on Webb's face. Maybe he should even have been concerned when Webb pivoted away and slammed the door behind him. And if it had been anyone else but Webb, maybe Fred would have felt differently.

He studied the children's faces when their father stormed away. He watched Margaret's expression relax when her husband left the house, and his own spirits lifted a little.

He looked toward the old oak dining table he used to hold family pictures and smiled at his favorite photo of Phoebe. She stood in front of their Christmas tree—it must have been five years ago or more. She'd been about to put the angel on the tree when Fred had surprised her by taking the picture. She wore an expression of surprise mixed with exasperation, and she'd had more than a few words to say about him framing the picture and displaying it on the table.

But it captured her essence and brought her vividly back to Fred whenever he looked at it. And he could almost hear her saying, as she'd said so often during troubled times, "You know, dear. I do believe everything is going to work out fine."

In that moment, Fred believed so, too.